RIVER PRINCE

'Kalki' is the pen name of Ramaswamy Krishnamurthy (1899–1954), whose career in writing and journalism began as activism during the struggle for Indian independence. He served as editor of the popular Tamil magazine *Ananda Vikatan* before launching *Kalki*. The magazine—and eventually its founder—was named for the mythological tenth avatar of Vishnu to symbolise a vision to 'destroy regressive regimes, express radical thoughts, take readers into new directions, and create a new era'. Kalki wrote several novels, including *Parthiban Kanavu* and *Sivakamiyin Sabadam*, as well as political essays, film reviews, dance and music critiques, and scholarly work.

Nandini Krishnan is the author of *Hitched: The Modern Woman and Arranged Marriage* and *Invisible Men: Inside India's Transmasculine Networks*. She has translated two of Perumal Murugan's works into English: *Estuary* and *Four Strokes of Luck*. She was shortlisted for the PEN Presents translation prize 2022 and the Ali Jawad Zaidi Memorial Prize for translation from Urdu 2022. She is an alumna of the Writer's Bloc playwrights' workshop by the Royal Court Theatre, London. Her novel-in-manuscript was a winner of the Caravan Writers of India Festival contest and showcased at the Writers of the World Festival, Paris, 2014.

PONNIYIN SELVAN BOOK 3

RIVER PRINCE

KALKI

TRANSLATED BY
NANDINI KRISHNAN

eka

eka

First published in Tamil as *Ponniyin Selvan*

Published in English in 2024 by Eka, an imprint of Westland Books, a division of Nasadiya Technologies Private Limited

No. 269/2B, First Floor, 'Irai Arul', Vimalraj Street, Nethaji Nagar, Alapakkam Main Road, Maduravoyal, Chennai 600095

Westland, the Westland logo, Eka and the Eka logo are the trademarks of Nasadiya Technologies Private Limited, or its affiliates.

Translation copyright © Nandini Krishnan, 2024

ISBN: 9789360454357

10 9 8 7 6 5 4 3 2 1

This is a work of fiction. Names, characters, organisations, places, events and incidents are either products of the author's imagination or used fictitiously.

All rights reserved

Type set by SÜRYA, New Delhi

Printed at HT Media Ltd, Greater Noida

No part of this book may be reproduced, or stored in a retrieval system, or transmitted in any form or by any means, electronic, mechanical, photocopying, recording, or otherwise, without express written permission of the publisher.

PONNIYIN SELVAN BOOK 3

RIVER PRINCE

KALKI

TRANSLATED BY
NANDINI KRISHNAN

eka

eka

First published in Tamil as *Ponniyin Selvan*

Published in English in 2024 by Eka, an imprint of Westland Books, a division of Nasadiya Technologies Private Limited

No. 269/2B, First Floor, 'Irai Arul', Vimalraj Street, Nethaji Nagar, Alapakkam Main Road, Maduravoyal, Chennai 600095

Westland, the Westland logo, Eka and the Eka logo are the trademarks of Nasadiya Technologies Private Limited, or its affiliates.

Translation copyright © Nandini Krishnan, 2024

ISBN: 9789360454357

10 9 8 7 6 5 4 3 2 1

This is a work of fiction. Names, characters, organisations, places, events and incidents are either products of the author's imagination or used fictitiously.

All rights reserved

Type set by SŪRYA, New Delhi

Printed at HT Media Ltd, Greater Noida

No part of this book may be reproduced, or stored in a retrieval system, or transmitted in any form or by any means, electronic, mechanical, photocopying, recording, or otherwise, without express written permission of the publisher.

CONTENTS

1. Poonguzhali — 1
2. Quicksand — 11
3. Delusions — 19
4. At Midnight — 26
5. At Sea — 34
6. An Ancient Ruin — 42
7. 'Samudra Kumari' — 55
8. Bhoota Theevu — 69
9. 'This is Lanka!' — 79
10. Aniruddha Brahmarayar — 86
11. Therinja Kaikola Army — 94
12. Guru and Shishya — 104
13. Ponniyin Selvan — 119
14. Two Full Moons — 127
15. A Primal Scream at Night — 134
16. The Hallucinations of Sundara Chozhar — 145
17. Do the Dead Come Back to Life? — 158

18. Which Is the Worst Form of Treachery?	173
19. 'The Spy Has Been Caught!'	182
20. A Clash of Tigresses	190
21. The Dungeon	196
22. Senthan Amudan in the Dungeon	206
23. Nandini's Letter	218
24. Like Wax in a Flame	227
25. The City of Mathottam	237
26. A Dagger Baying for Blood	244
27. The Forest Path	252
28. The Royal Path	261
29. The Mahout	272
30. The Duel	283
An Extract from Book 4: Wind Storm	291
Notes	304

1

POONGUZHALI

The dusk was infused with a sense of calm and peace. The waves along the Kodikkarai seashore had subsided into sleep. Catamarans and boats were making their ways back to the land. The birds that had gone to prey in the sea were coming home to roost. The shore housed a small beach of white sand. Beyond, for as far as the eye could see, was forest. The branches of the trees were still, as were their leaves. In whichever direction one turned, there was only silence. The Sun God, resplendent in the hue of the gloaming, was hurrying towards the point where sky and sea met. Clouds that had sought to hide the rays of Surya found themselves glowing with the brilliant colours of sunset instead.

A little boat was floating by the shore. The waves rocked the boat with their slender fingers, as gently as they would have a baby's cradle. A young woman was seated on the boat. Her appearance reminds us[1] of Senthan Amudan's ardent description of his uncle's daughter. Yes, this must be Poonguzhali.[2]

As if living up to her name, she has tucked the petals of a thazhampoo into the folds of her tresses. Tendrils of her long, thick hair curl against her sculpted shoulders. She wears a necklace of seashells that she has fashioned for herself. But one can't really call these ornaments. She was the ornament. The shells looked prettier for having been graced by her skin, as did the flower for having been honoured with a place in her hairdo. If beauty were to take human form, how could one hope to enhance it with ornaments?

Poonguzhali leaned back in her boat gracefully, and sang. Perhaps the waves had silenced themselves just so they could hear her song. Perhaps the wind too had stopped blowing and crawled through the air for this very purpose. Perhaps the trees in the distance had held their leaves in check so their rustling would not dampen the sound of her singing. Sky and earth forgot themselves and stood transfixed by her voice. The Sun God himself appeared to linger on the horizon so he could hear her sing before he sank into the sea.

Let us listen in, then, to her song with its honey-soaked notes floating through the air:

Alaikadalum oyindirukka
Agakkadaldaan ponguvaden?
Nilamagalum tuyilugaiyil
Nenjagandaan padaippadumen?

Kaattinil vaazh paravaigalum
Koodugalai thedinave!
Vettuvarum villiyarum
Veedunokki eguvaare
Vaanagamum naanilamum
Monamadil aazhndirukka
Maanvizhiyaal pennoruththi
Manaththil puyal adippadumen?
Vaaridiyam adangi nirkkum
Maarudamum tavazhndhu varum
Kaarigaiyaal ulandanile
Kaatru suzhandadippadumen?

While the sea drifts to sleep,
Why do waves crash within?
While the earth finds rest, why
This churning in the chest?
Birds that fly all day seek
Nests to roost for the night.
Huntsmen and bowmen crave,
Homes for exhausted feet.
When all contained in space,
And all the four landscapes,[3]
Soak in the silence, why
Must storms rage in the breast
Of this doe-eyed damsel?
The ocean has been tamed.
The wind crawls to a halt.
Yet, within this woman's heart,
Whirlwinds hold sway.

We can't tell what deep sadness haunts this young woman. What sweet sorrow has blended itself into her lovely voice? Why have tears seeped their way into the lyrics of her song? As we hear her sing, we feel our hearts brim over, our chests explode from pain.

Poonguzhali's song faded into silence. She steered her little boat towards the shore, and leapt on to land. She drew the boat onto the sands, and secured it so that it rested against the catamarans that were anchored already. She then climbed back into the boat, leaned against its side and looked about herself.

There, the fire had been lit atop the lighthouse. It would burn all night, warning the ships at sea not to come too close. The waters by the Kodikkarai shore were shallow. Only catamarans and small boats could approach without sinking into the silt. Ships could even be wrecked if they hit the seabed, which was why the lighthouse served such an important purpose.

There was a little temple by the lighthouse, housing the deity Kuzhagar[4]. About two hundred years earlier, Sundaramurti Nayanar[5] had visited Kodikkarai. He had had a darshan of Kuzhagar, who had isolated himself in the forest.

'Lord! You sit without company in this forest by the seashore! Could you find no other place to call home? When so many of your sthalams are teeming with droves of devotees, why did you see fit to find a temple in this forsaken place? What sin have I committed that my eyes should witness such a terrible sight?' he said, and then sang:

Kadidaai kadarkaatru vandetra karaimel
Kudidaanayale irundaal kutramaamo?
Kodiyen kangal kandana kodi kuzhageer
Adigel umakkar thunaiyaaga irundeere?
Madhdham malisoozh maraikkaadadanrenbaal
Bhaktar palar paadavirunda parama!
Koththaar pozhil soozhntharukodi kuzhaga
Eththaatraniye irundaai? Empiraane!

Is it not a grave injustice to reside
Where cruel winds slap the shores and rage through trees?
Whom do you have for company here, my lord,
My Kuzhagar, whom my sinner's eyes must see
In this forest that not a soul visits, when
Your devotees throng temples to sing your praise?
O why have you abandoned us all, my lord,
To make your home in this forgotten alcove?

Even two centuries after these words had been sung, Kodikkarai Kuzhagar was in that very same, isolated state (and continues to be, a thousand years after).[6] If at all, the forest had grown even more dense. The trees were populated by owls and whimbrels. The only human denizens of that place were hunters whose very appearance was menacing. They had fashioned dwellings under those looming trees.

But, wait. There was one difference. There had been no lighthouse to guide the seacraft when Sundaramurti Nayanar had made his way there. It was during the rule of Parantakar I that this structure had been constructed, along with cottages for the families of the men who were tasked with the quotidian job of lighting the fire on top. The priest who served at the Kuzhagar temple had also been allotted a house.

Poonguzhali wondered whether she should go back to her home by the lighthouse. Then, her eyes fell on the kalasam of the Kuzhagar temple gopuram. At that very moment, the temple bell rang, and Poonguzhali made a decision. What was the point in rushing home now? She might as well go to the temple, and request the priest to sing verses from the Devaram. She could eat the prasadam too.

She jumped off the boat and started towards the temple, singing to herself as she skipped along the path. She chanced upon a herd of deer, who were crossing the sands to go into the forest. Among the seven–eight grown deer was a little fawn.

Poonguzhali felt her spirits soar as she watched the deer run. She made as if to chase them. She was quick on her feet, but could anyone hope to keep up with deer? They ran even faster, and were soon far ahead of her.

At one point, the deer came to a halt and then soared into the sky one by one, leaping across something to the other side. Poonguzhali guessed there must be quicksand at that spot. The grown deer got across without effort. But the fawn fell just short, its hind legs sinking into the quicksand. The fawn tried to propel itself on to the shore by leaning on its forelegs.

But its hind legs were sinking fast. The mother looked on anxiously from the shore, helpless to go to her baby's aid.

Poonguzhali took all this in within seconds, and gauged where the quicksand ended. She ran as fast as she could, while staying on firm ground. It didn't take her long to reach the place where the fawn was stuck. The mother looked at her in fright. But perhaps Poonguzhali knew the language of deer, for she said something that calmed the mother down. Poonguzhali seated herself by the shore, planting her knees into the soil, and then reached for the fawn. Grasping the baby's forelegs, she pulled hard until she was able to overcome the force of the quicksand and get the fawn to safety. For some time, the little one's body quaked and shook. The mother approached. Perhaps she whispered words of courage, for the very next moment, the baby took off into the forest, along with the mother.

'Tchah! Ungrateful beasts!' Poonguzhali said to herself. 'Well, not that they're any worse than humans,' she added, by way of consolation.

Then, she headed for the temple. The undergrowth was thick, the forest floor uneven. One had to climb for several metres, and then negotiate past sudden, gaping pits. This particular forest must be acknowledged as a wonder of nature. The hills and valleys within its body had not been raised and carved by rock or water. There had been only sand. Over time, plants that had determined to live in those unfriendly surrounds had taken root, and had pushed and pulled against the sand until it had been raised into mounds and beaten into troughs. It was no easy task to find one's way through such a landscape. One might feel one had walked a long distance, only to find oneself back at the starting point.

Poonguzhali, though, had little difficulty in walking through the brush. She arrived at the temple in no time. The breeze carried the fragrance of flowers from the konnai and panneer trees[7].

When she entered, the priest beamed. It was on the rare occasion that the temple had visitors, and so the arrival of anyone was cause for great joy.

He brought Poonguzhali the prasadam, along with one half of a coconut.

'Amma, will you wait for a while? I'm about to close up and leave,' he said. He tended to find it rather hard to walk through the forest at night. But with Poonguzhali for a guide, he would have no cause for worry.

'I'll wait, aiya,' she said. 'I'm in no hurry. Do take your time.'

She went to the temple courtyard, and swung herself on to the boundary wall with the help of a tree branch. A statue of Nandi stood abutting the wall. Poonguzhali stretched herself on the wall, leaning against the statue, and bit into the flesh of the coconut.

As she was marvelling at the speed with which

the dusk swallowed the surroundings into itself, she heard the sound of hooves. She turned eagerly in the direction from which it came. The arrival of a horse in these parts seems to have stirred a memory in her, and carried her into a dreamworld of sorts. Yet, her heart was filled with a sorrow she couldn't quite place. Who could the rider be? What did it matter to her, anyway? For some time now, strangers had been coming this way more often than ever before. They were all apparently here on royal assignment.

Just the day before, two men had arrived. Their very mien had filled her with revulsion. They had asked her elder brother to ferry them to Lanka. They had offered him a lot of money for this. *To hell with their money*, she thought. *What did one care for money? What value did it have in the middle of this forest, anyway?* But her brother and his wife were obsessed with money. She wondered why. They collected it, hoarded it and hid it away.

The horse was nearing her now. It wasn't just one horse, she thought. It sounded like there were two. There they were, climbing laboriously up the slope of a pit. The horses were evidently tired from a long journey. Each horse carried a rider. The first was a young man of pleasing appearance. He had a strong physique and a handsome countenance. There was something regal about his face. But what was this face to the one that had captured her heart? Could anyone match the handsomeness of that beloved face, the regal contours of that beloved jaw? By comparison, this man had the face of an owl.

Of course, the first rider was our old friend Vallavarayan Vandiyadevan. The other rider was the son of the physician. They were both exhausted from their journey.

However, once he set eyes on Poonguzhali, Vandiyadevan's face brightened. He realised she was staring at him, and the idea rejuvenated him. He reined in his horse so he could drink in her face, blissfully unaware that she had just dismissed his face as that of an owl. That might have dampened his spirits. It is a blessing, isn't it, that we can't divine another's thoughts?

Poonguzhali realised that the rider was looking at her. It struck her that she was biting into a coconut and leaning against a statue. She felt a sudden sense of embarrassment. She leapt off the wall and began to run along the temple boundary.

For some reason, this prompted Vandiyadevan to leap off his horse. Something made him want to chase Poonguzhali down. He wasn't one to disobey his gut, and so he took off after her. Who could rationalise such an illogical act? We must put it all down to the human instinct, learnt over millennia. It was human instinct that made Poonguzhali run away, and it was human instinct that made Vandiyadevan give chase.

2

QUICKSAND

Vandiyadevan ran through brush and climbed over sand mounds, he jumped over stones and grazed his feet on thorns, all in pursuit of the woman. Now he could see her, now he couldn't. Every time he was about to give up, she appeared on the horizon. Vandiyadevan was reminded of the story of Rama chasing Maya Maricha.[1] But she was no illusion. And she was no Maricha either. She did have the fleet-footedness of a deer, though. Ammamma! How fast she ran!

Why on earth am I chasing after this woman, what insanity is this? Vandiyadevan thought to himself.

He went on to rationalise it right away.

On his way to Kodikkarai, Vandiyadevan had often thought of Senthan Amudan's description of the woman with whom he was in love. This must be her. It would be prudent to get to know her. She might be of help on his assignment. And he could also ask her the way to the lighthouse.

He and his companion had been able to spot the top of the lighthouse from some distance away, but they hadn't been able to figure out how to get there. The moment they had entered the forest, the lighthouse had disappeared from view. They had ended up going round and round in circles, without finding their way to it.

It was on one of these meandering, exhausting rounds that Vandiyadevan had spotted Poonguzhali leaning against the wall of the Kuzhagar temple.

All he'd wanted to do was ask her the way, and here she was, running like an enchanted deer. There was little point in trying to catch up. He might as well give up. But the ignominy of losing to a woman in a chase ... the prospect didn't appeal to him one bit.

Ah! There, she was on open ground. The azure waves of the sea gently lapped the sky. They were right by the shore. How lovely the sea was, a serene blue blanket spread out as far as the eye could see! And there, he could finally see the lighthouse in its entirety. There was a flare at the top of the lighthouse now. Its amber rays darted out in every direction and played tricks on the eye as they hit the clouds.

Should he simply stop his pointless pursuit and head for the lighthouse? No! No! She was on open ground, without brush and undergrowth to hide behind. He could catch her easily enough. The terrain was not too challenging. His feet were no longer sinking into the sand. Grass had grown on this part of the shore, and firmed up the land. In some places, the mud from earlier rains had dried in the sun, and he was sure he wouldn't lose his footing. There was no obstacle here. He would catch that girl for sure.

Besides, she was headed for the sea, wasn't she? Whichever direction she chose, she would at some point arrive at the water and would have to stop, wouldn't she? But what if this wonder woman walked right into the sea and disappeared? Adada! Why hadn't he thought to pursue her on horseback? It would have taken him no time at all to catch up with her on this landscape, if only he'd been able to gallop up to her.

There. She was hesitating a bit. She seemed to have decided to switch paths—instead of making for the sea, she now turned to her right. She intended to give him the slip by running into the forest that was some distance away, in that direction. If he allowed her to reach the forest, he would have no hope of catching her. The chase would have been in vain. All the energy he had expended, all the time he had spent, would amount to nothing. Vandiyadevan's legs were begging for mercy now ...

What was this? She seemed to have changed her mind yet again. She'd abandoned the thought of running into the forest. She looped right back, like a spinning top, and appeared to be making for the lighthouse now.

All it would take now was a couple of grand leaps, and he could catch hold of her. He would grip her arms and say, 'Woman! Why have you taken such a fright and started running away from me? I have a message for you from your beloved!' What a shock it would be for the girl, he thought. Of course, Senthan Amudan hadn't entrusted him with a message for her. So what? He could make something up.

Vandiyadevan summoned every bit of strength left in his body, and leapt into the air. Four leaps, and he'd be right by her side.

Instead, he surprised himself by yelling, 'Aiyo!'

His body realised what had happened to him before his mind did. And then it struck him that his legs were trapped. First, his feet sank into the slush, and then his ankles. Next thing he knew, he was knee deep in mud.

Adada! The landscape had played a trick on him. What had appeared to be an even surface had only been a thin layer of solidified mud. Under it was thick marsh.

Vandiyadevan had heard of quicksand, pockets of mud that never fully dried. Cattle, horses, even elephants were known to have been sucked into the mud, bit by bit, until they were entirely submerged, and eventually died terrible deaths.

Could this be that sort of morass? It certainly appeared so. His knees were now well below the surface of the mud. Would he continue to sink into it? His thighs were disappearing fast. This quicksand, which had swallowed horses and elephants whole without so much as a burp, would not spare him, would it? Aiyo! Was this how he was fated to meet his end? Were all his daydreams and all the castles he had built in the air destined to be decimated by a sinkhole?

The only hope he had of escape at this desperate time was this strange girl taking pity on him and pulling him to safety. No one else could rescue him. Vandiyadevan decided to yell as loudly as he could. 'Aiyo! I am dead! I am being sucked into the slush! I'm going to my death! Is there no one who will save me?'

Poonguzhali heard his cry. She stopped running, and hesitated for a moment. She turned, and took in the perilous situation in which Vandiyadevan had landed himself.

The next moment, her eyes fell upon a boat that was partly anchored on the sand and partly jutting into the slush. The boat must have been in use when this marshy mess had been a body of clear, deep water. She manoeuvred herself onto the boat in a series of adroit moves, took the oars and tried pushing them against the slush. Adada! What a wonder! The boat was gliding across the slush with the elegance of a swan on a stream!

It didn't take long to get to the other side of the quicksand. Poonguzhali jumped on to solid ground. She planted her feet firmly into the sand, leaned forward to catch hold of Vandiyadevan's arms and pulled him to safety.

Ammamma! How much strength this waif had hidden in those arms! It struck Vandiyadevan that her grip was even more ironlike than that of the Thalapathi of Thanjai Fort.

As soon as he had reached the safety of the shore, Vandiyadevan broke into a laugh. His legs alone were still shaking.

'You seem to think you've saved my life. Do you imagine that I wouldn't have pulled myself to safety if you hadn't come to my aid?'

'Then, what did you scream "Aiyo! Aiyo!" for?' Poonguzhali demanded.

'To stop you from running away.'

'Then, I'm happy to push you right back into the pit. Let's see you use your smarts to get back ashore!' and Poonguzhali made as if to push him back in.

'Aiyayo!' said Vandiyadevan, and jumped aside.

'Why are you panicking now?'

'I'm not afraid for my life. I'm afraid of the filth. I'm already muddied right up to the thigh.'

Poonguzhali's lips parted in a smile. She looked Vandiyadevan up and down.

'There, the sea is right here. You can wash the mud away,' she said.

'You'll have to show me the way,' he said.

The two of them made their way to the shore, skirting past the quicksand.

'Why did you take off at such a run the moment you saw me? Do I look like a ghost or ghoul?' Vandiyadevan asked.

'No, not like a ghost or ghoul. You look like

an owl. Your features are exactly those of an owl,' Poonguzhali said, and laughed.

Vandiyadevan was not exempt from vanity. He was particularly proud of his good looks. To be told his face resembled that of an owl was deeply offensive. He found the remark infuriating.

'Like my owl face is any worse than your monkey face,' he muttered under his breath.

'What did you say?'

'Nothing. I asked why you decided to run like your life depended on it the moment you saw me.'

'Why did you decide to chase me like *your* life depended on it?"

'I wanted to ask you the way to the lighthouse.'

'It's right there. How silly of you to ask.'

'It disappeared from view once we entered the forest, that's why. Now, tell me—why did you take off at a run when you saw me?'

'Men are all evil. I don't like them one bit.'

'Senthan Amudan too?' Vandiyadevan asked, sotto voce.

'Who?'

'Senthan Amudan of Thanjavur.'

'What do you know about him?'

'I do know that he's your beloved.'

'What? What?'

'Your name is Poonguzhali, isn't it?'

'Yes, my name *is* Poonguzhali. What did you say about Senthan Amudan? He is my ...?'

'I said he's your beloved.'

Poonguzhali fell into paroxysms of laughter. 'Who ever told you that?' she asked, wiping away tears of mirth.

'Who else? Senthan Amudan himself.'

'Thanjavur is a fair distance away. That's why he's got away with it.'

'Or ...?'

'If he'd said that within my earshot, I'd have thrown him into that pit of quicksand.'

'So? There's plenty of water in the sea to wash the mud off.'

'That pit into which you fell, cows and horses have died in there. It can suck in elephants themselves.'

Vandiyadevan's hair stood on end. He relived how he had felt as he was being slowly sucked into the sand. If she hadn't come to his aid, by now he would have been ... the thought made him shudder.

'What else did Senthan Amudan say about me?' Poonguzhali asked.

'That you are his uncle's daughter. That not even Devalokam has such a beauty as you ...'

'So he's gone to Devalokam to see for himself, eh?'

'And that you sing like a dream. He said even the sea falls silent so it can hear you sing. Is that true?'

'Why don't you find out for yourself? Here, we're at the sea.'

The two of them stopped by the edge of the sand.

3

DELUSIONS

The stars twinkled in the sky. The crescent moon drifted across the clouds like a silver boat on water.

The wind gathered speed, and the seawater rippled. The ocean sent forth arms of white foam to pull the people on the shore closer to its bosom.

'What are you standing still for? Wash off the mud quickly. I need to get back home right away, or I'll have to go without dinner. My Anni[1] will clean out the pot and put it upside down to dry, if I take much longer,' Poonguzhali said.

'Is the water deep here?' Vandiyadevan asked.

'I've never met a coward like you. The water is shallow for a great distance from here. You could go half a kaadham[2] into the sea, and you'll still only be hip-deep in water. That is why we have to beam a flare from the lighthouse every night.'

Vandiyadevan entered the water gingerly, taking one little step at a time. He washed the mud off his arms and legs, and finally walked ashore. He spotted the physician's son approaching on his horse from some distance away. His own horse trotted by them.

'Aiyayo! The horses might slip into the quicksand!' Vandiyadevan gasped.

'No, they won't. They're a fair bit wiser than humans,' Poonguzhali said.

'But the horse is being ridden by a man. And he's got mine in tow as well. What if he forces them forward?'

'You have a point. There *is* danger of that happening. Go, run to warn him!'

'Stop! Stop!' Vandiyadevan yelled, running to stop his companion before the latter could lead the horses to their death.

Soon enough, Poonguzhali had joined the group. The three headed for the lighthouse, along with the horses.

'Why don't you get on your horse?' Poonguzhali asked.

'I'd rather walk with you,' Vandiyadevan replied.

Poonguzhali went up to Vandiyadevan's horse and stroked the animal's face gently. The horse nuzzled against her hand and whinnied gently.

'My horse likes you. That's a good thing.'

'Why is it a good thing?'

'I have to head for Lanka. I'm thinking of leaving the horse with you. Will you look after him for me?'

'Happily. All animals take to me right away. It is only humans who don't like me.'

'Why do you say that? Do you know how much Senthan Amudan ...'

'I like only animals myself. I don't like humans.'

'What have humans done to you to deserve such derision?'

'Humans are evil. They're full of lies and schemes and deceit.'

'You can't dismiss everyone like that. Senthan Amudan is a good man. This chap, the physician's son, is a good man ...'

'And you?'

'I, too, am a good man. But I shouldn't be blowing my own trumpet, no?'

'Why have the two of you come here?'

'You know our emperor is ailing, don't you? The royal physician has asked for some herbs to cure him. Apparently, there are powerful medicinal plants in this forest. That's why the two of us are here.'

'You said just now that you were headed for Lanka?'

'Yes, I'll have to source the herbs I can't find here from Lanka. I believe the Sanjeevi mountain[3] Hanuman carried to Lanka is still there.'

'Yes, absolutely. That's why people are dying of disease by the thousands down there.'

'Is that so? I have no news of this. Neither does the royal physician ...'

'I've never seen anyone else lie like men do. Two days ago, a couple of men came here. They had some similar tall story to tell. But at least their lie was somewhat believable.'

'Who were they? And what lie did they tell you?'

'They said a mantravadi had sent them. Apparently, he needed tiger claws and hair from an elephant's tail to make some sort of talisman for the emperor. My brother has taken them to Lanka by boat.'

'Oh! Oh! Is that so?' Vandiyadevan said.

The terrible mantravadi Ravidasan came to mind, as did the awful experience of that night in the ruin. *Dear God,* he thought, *why did I ever get involved in these dangerous missions? I was made for the battlefield, where one confronts an enemy face-to-face and proves his valour and virtuosity. Why did I get drawn into these plots and schemes and conspiracies?*

Then, his thoughts turned to the men who had preceded them to Kodikkarai. Who could they be? How much could he trust this woman? Perhaps she was part of the gang of conspirators too? ... No, no, that was impossible. Anyone could tell she was entirely without wiles. It would be a good idea to forge a friendship with her.

'Poonguzhali, I'll be honest with you now. I did lie about going to Lanka to fetch herbs. I'm going there on a crucial secret mission. I'll tell you what it is now.'

'No, don't! Haven't you heard that you should never trust a woman to keep a secret? Please don't tell me anything.'

'They say that about ordinary women. You're

quite extraordinary. There's no danger in my making you party to a secret.'

'How do you know I'm no ordinary woman? Not even one naazhigai[4] has passed since you met me.'

'Poonguzhali! The moment I laid eyes on you, as you were leaning against the wall of the temple, I liked you. Let me ask you something. Will you give me an honest answer?'

'You won't know till you ask.'

'Is it true that Senthan Amudan is your beloved? Are you going to marry him?'

'Why do you want to know?'

'Senthan Amudan is my friend. It would be wrong for me to do anything that would work against him. But if there is nothing between the two of you ...' Vandiyadevan trailed off.

'Go on. Why do you hesitate?'

'I'd like to apply for the post of your beloved, if there's a vacancy. Poonguzhali! I don't like your contempt for love. There is no power as divine as love in the entire world. Appar, Sundarar, Sambandar have all composed devotional songs where they have imagined god as a lover. Tholkaappiyar, Valluvar and all the other great Tamil poets have sung of love. Kalidasa has written of love. In Brindavan, Krishna was slave to the love of the gopis ...'

'Aiya! I'll say this once. And I'd like you to hear it and understand it and remember it.'

'What is this great revelation you wish to make?'

'I like you too. I don't feel the same revulsion towards you that I felt for those two men who came here a couple of days ago.'

'Oh, what a lucky man I am!'

'But please don't speak of this love-shove again.'

'Why? Why?'

'Senthan Amudan is not my beloved. But I do have other lovers ...'

'Adadaa! Adadaa! Other *lovers*? Who? And how many?'

'I'll leave the house at midnight. If you follow me, you'll be able to see them for yourself.'

And with that, Poonguzhali broke into peals of laughter.

Her laughter troubled Vandiyadevan deeply.

Poor girl. It appears she is delusional. Perhaps insane. There's no point in hoping for any help from her. It's best I don't take her into my confidence, he thought to himself.

They arrived at the cottage by the lighthouse. An elderly couple appeared in the doorway. The man looked startled when he saw Poonguzhali approaching with two men and their horses.

'Poonguzhali! Who are these men? Where did you go and find them?' he asked.

'I didn't find them, Appa. They found me,' Poonguzhali said.

'It's the same thing. You never listen when I ask you to come home before dusk falls. The day before yesterday, you brought two men here. And now, two others. What are they here for?'

'They're here to fetch herbs to cure the emperor's illness, Appa.'

'Aiya, is this girl telling the truth?' asked the man, turning to Vandiyadevan.

'Yes, sir. Here's the evidence,' Vandiyadevan said, and brandished an olai[5] that he had tucked into his waistcloth.

Another scroll tumbled out of the cloth. He hurriedly bent down to pick it up and tucked it away safely.

What an idiot I am, he muttered to himself, *I've learnt nothing from having made this very same mistake earlier.*

The elderly man took the first scroll and went closer to the flare to read it. His face shone as he turned to his wife and said, 'Ilaiya Piraatti has written this. We must give them a meal. Go inside and tell your daughter-in-law before she puts away the cooking pot!'

4

AT MIDNIGHT

After dinner, Vandiyadevan spoke to Poonguzhali's father Tyagavidanga Karaiyar, who had been entrusted with the maintenance of the lighthouse. Vandiyadevan told the elderly man that he had to leave for Lanka urgently.

Tyagavidanga Karaiyar said, regretfully, 'Once upon a time, there were dozens of boats of various kinds and sizes plying from this shore. But now, they have all left for Sethukarai. All to help our army in Lanka, of course. I do have two boats of my own. My son has taken one to ferry those men who came here yesterday, to Lanka. I don't know when he will return. What can we do now?'

'Who were those two men? Your daughter said they seemed strange, even repulsive.'

'Yes. I didn't like them at first sight myself. I don't know who they are or why they wanted to go to Lanka. They were carrying the Pazhuvettaraiyars' palm tree insignia. Even so, I would not have asked my son to ferry them. But my daughter-in-law is terribly money-minded. They offered a bagful of money, and she persuaded her husband to go.'

'What sort of charade is this, aiya? Why would your son listen to a young woman who has no worldly experience?' Vandiyadevan asked. Then, he added with some hesitation, 'I'm sorry, please forgive me. That is a personal matter, concerning your family, and I should not have spoken as I did.'

'Appane! You haven't erred by asking the question you did. You see, my family carries a curse. My son ...' Tyagavidanga Karaiyar hesitated.

Vandiyadevan suddenly remembered what Senthan Amudan had said about this family.

'Is your son ... can he not speak?' he asked.

'Yes. How did you know?' the elderly man asked.

Vandiyadevan told him of his stay with Senthan Amudan, and the hospitality of the latter's mother.

'Aha! So that was you, was it? Your reputation preceded your arrival on these shores. Apparently, the entire empire is being scoured for you?'

'Perhaps. I am not aware of the latest news on that.'

'Now I see why your departure to Lanka is so urgent.'

'Periyavare[1]! Things are not as you assume. It is not for fear of my life that I must leave for Lanka. I carry a very important scroll that has to be delivered urgently to someone there. You may read it if you so wish.'

'There is no need for that. The fact that Ilaiya Piraatti has given you a letter of introduction is enough. But I'm afraid I'm not able to help you at this time.'

'You said you had *two* boats?'

'Yes, there *is* another boat. But there is no one to man it. If you and your friend can handle the boat, I'm happy to lend it to you so you can row yourselves to Lanka.'

'Neither of us can row a boat. In fact, I'm rather afraid of water. And the sea is even scarier than ...'

'Even if you know how to row a boat, you can't take it out on the open seas without experience. The land disappears from view almost right after you paddle out to sea, and then you will lose all sense of direction,' Tyagavidanga Karaiyar said.

'Moreover, I can't take my companion along. He has work here. He has been assigned to gather the herbs his father needs for the emperor, and return as soon as possible. You must come up with a solution for me.'

'Well ... there *is* one way you can get to Lanka. But that is no easy task. I suppose you might give it a shot. Luck just may be on your side.'

'What should I do? Periyavare, tell me, and I'll certainly do all I can to get there,' Vandiyadevan said.

'There is no one around these parts who can handle a boat as deftly as Poonguzhali. She's gone back and forth to Lanka so very often. I'll ask her on your behalf. You put in an appeal too.'

'Call her right away, won't you? Let's ask her.'

'No, no. She's extremely adamant. If she refuses right away, then there will be no changing her mind. I'll try to catch her in a good mood tomorrow, and put in the request. It would be a good idea for you to do that too, independent of my efforts.'

With that, Tyagavidanga Karaiyar headed for the lighthouse.

Vandiyadevan settled down on the thinnai[2] of the house. The physician's son was already asleep. Vandiyadevan was exhausted from the exertions of the journey. His eyes were closing even as he lay down. He fell into a deep slumber in no time.

Suddenly, he was woken from sleep. He heard something—it sounded like a door being pushed open. Vandiyadevan forced open his eyelids to see what was happening. A figure was stepping out of the house. He squinted, and realised it was a woman. The light from the flare now fell on the figure. Ah! It was Poonguzhali. There was no doubt.

What was it she had told him earlier? *Follow me at midnight. You can see my lovers for yourself.* Surely, she had been joking? But now she was setting off in the middle of the night. Where was she going? It could not be to meet a lover or lovers, surely? She wouldn't have said such a thing if that were really the case. Or would she? No, there was some mystery here. Or was there ...?

Whatever it was, nothing was stopping him from following her. He had a formidable task ahead of him—persuading her to ferry him to Lanka. Learning what she was up to at night could come in handy when he had to negotiate with her. Or, she might find herself in some danger that night He could play the hero, and she would then owe him a favour.

Vandiyadevan got up silently. He kept Poonguzhali within his sights. The memory of the trauma he had experienced that evening was vivid. He had no intention of getting caught in another quicksand. And so, it would not be prudent to lose her.

For some time after they left the lighthouse, the flare lit the way. He was able to see Poonguzhali, and had no trouble following her. But soon enough, she seemed to walk faster, even though she showed no sign of having noticed him follow her. She went towards the forest, but skirted around the grassy mound that he had expected her to climb. She turned a corner, and Vandiyadevan lost sight of her. He hurried after her, and almost ran around the corner. He could see her ahead of him, and thanked his stars.

But the next moment, she was gone.

How had she disappeared? What sort of magic was this? Was there a pit he couldn't see at that spot? Vandiyadevan hurried to the place where he had last seen her, and looked around. Of the four directions that she could have taken, three led to open ground. She could not have disappeared from view if she had taken any of those. There was no quicksand here, so she could not have sunk into the earth. That left only one possibility—she must have climbed the mound after all, and gone into the forest.

When he scrutinised the mound, with its thorny bushes, he realised there was a little path leading through the shrubs. Vandiyadevan followed this path, his heart beating fast. The lighthouse was far behind him, and not one stray ray of light lit his way. The crescent moon had sunk into the sky some time ago, and the distant stars barely sent a twinkle towards him. The thorny brush and the dwarf trees took on monstrous proportions in his mind. The shadows they cast appeared as dark ghosts and ghouls. When their leaves rustled, the shadows moved. What perils awaited him in this darkness and among those shadows? Venomous creatures and wild animals might be hiding in the bushes. Something could swoop down on him from above, or slink up behind him, or assault him from either side. Adadaa! What had prompted him to fall into such a trap? He hadn't even thought to bring his spear along for protection.

What was that susurrous sound? What was the black form he could spot on that tree there? And what were those two shiny dots by the bush?

Vandiyadevan's legs began to tremble. Enough was enough. What was the point in staying on? Why had he even come here? What foolishness this was! He must go right back to the lighthouse.

Just as he turned, he heard a voice. A voice that could capture the heart, a woman's voice. A sob. And then this song:

Alaikadalum oyindirukka
Agakkadaldaan ponguvaden?
Nilamagalum tuyilugaiyil
Nenjagandaan vimmuvaden?

While the sea drifts to sleep,
Why do waves crash within?
While the earth finds rest,
Why do sobs rise in my chest?

Vandiyadevan abandoned all thoughts of return. He climbed higher, towards the voice. Not long after, he could see the peak of the mound. She was standing there. Yes, it was indeed Poonguzhali. It was she who had been singing. She was staring at the sky, at the stars shimmering in the vastness of space. Perhaps that was her grand audience.

Suddenly, a shooting star danced across the sky. Its light fanned out and silhouetted the woman standing on the mound. The woman, her voice, the shooting star ... Vandiyadevan lost all sense of reality. Entranced, he found his legs walking of their own accord right up to the woman. He stood before her. Far away, over her shoulder, he could see the red rays emanating from the flare of the lighthouse they had left behind. The sea spread out even further behind, outlined by the curve of the horizon.

'So you've come, have you? You were sleeping like Kumbhakarna on the thinnai.'

'I woke to the sound of the front door opening. You came here almost at a run, without so much as glancing behind you. Ammamma! Do you know what a task it was to catch up with you?'

'Why did you want to catch up with me?'

'What a question! Wasn't it you who asked me to follow you? Have you forgotten?'

'Why did I ask you to follow me? Do you remember?'

'How could I not? You said you would show me your lovers. Where are they? Show me, let me meet them?'

'There, look behind you,' Poonguzhali said.

5

AT SEA

Vandiyadevan turned. His insides churned. It was as if his gut was climbing into his chest, and then further up into his throat. A thousand bolts of lightning hit him all at once, and a hundred thousand needles pierced every pore of his body. So horrific was the sight that greeted his eyes.

In the darkness that seemed to stretch to the limits of all land and for all time, ten, twenty, a hundred tongues of fire rose high into the air. They emitted no smoke and gave off no light. There was no wood burning below. They loomed in the air, without origin it seemed. Suddenly, some went out; suddenly, others sprang afresh.

A terrifying black asura, with no head but with a fearsome mouth embedded in his stomach like the demon Kabandha[1] appeared. But he had not just one mouth on his stomach but hundreds of mouths, which he opened and closed in turns. Every time he opened a mouth, a flame shot out of the space where his head ought to have been, and every time he closed those jaws, the flame was snuffed out.

Vandiyadevan felt the blood leave his body through each of his follicles. He had never known such intense fear as he knew at that moment, not even when he had found himself in that subterranean vault at Periya Pazhuvettaraiyar's palace.

He heard a laugh break out behind him, and turned.

It was Poonguzhali! Under any other circumstances, her loud 'Ha, ha, ha!' would have scared the daylights out of him. But now, he felt emboldened by her presence—by the presence of another human being, made of flesh and blood, who had life and limb.

'So, you've met my lovers, have you?' Poonguzhali asked. 'These kolli vaai pisaasus[2] are my lovers. I come here at midnight to exchange sweet nothings with them.'

There could be no doubt that this woman was insane. Was it pragmatic to trust his life to her and ask her to row him to Lanka? But something else was struggling to surface in his consciousness. What was it? Something to do with the kolli vaai pisaasus …

'Can your friend Senthan Amudan compete with such lovers?' Poonguzhali asked.

Her voice came to him as if from the depths of a well. Because, at that very moment, he was struggling to remember something. Ah! *There* was the elusive memory! He had heard that when water stagnated on land that had sulphur deposits and turned it marshy, it could spark off this nightly phenomenon. The sulphur dust that emerged from the earth could light up and give the appearance of fire when it made contact with air. The tongues of flame might last for hours, or die out in seconds. The ignorant were frightened by the sight and ascribed it to spirits. They'd even created a genre of ghost for the purpose, the kolli vaai pisaasu. Now, Vandiyadevan's rational and irrational sides were at war with each other. The rational brain won out. But there was little point in talking science with this hallucinating woman. He would have to cajole her into going back to the safety of her home now.

'Penne! Your lovers aren't going anywhere. They'll be here tomorrow, waiting for you. Why don't you come see them then? Let's go home now, come,' he said.

Poonguzhali did not reply. Instead, she began to sob.

What kind of nonsense had he got involved in? Vandiyadevan sighed, and then waited in silence.

'Penne! Shall we go?' he asked.

The sobs would not stop.

Vandiyadevan's patience was exhausted.

'All right. I'm leaving you to your own devices. Do as you will. I feel sleepy. I'm going.' With that, he began to climb down the mound.

Poonguzhali stopped sobbing at once. She started down the slope too. In four agile leaps, she had overtaken him. Vandiyadevan had to run to catch up with her. The two of them began to walk towards the lighthouse.

Was it wise to get on a boat and row out to sea with this crazy woman, Vandiyadevan thought again. But there was no other option. Perhaps he should make conversation and befriend her?

'You see that comet in the sky? What is your opinion about it?' Poonguzhali asked.

'I have no opinion. The comet appears. That's all I see,' Vandiyadevan said.

'They say a comet in the sky bodes evil on earth.'

'Some do say that.'

'What do you say?'

'I have no knowledge of astrology. All I know is that people say this.'

They walked in silence for a time.

Then, Poonguzhali said, 'The word on the street is that the emperor is ill. Is that true?'

Perhaps she had not entirely taken leave of her senses, Vandiyadevan thought. There might be some hope after all.

'I saw for myself. The emperor is confined to his bed. He has lost the use of both his legs. The purpose of my journey is to procure herbs to cure him, isn't it? Penne! Will you do me a favour?' Vandiyadevan asked.

Poonguzhali went on without acknowledging his question, 'They say the emperor won't live long. Is that true?'

'If you don't help me now, that just may happen. There is some magical herb on the Sanjeevi mountain in Lanka, I believe. That could save the emperor's life. Tell me, will you row me to Lanka?'

'If the emperor were to die, who will be crowned king in his stead?' Poonguzhali asked.

Vandiyadevan nearly jumped out of his skin.

'Penne! Why does that concern you or me? What difference would it make to either of us who is crowned king?'

'Why would that not concern us? We are subjects of this kingdom, are we not?'

This woman was no lunatic, he thought. He would have to watch his words around her. There must be some explanation for her odd behaviour.

'Why are you silent? Who will be crowned the next king?' Poonguzhali asked again.

'Aditya Karikalar has been announced as the heir. He should be the one who inherits the title.'

'How about Madurantakar? Does he have no right to the throne?'

'But he has said he has no interest in governance.'

'He did say that, earlier. But, apparently, he has changed his mind now?'

'So what if he has changed his mind? Unless he has the support of the subjects of the kingdom, what difference will it make?'

'I hear some of the most influential people in the land are on his side?'

'I hear that too. But it surprises me that such news has travelled to you.'

'What will happen if Sundara Chozhar were to die suddenly?'

'There will be chaos throughout the land. That is why I need your help now.'

'In what way could I possibly help prevent such a thing?'

'I've already told you. I need to make an urgent trip to Lanka to procure herbs that could cure the emperor. Will you row me there?'

'Why do you need me? Aren't you embarrassed to have to ask a girl to ferry you across the sea?'

'Your father says there is no one else. I believe your brother left for Lanka yesterday?'

'So what if my brother's not here? Don't you have arms? Doesn't your companion have arms?'

'But we don't know how to row a boat.'

'What is there to know? As if it involves magic spells! You pull the oar, the boat moves forward. That's all!'

'But how will we go without knowing which direction to take? What if we lose our bearings out at sea?'

'Then go drown and die. What do I care?'

They had neared the lighthouse. Vandiyadevan thought it prudent to hold his tongue now. He didn't want Poonguzhali to refuse outright. There was a note in her voice and something about the inflection of her words that suggested she wasn't averse to ferrying him to Lanka, in spite of the words themselves. A tiny ray of hope had been ignited in Vandiyadevan's heart.

When he went back to bed, Vandiyadevan found himself tossing and turning, unable to sleep. His mind was troubled. Strange thoughts disturbed him every time he thought he might fall asleep. It wasn't until the fourth jaamam had begun that he dozed off.

And then, he had a dream. He and Poonguzhali were sitting across from each other in a little boat, with its sails unfurled. The sea surrounded them. Everywhere he looked, there was nothing but the deep blue of the ocean water. A pleasant breeze carried the boat over the waves. Poonguzhali's face was beauty incarnate. Tendrils of hair curled over her forehead. The pallu of her sari was flying in the wind. Vandiyadevan had forgotten where they were going and why they were going there. It was as if he had made this long journey just so he could sit in a boat with Poonguzhali. Something was missing, though. Just one thing was missing. What was that? Oh, yes! Song! Her voice! Senthan Amudan had spoken of her singing.

'Penne! Won't you open those coral lips and sing me a song?' Vandiyadevan asked.

'What did you say?' Poonguzhali asked, smiling at him.

Aha! That smile could win over all seven worlds.

'Won't you open that sweet mouth and sing a song?'

'What will you give me if I sing?'

'I will come close to you, and on those lovely cheeks of yours, I will ...'

Poonguzhali brandished a knife out of nowhere. She raised her hand, poised to plunge the knife.

'Look here! You take one step on this side of the mast, and I will stab you. The fish are starving,' she said.

6

AN ANCIENT RUIN

The next morning, the red rays of the sun woke Vandiyadevan with a series of sharp taps on the shoulder. It took him a while to come to his senses even after he had shaken off his sleep. He wasn't sure whether the light that was falling on his eyes was from the sun or the flare of the lighthouse. He wasn't sure which of the experiences of the previous day were dreams and which were memories. Only the elderly lighthouse keeper's wife and daughter-in-law were at home. They told him Poonguzhali's father had gone to the temple to decorate the deity with flowers. He didn't dare ask them about Poonguzhali herself.

Having had his breakfast, he set off to look for her. He searched in the vicinity of the house. She was nowhere to be seen. Perhaps she would be at the temple? He went to look, and met her father there. Tyagavidanga Karaiyar was plucking flowers from the trees for the deity. He told Vandiyadevan that Poonguzhali sometimes accompanied him to the temple to weave the flowers into garlands, but that she hadn't come that day.

'She's probably chasing deer in the forest, or wandering along the shore. Find her and ask her about ferrying you to Lanka,' he said. 'But, thambi, be careful. She's unpredictable. Don't say anything that could be mistaken for brazenness. Don't get cheeky with her. Don't take a cue from our epics and try the sringara rasa[1] with her. She'll turn into Bhadrakali, and then your life won't be yours anymore.'

The dream of the previous night came back to Vandiyadevan. He felt his nerves tingle. Then, he headed for the forest to look for Poonguzhali. But where did one even begin to look? It wasn't long before Vandiyadevan found himself so frustrated; all he wanted to do was to get out of the forest.

He now made for the shore. He walked quite a distance, with no luck.

Well, she would have to come home for lunch. He would meet her then. There was no point in trying to find her now.

Vandiyadevan was just turning back, when a thought struck him. The waters were calm now, almost still. He was tempted to bathe in that serene sea. He'd already been told the waters were shallow here. What danger could possibly present itself? It was also crucial that he overcome his fear of water. He would have to make the journey to Lanka, and that would entail sailing on a boat. He couldn't afford to be scared of the ocean.

He divested himself of his waistcloth and the dagger he'd tucked into it, and left them safely by the shore. He then set one foot in the water, gingerly. He walked a little further, taking one step at a time. He went a fair distance, but the water only lapped at his knees. Small waves splashed him up to the thigh, and very occasionally, up to the hip.

Some ocean, he thought to himself. *The water's not even deep enough for me to bathe!*

He walked a little further, and then wondered whether he had come too far from the shore, emboldened by the fact that he could feel solid ground beneath his feet. What if the sea decided to swell all of a sudden? What if giant waves washed over him? He turned to gauge how much time it would take him to get back to land.

'Adade!' he said out loud. His fears were indeed founded. He was a long way from shore. Should he go back? But no, what were the chances that the sea would swell, anyway?

Wait, what was that? Poonguzhali! Walking along the shore! He would get out of the water right away and catch hold of her before she traipsed off. He would choose his words carefully, and charm her into ferrying him to Lanka. She seemed to have caught sight of him as well. It appeared she was walking towards him. She was signalling something.

Oh! Oh! She was looking at something on the ground. Now, she was picking it up. What was that? No! Were those his clothes?

'No, woman, no! Don't take that! That's mine!' he yelled.

But the gurgling water drowned him out. She hadn't heard him.

He shouted louder. She seemed to have heard him. She was saying something too.

'Poonguzhali! That's mine! Don't take that. Put it back down ... Listen! Can't you hear me? What are you doing? You're taking my things as if they were yours! And you're making off with them! No, no! Stop!'

Vandiyadevan began to run towards the shore. Poonguzhali turned back to see him once. Then, she began to run too. She was going in the opposite direction to that in which her home and the lighthouse lay. She was headed into the forest.

Aha! What a wicked woman this one was! Or was she just plain mad? He would have to beg a lunatic for his clothes back now.

He slipped twice in the sea and drank a mouthful of salty water before he reached the shore. And then he chased after Poonguzhali as best as he could. But she only seemed to gain ground on him. Not far away, a group of fifty or sixty running deer emerged.

What a sight it is, to see these deer prance and run! How beautiful they look as they jump high into the air and land so gracefully! Why, that girl isn't any different! To see her leap and run is just as beautiful. A woman who lives as one with nature, who does everything of her own free will ... how lovely such a woman is! But I should never, ever tell her that. It would ruin my plans. Her father has already warned me. Why is she running as if she's been possessed, though? How will I find her once she runs into the forest? There! Just as I feared. She's disappeared into the trees. Everything has gone to hell now. There can be no idiot in the world like me. Once a monkey has grabbed a garland of flowers, can one hope to get it back intact?

Vandiyadevan ran into the forest, even as these thoughts were running through his head. He was in such a hurry that he didn't push the vegetation in his way aside, and ended up with scratches all over his body.

'Poonguzhali! Poonguzhali!' he called. Then, he began to address questions to his audience. 'O tree! Have you seen Poonguzhali? O crow! Have you seen Poonguzhali?'

Right. So he had gone insane too. Just as that thought occurred to him, something fell on him from the tree under which he was standing.

Ah! It was his waistcloth. He undid the knot in it eagerly. Yes, the scroll and the gold coins were safely tucked in.

'Is your money all there?' a voice called from above.

Vandiyadevan looked up. Poonguzhali was seated on a branch of the tree.

Hot and sweaty as he was, he flew into a temper at the sight.

'I've never seen a mandhi[2] like you!' he snapped.

'And *I've* never seen an aandhai[3] like you!' she said. 'How you stare and blink in turns!'

'Why did you drag me all the way here? If it was money you wanted ...'

'Chhi, chhi! Who wants money in these parts?'

'Then, why did you take my waistcloth and purse?'

'If I hadn't done that, you wouldn't have come into the forest. You'd have gone straight to my house.'

'And what if I had?'

'Climb the tree, and you'll see.'

'What will I see?'

'You'll see a group of horses, twelve or fifteen of them. And swords and spears glinting in the sun!'

Her expression suggested she wasn't making this up. But Vandiyadevan wanted to see for himself. He leapt on to the tree and began climbing to where she was. Before that, though, he made sure he had secured the waistcloth around himself and bound it tightly. What if she hadn't intended to throw it to him, and it had only slipped from her grasp? What if she was simply luring him on to the tree so she could grab it from him again?

Once he had climbed high enough, he looked towards the lighthouse. It was as Poonguzhali had said. A group of horses was assembled outside, carrying soldiers armed with spears and swords.

Who could they be? They must be Chinna Pazhuvettaraiyar's men, come to apprehend him. Well, Poonguzhali had saved him from great peril. But why had she bothered? What had moved her to look out for him? He couldn't be sure.

Once the two of them had got down, he said, 'Poonguzhali! You've saved me from a terrible fate. Thank you, more than I can say. I'm ever so grateful to you.'

'You're lying. Men and gratitude! Who ever heard of such a thing?'

'Don't think I'm like all other men.'

'No, you're unique.'

'Penne! May I ask you something?'

'By all means, you may. Whether I reply or not is, of course, my choice.'

'What made you put yourself out to save me? Why this sudden burst of compassion for me?'

Poonguzhali was silent. The question seemed to have startled her. After some time, she said, 'Idiots have always induced pity in me.'

'Good to know that. How did you know those men were looking for me?'

'One look at you, and it's obvious you're a fugitive. I guessed yesterday. My suspicions were confirmed thanks to your friend, the physician's son.'

'He blabbed to you, did he? What did he say?'

'The moment he woke up, he said he had to go look for herbs in the forest. I brought him here. As soon as we were alone, he started professing his love for me. I told him, "But your friend has beaten you to this," and ...'

'What did you say?' gasped Vandiyadevan, incredulously.

'Hold on. Have some patience. I told him you had professed your love for me already. That was when he told me of his suspicions about you. Apparently, your demeanour and a series of incidents on your way here had led him to believe you were running away from some punishment to which you had been sentenced by royal decree. "Don't trust someone like that and fall into ruin. Marry me!" he told me. I said, "You seem to be in a terrible hurry! Shouldn't we first consult the elders?" "No, no, let's elope. That would be in accordance with ancient Tamil custom!" your wonderful friend said. Would you believe it!'

'Ada sandaala paavi!'[4] Vandiyadevan shouted.

'We heard the sound of horses' hooves right then. I asked him to climb the tree and look. His legs shook so much as he tried to balance himself on the tree. It makes me laugh even to think of it,' Poonguzhali said, and began to giggle.

'Enough with the fun and games. What happened next?'

'He clambered down the tree and told me, "See! It's as I said. The royal guards are here to arrest him." I said they would arrest him, too, in that case, since he'd accompanied you. "You should run and hide somewhere," I told him. "Yes, I should," he said. And now, it's all just as I thought ... I knew this would happen.'

'What? What happened?'

'He told me he was going to run and hide, and then went straight to where those guards were, and got apprehended.'

'Aiyo! The poor fellow!'

'Don't waste all your pity on him. Hold on to some of it.'

'Why do you say that?'

'Hear me out, won't you? He went straight to them. They were astonished. They kept staring at him, and then began to whisper amongst themselves. "Who are you all?" your *poor fellow* asked. "We're huntsmen," one of them said. "We're here on a deer hunt." "No, I know exactly what hunt you're on," your friend said. They seemed surprised, but tried to provoke him into revealing what he knew. "You're here for Vandiyadevan," he said. "I'll take you to him. In return, will you promise to spare me?" They agreed. He then led them straight home.'

'The traitor! Sandaalan!'

'As soon as they left, I came looking for you. And you were bathing in the sea ...'

'Why didn't you tell me all this right there? Why take my clothes and make me run all the way here?'

'Would you have come running here if I hadn't done what I did? For all I know, you'd have insisted on taking on all those soldiers and set off right to your death. Or, you'd have refused to believe me. By the time I'd convinced you, they would have found you'

Vandiyadevan wondered how he had ever thought this brilliant young woman was insane. How foolish he had been. He could trust her with his very life. Anyway, he couldn't go to Lanka unless he sought her help. If he failed to persuade her, his entire journey so far would have been pointless, and he would likely end up at the receiving end of the Pazhuvettaraiyar brothers' tender mercies.

'Penne! I cannot tell you what a great favour you have done me. It's all up to you now. You have to help me complete my mission.'

'What are you asking of me?' Poonguzhali looked at him.

'You've now seen my friend's true colours, haven't you? You understand it's pointless trusting him, don't you? Now, it's up to you to ferry me to Lanka.'

Poonguzhali was silent.

'Do you have faith that I am trustworthy? That I have no evil intentions? Penne! I have a crucial mission in Lanka. I absolutely have to go there. You simply *must* help me ...'

'And what will you give me in return?' Poonguzhali asked.

Vandiyadevan looked at her. For the first time, there seemed to be a hint of shyness in her mien. A dimple played by the side of her lips. Her cheeks were slightly flushed. The glow that infused her face made her several times more beautiful than she already was.

She had asked that question in his dream. Vandiyadevan was tempted to reply as he had in the dream, but then bit it back, remembering the consequences his subconscious had furnished.

'Penne! If you help me out now, I will never forget it for as long as there is breath in my body. I will be forever indebted to you. I can't think how to repay you, but I will do anything you ask.'

Poonguzhali looked thoughtful. She appeared to be contemplating whether to tell him what was on her mind or not.

'If you have a return favour in mind, ask me right away. I'll do whatever it is you want.'

'Do I have your word?'

'Yes, you do. I promise.'

'In that case, I'll ask when the time comes. You won't forget by then, will you?'

'Never, ever. I will be waiting for the day I can clear my debt to you.'

Poonguzhali seemed to turn this over in her head.

'Hmm, all right, come with me. I'm going to take you to a spot in the forest. You must remain there until dusk. You'll have to starve.'

'Oh, that's no problem. Your anni[5] gave me stale rice this morning. I ate a lot of it just to irritate her. I won't be hungry until nighttime.'

'I can't promise you'll have food at night, either.

I'll try bring you some. Remember, you must not move until dusk. Once night falls, I will come for you. I'll give you a signal. Have you heard the koel's "koo ... koo ..."?'

'Yes, I have. Even if I hadn't, I'd recognise your voice anyway.'

'When you hear my voice, you must come out of the hiding spot I show you. We will only have a jaamam after dusk to get away in the boat.'

'I'll be waiting for the koel's call.'

Poonguzhali led him to a spot where the ground had swollen into a hillock of sorts, right in the middle of the forest. On the far side of the hillock, the foliage was abnormally dense. Poonguzhali moved the boughs aside with a practised hand and seemed to disappear through a tree into a hole in the ground. Vandiyadevan followed her. He could make out the outlines of what seemed to be an old ruin. When he peered into the dark, he could discern a couple of pillars. Trees and grass had grown over it all. No one could spot the ruin from anywhere around, unless one knew exactly how to get inside.

'A leopard used to live here. I'm the next occupant. I see it as my own home. When I want to get away from people, I come here. There's some water in that pot there. Make sure you stay here all day. Whether you hear voices or horses or whatever, don't so much as peek outside,' Poonguzhali said.

'Even once it gets dark? What if some wild animal,

a tiger or leopard, gets in here?' Vandiyadevan asked.

'There's no tiger or leopard here now. If at all, you'll come across foxes and wild boar. Are you scared of those?'

'I'm not scared. But what will I do if they pounce on me? I don't even have my spear here. I left it behind.'

'Here's a weapon for you,' Poonguzhali said, and turned to fetch something. It was a bizarre weapon. On both sides, it had thorns that were razor-sharp, and even stronger than iron. Perhaps this was how Indra's vajrayudha[6] would look.

'What kind of weapon is this? What material is it made of?' Vandiyadevan asked.

'This is the tail of a fish. When the leopard that used to live here attacked me, this is what I used to kill it,' Poonguzhali said.

7

'SAMUDRA KUMARI'

The day passed fairly quickly for Vandiyadevan. He spent half the daylight hours sleeping. The hours that he was awake, he devoted to reflecting on Poonguzhali's unique character.

What a wonder she was, he thought. What a lovely name she had, one that rolled off the tongue ... and yet, her nature appeared to be so very stern, even harsh. But was she simply harsh? Or did her abrasive behaviour hide a certain vulnerability? She had spoken so very casually of killing a leopard. And then, there were times when she acted like a lunatic. To what could this be attributed? Perhaps she had been through a particularly traumatic experience at some point in her life? Or, perhaps a particularly exhilarating experience? Either could have driven someone to insanity. Maybe he was overthinking it. Perhaps he was imagining a past that did not exist. This odd nature of hers might well be congenital.

Her parents seemed quite normal, pleasant and calm. How was her mental makeup so very different? Well, that's as may be, but what had driven her to care so much for him, to strike up such a rapport and form such a close bond? She had made supreme efforts to ensure he was not caught by the men from Pazhuvoor. And she had promised to row him to Lanka. Was she up to something? Was this a trap of some sort? No, he could never believe that. What had prompted her to change her mind, though? And what was this return favour she had made him promise he would do her? Why had she insisted she wouldn't tell him what it was until later? What could it possibly be?

Even as he was mulling this over, he realised Poonguzhali had predicted quite correctly that the forest would be filled with sounds of commotion through the day. He could hear raised human voices, the hooves of horses, running feet, the panicked cries of frightened animals, the screeches of birds ... these would rent the air for a while, and then the world would sink into absolute silence. Those sounds were surely owed to a manhunt for him? He thought often of the physician's son's betrayal.

What a moron! That idiot had decided he was in love with Poonguzhali at first sight, it seemed. It was as absurd as the stagnant water in a pond aspiring to subdue the Vadava Mugagni[1], the final conflagration that would subsume the earth. Or a mouse hoping to marry a lioness. And yet, this girl had put the man's foolishness to some use. How easily she had roused his jealousy! All it had taken to turn him into a traitor was half a naazhigai of conversation with her. It was incredible, the power a beautiful woman exercised.

Vandiyadeva, you must admit something to yourself. You thought you were quite the smart one. No one could match you for your wiles, you thought. And yet, this wild girl who has never known civilisation has beaten you hollow! Would anyone else have thought up a scheme to drag you from the open sea into this ancient, hidden ruin as she did? If she hadn't run away with your clothes, what would have become of you? You'd have been apprehended by the Pazhuvettaraiyar brothers' men, that's what. No, you cannot ever afford to be so cavalier about your own safety, not anymore.

The sun sank into the west end of the ocean. Even today, the sunset at Kodikkarai is a sight. The coastline, which runs along the South, takes a sharp turn towards the West at one point. So, if one stands at a height, one actually has a vision of the sea stretching in the eastern, southern *and* western directions all at once. During some months of the year, one can watch the sun set and moon rise together, one sinking in a molten ball into the ocean and the other lighting up the water as it ascends.

There were seasons when the sun appeared to grow out of the ocean to the East and then settle back into the waters in the West. Vandiyadevan ached to watch this storied sunset, but resisted—with great effort—the temptation to climb to the top of the hidden ruin.

The darkness was closing in. Sitting inside the ruin, where the light had been dim through the day, Vandiyadevan felt that the blackness had intensified manifold. Finally, unable to bear it any longer, he crept outside and stood on top of the mound that cloaked the ruin. He could see the flare from the lighthouse at a distance. The stars twinkled like diamonds glinting in sunlight. The forest produced strange sounds, vastly different from those of the day. The nocturnal sounds seemed to carry sinister notes, as if to induce fear in one's heart and raise goosebumps on one's flesh. One could come face to face with a tiger at daytime, and feel no fear or panic. But the tiniest stir among the twigs at nighttime, a rat scampering through the leaves, could startle one.

There it was, the 'koo-koo' of the koel. It felt like divine music to Vandiyadevan's ears. He walked in the direction from which the sound came. Poonguzhali was waiting for him.

She signalled to him to follow her in silence.

The seashore was nearer than he had thought.

Her boat was all rigged and ready. The sail and the ropes that bound it had been rolled into a neat package. There were two stout rods at an angle to the boat, with a wooden staff tied across to secure them.

Vandiyadevan stepped forward to help Poonguzhali push the boat onto the water. She signalled that he must move away, and leave her to it.

She manoeuvred the boat onto the water expertly. It didn't make a sound as it slid into the sea.

Vandiyadevan was preparing himself to jump onto the vessel, when Poonguzhali hissed, 'Ushhh! Hold on for a bit. You can get on once I've pushed the boat farther out.'

She was dragging the boat forward by the ropes. Vandiyadevan couldn't keep himself from helping her, and pushed the boat. It promptly got stuck in the silt.

'All I need is for you to keep from interfering,' Poonguzhali said.

Once they had crossed into deeper water, where the waves were more subdued, she said, 'Now, we can get on the boat.' She leapt into it first. Vandiyadevan followed her, and nearly toppled the boat. He thought he would fall into the water himself, but managed to hold on. His heart was pounding.

'Now we can talk, can't we?' he asked.

'Sure, we can. Once you stop trembling and are able to talk,' Poonguzhali said.

'Trembling? Who's trembling? Nothing of the sort.'

'Sure, if you say so.'

'Don't we need to rig the sail?'

'That could make us conspicuous. The people looking for you on the shore might come catch us.'

'If they approach, I'll deal with them. You don't have to worry anymore,' Vandiyadevan said, and readied to give her an account of his various valorous feats.

'The wind is against us now. If we rig the sail,

we'll go right back to the shore. The direction of the wind will change after midnight. The sail will be of use then,' Poonguzhali said.

'Oh, you really do know your craft. That's why your father said I should go with you.'

'My father? Whom are you talking about?'

'Your father, the lighthouse keeper Tyagavidanga Karaiyar.'

'He's my father only when I'm ashore. Once I'm out at sea ...'

'You can change fathers when you're out at sea?'

'Yes. Here, it is Samudra Raja who is my father. My other name is Samudra Kumari. Has no one told you?'

'No. What sort of name is that?'

'Don't some people call the emperor's younger son "Ponniyin Selvan"? This is quite like that.'

The moment she said the name, Vandiyadevan's hands reached instinctively for the pouch in his waistcloth, which held the scroll.

'It's safe, isn't it?' Poonguzhali, who had noticed this, asked.

'Is what safe?'

'Whatever you've tucked into your waistcloth.'

Vandiyadevan's heart skipped a beat. A gnawing suspicion troubled him.

Poonguzhali was rowing even as she spoke to him. The boat was gliding along.

'How long before we reach Lanka?' Vandiyadevan asked.

'If both of us row, we'll be there by dawn, provided the wind is in our favour,' Poonguzhali said.

'I'll row too. Would I leave you to do all the hard work?'

He took up the oar that was by his side and began to row. Ah! This was no easy task, he thought. It took immense effort to handle an oar. The boat turned round once, and then came to a complete stop.

'What is this? When you row, the boat moves. When I do, it stops,' he said.

'I'm Samudra Kumari, aren't I? That's why. I told you, all I need is for you to stay without interfering. I'll get you to Lanka one way or the other. Isn't that enough?'

Vandiyadevan felt embarrassed. He sat in silence for a time. Then, his eyes fell on the two rods and the wooden staff that secured them.

'What is this contraption for?' he asked.

'So that the boat won't rock too much.'

'It can rock more than this? It's already so unsteady. I feel dizzy.'

'You call this unsteady? You should see it in the months of Aippasi and Kartigai.'

From the shore, the sea had looked still as a plate. Now, Vandiyadevan knew that had been an illusion. The waves didn't froth, but they did rise. And they were rocking the boat like it was a cradle.

'What will happen to the staff when there are strong winds?'

'It depends on how strong the winds are. Usually, the staff keeps the boat steady even when the wind blows hard. But if there's a gale or something, and the boat were to capsize, the only use we can put the staff to is holding onto it for dear life until we can swim to safety.'

'Aiyo! The boat can capsize?'

'Enormous trees splinter into bits in a gale. What is this tiny boat going to do to fight it?'

'What exactly is a gale?'

'Are you really so clueless? When two opposing winds clash, it causes a gale. During the months of Thai and Maasi, we have the Kondal Kaatru, the wind which poses no danger at all. You can cross quite easily from Kodikkarai to Lanka. You can, in fact, go there and come back through the night. From the month of Vaigaasi, we have the Sozha Kaatru. It is a little harder to go to Lanka at the time. We're now between the time of the Sozha Kaatru and the Vaadai Kaatru. Sometimes, the winds can clash at sea. Then, the air churns the water like a whisk churns curd. You'll see waves higher than mountains, and enormous troughs in the sea. The water then begins to swirl inside the troughs, forming a whirlpool. If the boat gets caught in one of those, well, it's haro-hara[2].'

Vandiyadevan felt a surge of panic. He was besieged by doubt.

'Aiyo! I'm not coming! Take me back to shore!' he shouted.

'What are you on about? Shut up now. If you're scared, close your eyes. Or go to sleep.'

Now, Vandiyadevan's suspicions grew stronger. 'You're a traitor! You're planning to throw me overboard. That's why you've lured me out to sea. If I go to sleep, I'll make your job easy!'

'Are you out of your mind?'

'No, I'm not! Are you going to turn the boat around or not? If you don't, I'll jump into the sea!'

'By all means, jump. But before you do, give me the olai you're taking for Ponniyin Selvan.'

'How did you know about the olai?'

'By untying the knot you'd made in your waistcloth. Do you think I'd have consented to rowing you to Lanka without knowing who you were and what your mission was? When I was sitting up in the tree this morning, I read the scroll.'

'You evil woman! What a fool I am to have trusted you. Are you going to turn the boat around or not, now?'

Vandiyadevan's panic and rage had entirely consumed his power of reasoning. He began to scream, 'Turn! Turn the boat! Turn the boat!'

'If I'd been in Ilaiya Piraatti Kundavai Devi's place, I'd never have entrusted such an important scroll to a raving lunatic like you,' Poonguzhali said.

'Oho! So you know who gave me the scroll too, do you? There is no doubt now, you're the very embodiment of evil. Are you going to turn the boat around? Or shall I jump into the sea?'

'Jump, by all means,' Poonguzhali said again.

Vandiyadevan, who was by now all but possessed, jumped right into the sea. He had figured the water would be shallow, as it had been by the shore. He hadn't realised the boat was so far out as for him to go underwater. It was only after he jumped that he discovered this was far deeper than bathing distance. Now, he began to wail and howl.

He had, by this time, learnt to swim to some extent. Yet, his inborn fear of water weakened his limbs. When one was neck deep in lake—or even river—water, one could draw strength from looking at the shore. But in the ocean, there was no land in sight. The waves, although gentle, did nevertheless play about with him, throwing him into troughs one moment and carrying him up crests the next. When he was riding the crest of the wave, he could see the boat and yell out. When he was in its lap, he was surrounded by walls of water that closed in and strangled the screams in his throat.

The third time a wave carried him upwards, the boat seemed far away. Vandiyadevan was convinced this was it—he was destined for a watery death. And it was not just he who would drown. His waistcloth and the olai secured within would accompany him to his grave.

Kundavai Devi's face floated before his eyes. *How could you have gone and done this?* she seemed to be asking.

Aha! What dreams he had nursed! How many castles he had built in the air! He would restore the Vaanar clan to its former glory, and sit on a throne embedded with precious gems with Ilaiya Piraatti by his side, he'd thought. All those dreams had gone to hell. This terrible woman had ruined it all. She was no woman. She was a demon, an evil spirit, in the guise of a woman. She was an ally of the Pazhuvettaraiyars. No, no, she was an ally of that other Mohini Pisaasu, Nandini herself.

His death would be worth it, if only he could get hold of this demoness and strangle her before ... chhi, chhi, what sort of thinking was this? One should think positive thoughts, at least when one was dying. He would think of God. Umapati! Parameshwara! Lord of Pazhani! Lord Vishnu, who rests on the ocean of milk ...

Kundavai Devi, please forgive me. I have failed to complete my mission. There, I can see the boat. If only I could get my hands on that demoness.

For a while after Vandiyadevan had thrown himself into the sea, Poonguzhali remained unconcerned. He would swim—no, splash—his way to the safety of the boat, one way or another. Let him suffer a bit. She rowed some distance away to teach him a lesson.

But soon enough, she realised she had been wrong. He was a poor swimmer. His screams were not put on. He was genuinely terrified for his life. He was on the verge of swallowing the salty water. Then, he would sink without a trace. It would be impossible to retrieve even his body. Chhi, chhi! She had erred. She had taken the game too far. She would hold her peace until they reached the Lankan shore. She should never have let on that she knew his secret. But who could have predicted that this lunatic would do as he had done? Or that anyone could be so scared of water?

The next time Vandiyadevan appeared on the crest of a wave, Poonguzhali began to row towards him. She was by his side in no time.

'Come on, get on the boat!' she called.

But he did not seem to have heard. Even if he had, it didn't appear he was going to do as she had asked. He had lost his senses of hearing and sight. But the capacity to scream remained strong. He raised a hand, lifted his head up to the sky and howled.

Poonguzhali instinctively knew it was the howl of a man who had lost all hope and all faith, and had readied himself to die. The crescent moon cast a dim glow over his upturned face. He wore the expression of a madman. There was little point in hoping he would have the presence of mind to navigate to the boat. She would have to pull him aboard. She'd dug her own grave. The saying *Pennbudhi pinnbudhi*—women could only understand things retrospectively—was right, she thought.

She threw herself into action. She took hold of one end of the rope that was being used to secure the sail and tied it to the wooden staff, and wound the other end around her waist. She then jumped into the water, and sluiced through the waves to where Vandiyadevan was splashing about. She stopped at an arm's distance from him.

When Vandiyadevan noticed her, his face and eyes began to burn with an insane rage.

His murderous expression frightened Poonguzhali. She knew how much strength and how little sense one had when one was in the throes of death. Anyone in Vandiyadevan's place would hold onto the neck or shoulders of a prospective rescuer, immobilising the latter, from an instinct to cling to safety. The will to live would give them the strength of an elephant. They would use all that strength to hold down the rescuer, who would be helpless, able to neither get free nor stay afloat. Both of them would end up drowning.

Thinking at the speed of lightning, Poonguzhali made a decision. Vandiyadevan was trying to come closer. She navigated the waters so that she was right behind him. She then threw an almighty punch at his face. Her fist landed between his nose and forehead.

The impact, from arms grown sinewy through years of rowing on the choppy seas, hit Vandiyadevan like the vajrayudha itself. His head burst into a million pieces, and his eyes into ten million. Before each piece, a hundred thousand stars swam. And within each of these stars, Samudra Kumari's face appeared, laughing like a demon. His ears were splitting from the ghoulish laughter of a hundred million demons.

He could not hear. He could not see. He could not think. He could not remember. All that remained were absolute darkness and unbreakable silence.

8

BHOOTA THEEVU[1]

The Sky Goddess Vaana Mahadevi, seems to be just about as bright as the human species. Humans tend to let God, who is Paranjyoti—the Great Light—slip out of the firmament of their hearts, and then seek him out by lighting a hundred thousand lamps in the prakarams[2] of gloomy temples and musty sanctum sanctorums.

Vaana Mahadevi, too, commits just as intelligent an act every day. She lets the luminous Surya Bhagavan slip out of her grasp into the sea in the evening. Then, she feels the pangs of separation from her beloved, and she lights a hundred thousand lamps to search for him. Does she stop there? No, she lights millions of ever-flaring torches and stays up through the night to look for him.

When Vandiyadevan came to, and opened his eyes, he saw those lights from millions of torches flaring above him. He wondered which temple this was that had been so beautifully ornamented by the devoted. Then, he realised they were not lamps, but stars shining in the sky. He looked about himself, and understood he had been positioned to one side of the boat. A rope was tied across his waist, over his wet clothes. The cool wind sent little thrills down his spine, and filled him with a sense of comfort and calmness. The hum of the tranquil ocean sounded like the omkara to him, and brought with it peace of mind.

And yet, through that hum, he could hear a song. What song was this, and where had he heard it before?

> *Vaaridiyam adangi nirkka*
> *Maarudamum tavazhndhu vara*
> *Kaarigaiyen ulandanile*
> *Kaatru suzhandradippadumen?*
> *Alaikadalum oyindirukka*
> *Agakkadaldaan ponguvaden?*
>
> *While the ocean has been tamed.*
> *And the wind crawls to a halt,*
> *Why, within my woman's heart,*
> *Do whirlwinds hold sway?*
> *While the sea drifts to sleep,*
> *Why do waves crash within?*

Aha! It was that strange girl, Poonguzhali! He sat up and looked about the boat. Yes, it was indeed she. She was rowing the boat, singing that plaintive song. And then, like a sudden bolt of lightning that illuminates in an instant a world cloaked in darkness, the events of the previous night hit Vandiyadevan's memory all at once ... that is, up to the point where Poonguzhali had come to his rescue when he'd been floundering in the waves.

He couldn't remember a thing after. She must have pulled him out of the water, to the safety of the boat. She would then have secured him to the thwarts of the boat with rope, so he wouldn't fall overboard in case they ran into turbulent waters. And she had tied it over his waistcloth so that his skin wouldn't chafe from the rope. Vandiyadevan checked his pouch instinctively and made sure the scroll and his gold coins were safe.

Aha, what an error of judgment it had been to suspect this woman's intentions. She had had no cause to save him. She could have simply let him die, and would have if she'd nursed the evil thoughts of which he had accused her. How much effort it must have taken her to haul his lifeless body onto the boat! How had she done it all by herself? She was quite an incredible woman, he thought.

She had risen now. What for, Vandiyadevan wondered. Had she noticed that he had come to? What was she going to do once she had neared him? No, no, she was up to something else. She was going to hoist the sail on to the mast, all by herself! What a tough job she was taking on!

'Poonguzhali! Poonguzhali!'

'Oho. You're up, are you?'

'Untie me. I'll help you.'

'The greatest help you can give me is to do nothing. You can untie yourself if you want. But don't go and jump into the sea again.'

Vandiyadevan undid the ropes that bound him.

Poonguzhali raised the mast and fastened the sail. Now, the boat gathered speed as it sluiced through the waves.

'Samudra Kumari!'

'What, now?' asked Poonguzhali.

'I feel thirsty.'

'What do you expect, after swallowing all that salty water?'

She brought him a calabash filled with water.

'I'd packed food for you, too, but that toppled over when you jumped overboard. Thankfully, this calabash was spared,' she said, as she lifted the lid and showed him the water.

Vandiyadevan took it and drank his fill. He cleared his throat and found his voice again.

'I was mistaken about you. I feel embarrassed,' he said.

'That's of no consequence. Who are you and I to each other, anyway? Once the dawn breaks, we will be separated.'

'What hour is it now?'

'Look at the sky and figure it out. Look at the saptarishi mandala[3],' Poonguzhali said.

Vandiyadevan trained his eyes on the northern

sky. The saptarishi constellation had changed position since he had first got on the boat. The constellation had moved half a circle, he thought. How Arundhati trailed Vasishtha, never leaving his side![4] That *was* a wonder. And yet, the Dhruva Nakshatra[5] alone hadn't changed position. It never did. For how many epochs it had stood its ground, in that peculiar place where the sky and the sea met, and how many seafarers and traders had found their bearings through the offices of that star!

The Dhruva Nakshatra ... it had been compared to someone ... to whom? And who had made the comparison? Yes, he remembered now—it was the astrologer of Kudandai. He had compared Prince Arulmozhi Varmar to the Dhruva Nakshatra.

Am I really going to have the honour of meeting the prince? Vandiyadevan wondered. *Because of this woman's help?*

Poonguzhali went back to her seat.

'Have you figured out the hour? We're halfway through the third jaamam. The wind has changed direction. We'll be at Naga Theevu[6] by daybreak,' she said.

'Naga Theevu?' Vandiyadevan asked, startled.

'Yes. There are many islands in the northern part of Lanka. Naga Theevu is one of those islands. If you disembark there, you can reach the Lankan mainland by foot, without having to plead for a ride again.'

'What will you do once you've rowed me there?'

'What does it matter to you?' Poonguzhali asked.

'You've done me such a good turn. Do I not owe you thanks? You told me you'd ask me for a return favour. What is that?' he asked.

'I've changed my mind about that. I'm not going to ask you for anything. You're an ingrate.'

That was a fair observation, Vandiyadevan reflected. He felt his pouch once more, and ascertained that the scroll was safe.

'Samudra Kumari! I'm ashamed of my behaviour, of having suspected your intentions. Please forgive me,' he said.

'Right. And *you* forget about it. Think about what must be done next. What will you do once you disembark? How will you find the prince?'

'The very god who helped me cross these waters will help me find the prince.'

'You set great store by god. Do you think He invests Himself in the petty concerns of us insignificant mortals?'

'I haven't interrogated that issue. When I'm in trouble or in danger, I pray to god. He tends to send me timely help, for His part. Didn't He send you to row me across the ocean?'

'You think too highly of yourself. I didn't agree to row you across from concern for *you*. And god didn't appear to me in a dream with instructions to help you out, either ...'

'Then why did you save me? Why are you ferrying me across now?'

'That's no business of yours. It's a personal matter of mine.'

Vandiyadevan sank into silent contemplation. A thought cropped up in his conceited mind. Perhaps this woman was infatuated by his good looks and warrior's build? But he changed his mind about that in a moment. Her demeanour and words allowed no scope for such a thought. There was something else to it. He'd have to draw it out of her.

'There *is* something that worries me ...' he began.

'What is that? You're capable of worrying, are you?'

'They say Lanka is full of hills and forests ...'

'More than half of Lanka is hill and forest.'

'They say there are lots of wild animals about ...'

'There are herds upon herds of wild elephants in the forest. Sometimes, they even wander outside it.'

'I've heard that the people of Lanka are absolute savages.'

'That is entirely untrue.'

'Oh, all well, then. If you say so, it must be right. Now, I'll have to find Prince Arulmozhi Varmar in this wild, forested landscape.'

'You said just now that that would pose no difficulty?'

'Yes, I did. I had thought at first that one could have no trouble finding where the sun is.'

'And why do you think otherwise now?'

'The clouds could hide the sun. Or, he could have sunk into the sea.'

'No cloud or sea could possibly hide this sun. Any cloud that attempts to cover Ponniyin Selvar will glow; the sea, too, will shimmer.'

How fervent she sounded when she spoke of the prince! This woman, like so many other subjects of the Chozha empire, saw the prince as a god. What magnetic power did Arulmozhi Varmar wield that captured so many hearts? As these thoughts ran through his head, Vandiyadevan asked, 'So, you're saying I'll have no trouble finding the prince, are you?'

'If you go around enquiring where the Chozha army is, you'll find the prince at some point.'

'How is that? I've heard that the Chozha army is spread out across half of Lanka?'

'Yes. I, too, have heard that the Chozha army has taken over the entire swathe from Mathottam to the city of Pulastya.'

'What, then? Who knows where the prince is, in such an enormous swathe of land? It could take me a long time tracing him through the forest. You've read the scroll for yourself. You know how urgent this is, don't you?'

Samudra Kumari made no reply to this.

'If I knew where exactly the prince was, I could go straight to him without wasting precious time,' Vandiyadevan said.

'There *is* one way' Poonguzhali said.

'I knew you'd come up with something.'

'I said I'd drop you off at Naga Theevu in the morning, didn't I?'

'Yes!'

'There's another island by it, called Bhoota Theevu.'

'The very names of these islands inspire fear.'

'Don't be afraid. The island was actually named "Bodha Theevu". Legend has it that when the Buddha first came to Lanka, it was upon this island that he set foot. He sat under an arasu tree on the island, and began to preach Buddhism. That is how it got its name.'

'And then it got corrupted to "Bhoota Theevu"?'

'Yes. People like you are so daunted by the name that they avoid the island. Now, it's largely abandoned. Only people who are not afraid of bhootams go there.'

'In other words, bravehearts like you. You're not scared even of the kolli vaai pisaasu, no? Right. What were you going to say about Bhoota Theevu?'

'If you can wait a naazhigai by the Bhoota Theevu shore, I'll find out Ponniyin Selvar's whereabouts and tell you.'

'Whom will you ask, in Bhoota Theevu?'

'There's a bhootam in Bhoota Theevu. I'll ask it.'

'You'll introduce me to that bhootam, won't you?'

'I'm afraid I can't do that. You must not follow me onto the island. If you promise me you'll stay by the shore and watch the boat, I'll find out about Ponniyin Selvar and tell you.'

'Fine, as you wish,' Vandiyadevan said.

The wind was refreshing. The sail helped them

along considerably, and the boat flew through the waters. The omkara of the ocean echoed in their ears.

Vandiyadevan's lids were heavy with sleep. He slipped from wakefulness to stupor.

9

'THIS IS LANKA!'

When Vandiyadevan next slipped out of slumber and opened his eyes, the vista before and around him astounded his senses. To the East, the sun was rising. The sea, simmering in the early warmth, was of molten gold. Udayakumari, Lady Dawn, was radiant in her raiment of golden silk. An emerald island wearing the colours of the sea loomed right ahead, in the direction in which the boat was headed. Towards the right, another land mass in lush green attire appeared. From where he was, Vandiyadevan couldn't quite tell whether it was surrounded by water or was a part of a larger swathe of land. Between these two emerald islands, several others appeared in a varying palette of green. When he looked around himself, the world was awash with the seven colours of the rainbow and the seven thousand shades different proportions of those colours could produce. All in all, it was an incredible sight, which he found quite impossible to believe was real. It was as if the world's greatest artist had vowed to capture Swargalokam on his canvas and then stretched it across the world.

As Vandiyadevan stood, forgetting himself in the beauty in which he was immersed, the words, 'This is not swargam, this is Lanka!' brought him back to earth.

'Yes, it *is* true I was wondering if this was swargam,' Vandiyadevan said.

'This is not Swargabhoomi, but a piece of bhoomi in the guise of swargam. And for aeons, asuras in human disguise have been doing their best to turn this swargam into narakam, heaven into hell,' Poonguzhali said.

'Whom are you referring to as "asuras"?' he asked.

'People like you, whose vocation is war.'

'Ponniyin Selvar too?'

'Why are you asking me about him?'

'You said you'd make your enquiries about the prince, didn't you?'

'I said I'd make my enquiries about his whereabouts. I didn't say I'd enquire whether he was a man or an asura or a deva, did I?'

The boat was approaching the islands now. The omkara of the ocean had given way to the 'sala-sala' of waves lapping the shore.

'So, what do you want me to do? The island ahead of us is Bhoota Theevu, and the one to the right is Naga Theevu. Shall I let you off at Naga Theevu? Will you find your way to the prince yourself?'

'No, let's go to Bhoota Theevu. Even if it causes a bit of a delay, it's best to figure out where the prince is and then make directly for that place.'

'In that case, well ... make sure you don't forget your promise to me.'

She steered the boat towards the smaller of the islands. Asking Vandiyadevan to keep an eye on the boat, Poonguzhali disappeared into its emerald foliage.

As he watched her go, Vandiyadevan wondered how 'Bodha Theevu' had been corrupted to 'Bhoota Theevu'. Next, he wondered what kind of personality the resident bhootam might have. Then, he wondered what secret this inscrutable young woman carried in her heart.

Poonguzhali returned within a naazhigai, as promised. She got onto the boat, and asked Vandiyadevan to follow her. The boat now made for Naga Theevu.

'Were you able to find out?' Vandiyadevan asked.

'Apparently, Prime Minister Aniruddha Brahmarayar has gone to Mathottam to meet Ponniyin Selvar. The prince should have reached Mathottam yesterday. Can't say how long he'll stay. Go there and find out,' Poonguzhali said.

'How far is Mathottam from here?'

'Five or six kaadhams. And the path goes right through the forest. Don't think this is like the Kodikkarai forest. This is so dense the trees seem to reach right up to the sky. There are parts of the woods that are dark as night in broad daylight. Herds of elephant and other wild animals roam the forest. You must be careful.'

'If only a clever girl like you would guide me through the forest ...' Vandiyadevan sighed.

'Then what purpose do you serve? Give me the olai. I'll go hand it over ... no, no, I can't. I'm going on like a madwoman. No, there is no way I can. You promised Ilaiya Piraatti, didn't you? It is you who should deliver it,' she said.

'As you say, Poonguzhali. I'll deliver it myself. I won't hand it over even if someone else offers. You've helped me so much, that's enough,' he said.

The boat was nearing Naga Theevu. Poonguzhali's arms plied the oars effortlessly, but her expression made it obvious that her thoughts were elsewhere, in some dreamland.

'Samudra Kumari!' Vandiyadevan called.

She came back to earth with a start. 'Why did you call me?'

'You asked me for a return favour. We're almost at the shore. Tell me what it is now.'

Poonguzhali did not reply right away. She appeared to be in deep contemplation. This emboldened Vandiyadevan to say, 'You've done me a huge service. Not just me, you've rendered a service to the Chozha empire itself, to the clan of the Chozha emperor himself. If I don't return this favour in some way, my mind will never know peace.'

'Do you mean what you say? Or are you making false promises like all other men?'

'I swear before Samudra Raja.'

'So, just words on water, then.'

'I swear upon the goddesses of the sky and earth, Akashavani and Bhoomadevi, the palakas who guard the eight directions, the Sun God Suryan and the Moon God Chandran.'

'I'm saying this not because you've sworn an oath. Do the makers of false promises fear the consequences of breaking an oath? I'm telling you because you struck me as a good man the moment I set eyes upon you …' said Poonguzhali.

'The first impression is the best impression. There's no need for you to change yours.'

'Once you've met Ponniyin Selvar and handed over the scroll, and told him all there is to tell, find a time when he's in a relaxed mood and ask him if he remembers Samudra Kumari. If he says he does, tell him she was the one who ferried you to Lanka.'

Poonguzhali! How high you have set your sights! How far you seek to fly! Can a little sparrow hope to inhabit the same skies where the Gagana Raja Garuda, the mighty eagle who is king of the firmament, soars? This will not end well for you, will it? Vandiyadevan thought.

Aloud, he said, 'Is this what you hesitated so much to ask? I thought you were going to demand some huge labour of me. I'll tell the prince for sure. Even if the subject doesn't come up, I'll tell him!'

'Aiyayo! If the subject doesn't come up, you don't go and tell him anything.'

'Nothing doing. I *will* tell him!'

'What will you tell him?'

'I'll tell him what happened, as it happened. "Ilavarase! Ponniyin Selvare! You remember Samudra Kumari, don't you? Even if you don't, remember her from this moment on. She's the one who saved me from the Pazhuvettaraiyars' murderous men. It is she who ferried me to Lanka, rowing a boat all by herself. It is she who rescued me as I floundered about in the sea and carried me aboard to safety. If it weren't for Samudra Kumari's help, I could never have got here alive and met you. This scroll would never have reached you!" That is what I'll tell him. Is that all right?'

'What you've said so far is all right. But don't go and improvise anything else. Don't go and blab that I was the one who asked you to tell him all this!'

'Tchah, tchah. Do you think I'm entirely insane?'

'If the prince responds to your story, you must tell me exactly what he said, as he said it. Not a word less, not a word more.'

'How will I meet you again?'

'How difficult is it to meet me? I'll be in either Kodikkarai or Bhoota Theevu. Or on a boat between the two.'

'If I come this side on my way back, shall I look for you in Bhoota Theevu?'

'You must never go beyond the shore of Bhoota Theevu. Everything will go awry if you do. See if this boat is anchored off the island. If it is, then give me some kind of signal. I cooed like a koel yesterday, remember? Can you do that?'

'No, but I can caw like a peacock. Here, have a listen!'

And Vandiyadevan cupped his hands over his mouth and made a horrid screeching sound, exactly like a peacock. That sent Poonguzhali into a paroxysm of laughter.

The boat nudged the shore of Naga Theevu. They both alighted. Vandiyadevan bade Poonguzhali farewell as his feet touched land, and she began to manoeuvre the boat around. Vandiyadevan turned to watch her with longing. Wouldn't she say, 'I'll come along too?' and hop back on to the island? But she took no notice of him. Her face had already taken on the dreamy look it did when she slipped into her world of fantasy.

10

ANIRUDDHA BRAHMARAYAR

Our good friend with whom we've been acquainted since the very beginning of this story, Azhvarkadiyaan Nambi, has been ignored for a fair bit. The readers and Nambi are requested to forgive this trespass. It is crucial that we ask Nambi's forgiveness, for Azhvarkadiyaan is on the boil as we speak. His topknot is flying in the sea breeze by the Rameshwaram shore. His staff is swirling in circles over his head. He is surrounded by an army of Adi Shaivites and Veera Shaivites[1]. They seem to be creating quite the commotion, which makes us worry for the safety of Azhvarkadiyaan. But the speed with which he is whirling his stick and his appearance—evocative of the Narasimha avataram[2]—are somewhat reassuring.

Azhvarkadiyaan had left Pazhaiyarai right after eavesdropping on Vandiyadevan and Ilaiya Piraatti. He had rushed down south, not even stopping to enter into Shaiva–Vaishnava quarrels en route. He wanted to avoid all obstacles to his mission, so not only did he refrain from starting such quarrels but he also brushed off the ones that came his way. He halted in Madurai for some time. Once he'd learnt what he had set out to, he headed for Rameshwaram. The evening of the very day Vandiyadevan reached the shores of Lanka saw Azhvarkadiyaan enter Rameshwaram.

The moment he set foot on that hallowed earth, all the passion of Azhvarkadiyaan's Vaishnavism breached the fragile barriers he had erected and swelled to a flood. The flames of this passion were fanned by the Veerashaiva Bhattars swarming the streets of Rameshwaram. Their job was to escort pilgrims to the various tirthas, show them where they could take a holy dip, give them a darshan of the temple deity and speak of the uniqueness of that particular tirtha and deity. So, the moment they spotted a newly-arrived pilgrim, they would crowd around him, peddling their faith. Azhvarkadiyaan, thus, found himself at the receiving end of their zeal.

'Appane! Come, come! Take a holy dip in each of the sixty-four tirthas in this sthalam and wash off the Vaishnavite marks from your body. Isn't this the place where Lord Rama washed off the sin of Brahmahathi[3]? You, too, can wash off the sin of wearing this horrendous Vaishnavite mark all over your body,' one of the Bhattars said mockingly.

Another interrupted with, 'There are sixty-four tirthas named after Rama, Lakshmana, Anjaneya,

Sugreeva and the rest—each tirtha is named after the person who washed off his doshams[4] there. Come to the Anjaneya Tirtha with me, and I'll do the right sankalpam[5] and resolve the dosham of the Vaishnavite caste mark.'

Yet another said, 'Appane! Don't listen to them! I'll take you to the very spot where Rama fashioned a Shivalingam from beach sand, and prayed for forgiveness and release from the Brahmahathi dosham he had invited by killing the brahmin Ravana.'

Sparks flew from Azhvarkadiyaan's eyes as he glared at each one in turn and said, 'Enough! Stop your heretic rants. Go wash your tongues in the very tirthas you mentioned and rid yourself of the sins of your words.'

'Oho! You think we've accumulated sin by speaking the names of Rama and Lakshmana, do you? No, no, don't worry on that account. This place is called "Rameshwaram"; this is the kshetra where Rama prayed to Eeshwara—Shiva—and rid himself of his sins. And so the dosham associated with the name "Rama" has also been washed away,' a Veerashaiva Bhattar said mockingly.

'O you manifestations of ignorance! Each of you makes less sense than the other. Do you really not know the meaning of the name of this place?' asked Azhvarkadiyaan.

'Do enlighten us, then!'

'Shiva incurred the Brahmahathi dosham by lopping

off one of Brahma's heads. He came to this place, the earth hallowed by the touch of Tirumaal's purest avataram Rama, to free himself from that Brahmahathi dosham. It is called Rameshwaram because this is where Eeshwara prayed to Rama. Do you understand now, you beacons of foolishness?' Azhvarkadiyaan roared.

'Who is that who dares call us "beacons of foolishness"? Dei thadiya[6]! Think you've grown kombu on your head?'[7] a Bhattar seethed.

'No, aiya, Bhattare! I haven't grown kombu on my head. I only carry a kombu in my hands. You asked who I am, didn't you? I'll tell you. You know Nammazhvar, who was born in Tirukuroor, and translated the Vedas into Tamil? I'm the devotee of his devotee, the adiyaan of his adiyaan! And I'm a thadiyaan, too, who uses his thadi to break the heads of heretics!' Azhvarkadiyaan declared, swinging his stick over his head.

'Azhvarkadiyaarkadiyaane![8] Why do you have a tuft in front of your head? If you shave it off, your head will be in harmony—empty inside and empty outside,' another Shaivar said.

'Bhattargale! I had planned to tonsure my head at this holy site. You've reminded me just in time.'

'Ade! Go to the Navidar street and bring a Navidan[9] along. Ask him to sharpen his knife and come prepared to yank this man's tuft out by its very roots,' called out one of the Bhattars.

'Why bother the Navidan? Let's do the honours

ourselves. Bring a sharp knife, now!' another Shaivar chimed in.

'Hold your horses. You see, once upon a time, I had a full head of hair. I then swore an oath that I would pluck off one hair for each Shaivite whose crown I broke. So, most of my hair is now gone, and three-quarters and a half-quarter of my head is bald. I plan to pluck out the rest before I leave, so that I fulfil my oath. So, why don't you line up and offer up your heads in turn, you Shaivite numbskulls?' Azhvarkadiyaan said, holding his stick as if poised to break a proffered head.

'Adade! Will you look at the gall of this Vaishnavite!'

'You'll break all our heads, eh? You think you can do that, eh?'

'Would I have rid myself of the hair on three-quarters and a half-quarter of my head if I couldn't?' Azhvarkadiyaan asked, and began to swing the staff around his head again.

'Hit him! Catch him! Bind him! Hack him!' the assembly cried, but not one of them stepped close enough for Azhvarkadiyaan to hit.

At that moment, a commotion broke out so close to them that everyone's attention was diverted.

'All hail Tribhuvana Chakravarti Sundara Chozhar's most honoured prime minister, Aniruddha Brahmadi Rajar! Paraak! Paraak!'

The startled assembly turned as one towards the source of the sound. Azhvarkadiyaan, most startled of all, tucked his staff under his arm and looked on too.

The site of their quarrel was a corner by the walls of the Rameshwaram temple. Once one turned that corner, the ocean spread out as far as the eye could see. It was among the most wondrous sights one could imagine. Enormous freighters, large passenger vessels, cruise ships, pleasure boats, dinghies, catamarans, rafts and coracles dotted the waters. The huge sails swollen with the wind were as clouds that blocked out one's vision of the sea and the sky and the islands beyond.

Surrounded by boats carrying criers who announced his arrival, the Chozha empire's renowned prime minister, Anbil Aniruddha Brahmarayar, stood regally on a vessel making for the shore.

Once he had disembarked, he noticed the crowd gathered by the temple and sensed something was afoot. He singled out Azhvarkadiyaan, who was standing with the appearance of an ascetic, his staff tucked meekly under his arm, and gestured for him to come forward.

Azhvarkadiyaan approached the prime minister, his hands folded and head bowed in reverence.

'Tirumalai! To what do we owe the therukoothu[10]?' Aniruddhar asked.

'My guru! This is all the tirukoothu[11] of Krishna, the sutradhar of deception. I am not sure whether to believe what I see before my eyes. Is this a dream? Or is it all illusion, maya?'

'Tirumalai, I thought you were a devout Vaishnavite.

Since when have you turned into a Mayavadi who goes on about illusion, saying all the world is maya?'

'O guru! When you, who were born into a staunch Vaishnavite tradition, can embrace Shaivism, why should I not be a Mayavadi? I'm going to change my name to Shri Shankara Bhagavad Padachariyin Adiyaarkadiyaan ...'¹²

'Hold on, hold on. Who told you I have embraced Shaivism?'

'The marks on your hallowed skin told me.'

'Aha! Tirumalai! You haven't changed a bit. You've always given too much importance to appearances. Why does it matter whether I apply the caste mark horizontally or vertically? It's three lines one way or the other, isn't it?'

'O guru, I'm an ignoramus. I don't know what is important and what is unimportant. It is you who must undertake to clarify things for me.'

'I'll make everything crystal clear. Now, come see me where I'll be staying. You see that little island in the sea? There's a mandapam there. Come there.'

'My guru! These Shaivites who are spoiling for a fight must let me pass,' Azhvarkadiyaan said, sweeping his arm to indicate the might of the army that opposed him.

The Shaivites, who had been mute spectators thus far, now stepped forward.

'Brahmadi Rajare! This Vaishnavite claims he will break our heads! He must be given the punishment he deserves,' one of them said.

All at once, everyone else began to speak.

Aniruddhar broke through the cacophony of voices with, 'I'll punish him, don't worry. You may disperse.'

But that did not mollify them.

'Can we not do the honours ourselves? We'll chop off his munkudumi[13], wipe off his Vaishnavite marks, dunk him in the well and ...' began one.

'What did you say?' Azhvarkadiyaan said, sparks flying from his eyes again.

Aniruddha Brahmarayar intervened to tell the Shaivite, 'You may be the bravest among Bhattars, but this man is a terrible rogue and ruffian. There is no way you can handle him. Leave it to me.' He then turned to the posse of soldiers accompanying him and said, 'Eight of you escort this man to our mandapam.'

At his word, eight soldiers leapt on to the shore from the guard boat and surrounded Azhvarkadiyaan.

Aniruddhar's boat departed for the island.

Azhvarkadiyaan wordlessly allowed his escort to walk him to one of the other boats.

The gaggle of Bhattars dispersed, muttering to themselves about the Vaishnavite's demeanour and lack of decorum.

11

THERINJA KAIKOLA ARMY

In one of the little islands that dotted the sea by the coastline along the grand port of Rameshwaram was an ancient mandapam, in which Aniruddha Brahmarayar held court. Around him were the various aids and aides that a minister needed to go about his work. The accountants who maintained the books, the Tirumantra Nayagars in charge of inscribing decrees on palm leaves, the in-house bodyguards, all stood at the ready to take orders.

Not long after Aniruddhar had disembarked and settled down in the mandapam, he ordered that those who were waiting to see him be called in.

First in the queue were five men whose appearance suggested they were traders with considerable prosperity and influence. As their offering, they had brought a navaratna malai[1] on a plate.

Aniruddha Brahmarayar received it, handed it over to one of the accountants and said, 'Please do write that this must be used for Sembiyan Mahadevi's divine altruism.' He then turned to his guests and asked, 'Who are you?'

'We are here on behalf of the Nanadesa Disaiaayirathu Ainootruvar[2],' one of them responded.

'I'm glad to welcome you. I believe your trade is going well in Pandiya Naadu?'

'Yes, it grows by the day.'

'What is the word among the people of Pandiya Naadu?'

'They say the rule of the Chozha clan is far superior to that of the Pandiya dynasty. Most importantly, they are all praise for the compassion of Prince Arulmozhi Varmar. Word of all that is happening in Lanka has reached the people of this region.'

'And how is your trade with the countries across the Eastern seas going?'

'We lack for nothing under Sundara Chozha Chakravarti's rule. Through the last year, every ship we have sent from here has returned safely. We haven't lost a single one to shipwreck or other damage.'

'And there is no problem from the sea pirates?'

'Not in the last year. Since the Chozha naval force defeated the pirates who would attack us off the Maanakkavaara island, we have no reason to fear for the safety of our ships on the Eastern seas.'

'Good. And what arrangements have you made with regard to what we'd mentioned in the scroll we had sent across to you?'

'We've done as we were commanded to. We've brought a thousand bags of rice, our corn harvest and a hundred sacks of pulses to be sent to the Chozha army in Lanka. Arrangements must be made to ferry them from Rameshwaram to Lanka.'

'Can you send them on your own ships?'

'If that is your command. We would like to know when the war in Lanka will end.'

'Ah! Who can answer that question? Your union has an astrologer, doesn't it? Why don't you ask him and let me know what he says?'

'Brahma Rajare! We ourselves are hard put to believe what our astrologer says.'

'What has he said that is so incredible?'

'He says victory is assured everywhere that Arulmozhi Varmar goes. That, under his rule, the Chozha navy will cross the seas and win great victories. That the tiger flag will fly in far-off countries.'

'In that case, you have plenty to celebrate.'

'True. He has also said our trade will prosper even further.'

'I'm delighted. With Lord Sriranganathar's blessings, it will all happen as he says. Until the war in Lanka is over, you must send the same food stock to Lanka every month. Do come to see me again.'

'We will do as you command. We take your leave.'

Once the representatives of the Ainootruvar Sabha had left, a soldier came in and said, 'The generals of the Therinja Kaikola Army are waiting. They wish to meet you.'

'Ask them to come in,' said the prime minister.

Three strapping warriors entered. In the face and mien of each, Veeralakshmi had made her home. One glance at them, and you could tell they knew no fear.

If our readers will permit a diversion, the Kaikolas—who have been reduced to eking out a living as handloom weavers in today's Tamil Nadu, battling shortages of material—come from a lineage of great warriors who battled enemies of the Chozha empire. Handpicked from among them were elite soldiers who were then drafted into the emperor's personal guard, or the 'Aga Parivara Army'. This army was also known as the 'Therinja Kaikola Army', usually prefixed by the name of the emperor whom the warriors served. And now, let us get back to Aniruddha Brahmarayar's court.

'You are the Sundara Chozha Therinja Kaikola Padaiyaar,[3] yes?' Aniruddhar asked.

'Yes, aiya! But we are ashamed to call ourselves by that name.'

'Why so?'

'We've wasted the last six months here, fattening ourselves on the emperor's largesse.'

'How many warriors does your army comprise?'

'Ours is a three-pronged army. He is the commander of the Idangai, and he the commander of the Valangai. I am the commander of the Naduvirgai[4] army. In each of these divisions are two thousand warriors, all of whom have done nothing but eat and sleep since we were stationed here. It won't be long before we forget the art of war.'

'What is your request to me?'

'We request you to send us to Lanka. We wish to be part of the army that Arulmozhi Varmar commands as Mahatanda Nayagar[5].'

'As you wish. I will meet the emperor and ask his consent when I go to Thanjavur and let you know.'

'Brahma Rajare! What if the war in Lanka ends before then?'

'You need have no fear on that count. The war shows no sign of ending anytime soon.'

'Oho, so the soldiers of Eezham are so very formidable, eh? Send us over! We'll show them what's what.'[6]

'You'll show them what's what thrice over. Does one even have to guess the fate of the opposition once the Therinja Kaikola Army steps in? The Naduvirgai army will attack the opposition's middle regiment. The Idangai soldiers will take on the left flank at the same time, while the Valangai soldiers will ambush them from the right. You'll fall on them like thunder and smite them like lightning.'

'That was how we put paid to the Pandiya army and decimated the Cheras.'

'You took on the Pandiyas and Cheras in the battlefield. Unless you have your opposition in your sights, how will you show them what's what, be it once or thrice?'

'Why, have the soldiers of today's Lanka done as the asuras of Ravana's time and turned into Mayavis who disappear into thin air? Are they fighting the war from the celestial skies?'

'They have disappeared into thin air as Mayavis do, all right! But they are not fighting a war. If they were, we'd know where they were, wouldn't we? The Lankan king Mahinda is nowhere to be seen, and neither are his soldiers. We don't know where they are hiding, in the forests or the hills. And so, the last six months have seen a stalemate. What would we achieve by sending you there to join our men?'

'Mahamantri! Give us a chance. Send us over, and see what we do. Mahinda and his men could be hiding in the hills and forests. Or they could be hiding in the celestial skies. But we'll smoke them out and drag them to the prince, and throw them at his feet. If we don't do this, we will change our name from "Therinja Kaikola Army" to "Velaalar's[7] Slave Army".'

'No, no, please don't swear such oaths. Who in Jambudvipa can claim to be unaware of the Therinja Kaikola Army's heroism and fidelity? I will ask the emperor the moment I reach Thanjavur and send word to you. Please be patient until then. Keep the enemies at bay in Pandiya Naadu and ensure that there is peace.'

'Mahamantri! There is no enemy to keep at bay in

Pandiya Naadu. The people are glad the war is over. They lead peaceful lives as farmers and traders and artisans. The Pandiya dynasty has been decimated.'

'Oh, no, please don't think the dynasty has ended with Veerapandiyan. That is wrong. There are those who lay claim to the Pandiya throne, and those who conspire on their behalf too.'

'Aha! Where are those conspirators? Tell us! Take us into confidence!'

'You will learn by yourselves when the time comes. The ancient jewelled crown of the Pandiya dynasty, the ratnamala that was given to them by Lord Indra, and the diamond-studded sword are all hidden away in Lanka even now, somewhere in the hill kingdom of Rohana. Unless those are retrieved and secured here, the Pandiya war cannot be said to have ended.'

'So, the treasures must be retrieved. And Prince Arulmozhi Varmar must be seated on the throne in Madurai, wearing the ancient jewelled crown and the ratnamala and the diamond-studded sword.'

'Aha! What is this talk now?'

'It is the articulation of what is on the people's tongues and in the soldiers' hearts.'

'These are huge decisions that must be made by the royals, and commoners like us should not speak of such things. I'm going to tell you something else of importance now, something that will gladden your hearts.'

'We are all ears, Mahamantri.'

'The war will not end with victory in Lanka. Once we win that war, Prince Arulmozhi Varmar will leave on expeditions of conquest in every direction. He will take a thousand ships filled with soldiers and sail the Eastern seas. Manakkavaram, Mabappalam, Mayirudingam, Kadaram, Ilamuri, Srivisayam, Savagam, Pushpakam will all bow down to that great warrior. He will then head South and bring all of Munneerpazhanteevu under the Chozha domain. He will go West and bring Keralam, Kudamalai, Kollam and other kingdoms to their knees. He will turn his sights to the North, and take his armies to Vengi, Kalinga, Irattapadi, Chakrakottam, Angam, Vangam, Kosala, Videgam, Koorjaram and Panjalam. He will equal the feats of our legendary Karikala Valavan and fly the Tiger Flag from the Himalayas. O brave commanders! These are the plans of the Mahatanda Nayagar of our Southern Front. All the men through whose veins flows heroic blood and in whose chests beat the hearts of the strongest diamond will find plenty of work. Each of these men will have a chance to show his valour on the battlefield. So, there is no need for you and your Therinja Kaikola Army to lose your patience.'

The three commanders chanted in one voice, 'Long live Sundara Chozha Chakravarti! Long live Prince Arulmozhi Varmar! Long live Mahamantri Aniruddhar!'

Then, one of them spoke again. 'Mahamantri!

There is just one other appeal we wish to make to you. You know we go by the name "Sundara Chozha Therinja Kaikola Army".'

'Yes, this is a fact.'

'We have pledged with hands reddened by the blood of our enemies that we will even give up our lives in serving Sundara Chozha Chakravarti.'

'I'm aware.'

'And so, we will not serve anyone but the emperor. And we will not obey anyone else's command either.'

'Yes, and it must be so.'

'Once upon a time, we made up a division of the Pazhuvettaraiyars' grand army. That should not give anyone reason to suspect us now.'

'Aha! What kind of utterance is this? Who has ever suspected you?'

'All manner of rumour reaches us about what is going on in Thanjavur. The wind whispers things.'

'Let the whispers of the wind fly away with that very wind! There is no call to believe these rumours. Or repeat them.'

'The Kodumbalur Velaalars might rake up some suspicion against us …'

'They will not. Even if they do, no one will pay any attention.'

'Mortal life is not everlasting …'

'That should give true warriors no cause to fear for their lives.'

'Even the Emperor of the Three Worlds must one day …'

'Reach the lotus feet of God.'

'And the emperor's health is not promising ...'

'A comet has been spotted in the skies!'

'If something bad were to happen to the emperor, our army wishes to be part of the Aga Parivaram of Arulmozhi Varmar.'

'It is your duty to let us know the emperor's will and wish. Please take on the responsibility of telling us what he commands us to do. Or, allow us to go meet him in Thanjai!'

'No, it would not be prudent for you to go to Thanjai. It will create unnecessary trouble. I will take it upon myself to meet the emperor and let him know your wishes. You can relax on that count,' said Aniruddha Bramarayar.

'The burden in our hearts has disappeared, now that we have told you what is on our minds. We take your leave.'

And with that, the three commanders of the Therinja Kaikola Army left.

'Aha! What is this strange power Ponniyin Selvar wields that draws everyone to him? Even those who have met him only once are quite mad for him,' Aniruddha Brahmarayar said under his breath.

Then, he said aloud, 'Ask that militant Vaishnavite to come in now!'

12

GURU AND SHISHYA

At this juncture, we'd like to tell our readers about a particular incident from the history of this Tamil land's governance. In the zila of Tiruchirapalli, in the taluk of Lalgudi, was a village called 'Anbil'[1]. Those who came in from the northern lands translated this into 'Premapuri'. About forty-five years ago,[2] a farmer from this village decided to demolish his old home and rebuild it from scratch. As the ground was being dug up for the foundations to be laid, a strange item was uncovered. A number of copper plates with inscriptions were loosely bound by a ring running through a hole punched into a corner of each plate. These were enormous plates, so heavy that they could hardly be carried by two men. The farmer held on to them for a while.

Then, R.S.L. Lakshmana Chettiar arrived at this village to take on the devotional task of temple renovation. The farmer handed over the copper plates to him. Lakshmana Chettiar figured that the inscriptions on the plates might reveal valuable historical information, and so he took them to Mahamahopadhyaya Swaminatha Iyer, who in turn realised that the inscriptions were of critical importance and gave them to T.A. Gopinatha Rao, who was involved in epigraphic research at the time. The epigraphist was beside himself with joy— the inscriptions contained hitherto unknown details about the Chozha royal dynasty.

Within four years of his ascension to the throne, Sundara Chozha Chakravarti had given his 'Maanya Mantri' Aniruddha Brahmarayar ten velis[3] of land, and the details of this grant had been inscribed on the copper plates. The scribe who had etched these details, Madhava Bhattar, had also named the Chozha rulers right up to Sundara Chozhar. Along with this, he had written about Aniruddha Brahmarayar's Vaishnava heritage and the stellar service his father, mother, grandfather and great grandfather had rendered at the Sriranganatha temple.

This information not only reiterated what had been etched into the copper plates unearthed at Anaimangalam and Tiruvalangadu, thereby establishing the historical accuracy of the recorded events, but also contained certain details that were missing from the other two sets of plates. So, the Anbil copper plates have a place of great prominence in the historical research of the Tamil lands.

We ask that our readers go ahead with the

story, equipped with the knowledge that Aniruddha Brahmarayar was such a distinguished personage as to have had a royal inscription devoted to his lineage.

~*~

Azhvarkadiyaan entered the hall where Aniruddha Brahmarayar was seated. He went around the seat thrice, and then fell prostrate at the minister's feet.

He then shouted 'Om Hraam Hreem Vashattu'[4] four times, his voice echoing round the chambers, and then said, 'Gurudeva! Please allow me to take leave of you.'

Aniruddhar smiled and said, 'Tirumalai! To what do we owe this grand show? And why are you asking to leave?'

'I intend to wash off the Sri Vaishnava samprudayam[5], the name "Azhvarkadiyaan", and the honour of serving you in this great sea, and embrace the Veera Shaiva Kalamugam[6] samprudayam instead. I'll wander the earth with a skull in hand, chanting the holy mantra "Om Hraam Hreem Vashattu". I will grow my hair into matted locks and I will sprout a thick beard on my face, and split the skull of every Sri Vaishnavite I see with this staff ...'

'Appane! Stop! Stop! Is that the end my own skull is fated to meet?'

'Guru! Do you still follow the Sri Vaishnava samprudayam?'

'Tirumalai? Why would you think otherwise? Whom have you taken me for?'

'Whom should I take you for? This is the issue that's troubling me. You are the great grandson of Anbil Anantazhvar Swamigal[7] who made it his life's mission to serve Sri Ranganatha, who guards all the worlds in our cosmos from between two rivers, yes?'

'Yes, appane. I am, indeed.'

'And you are the illustrious grandson of Anbil Aniruddha Bhattacharyar[8] who took it upon himself to spread knowledge of the greatness of Srimad Narayana across the entire land?'

'Yes. I am, indeed. I was named after that great man, wasn't I?'

'And the very own son of Narayana Bhattachari, who sang the beautifully sweet songs of the Azhvars, dripping honey into the ears of crores of devotees and bringing them to a state of ecstasy?'

'Yes, appa, yes!'

'And the son of that iconic woman who lit the nunda vilakku[9] every day in the temple with the golden hall where Sri Ranganathar lies on his snake bed in the ocean of milk, and who served devotees food on silver plates, and who performed stellar service to the Lord?'

'Without a doubt.'

'In that case, do my eyes betray me? Is what I see before me a lie? Is what my two ears have heard a lie?'

'What are you referring to, appane? What has occurred to make you suspect your own eyes and ears?'

'I heard with my ears that you had gone to the Shiva temple in this town and done an abhishekam-archanai[10] at the shrine.'

'That is true enough. Your ears haven't betrayed you.'

'Then, perhaps the marks of your having been to a Shiva temple, which my eyes discern on your gracious self, are not an illusion either.'

'That is, indeed, the case.'

'Are you not my guru, who taught me that in this Kaliyugam, Srimad Narayana is the one true God, and that the pasurams of the Azhvars are our vedas, and that the naamasankeertanam[11] of Hari alone will allow one to attain moksha?'

'Yes. What of it?'

'If the guru says one thing and does something else, something that is the very opposite of what he preaches, to what path does the shishya have recourse?'

'Tirumalai! You're referring to my darshan at the Shiva temple, I presume?'

'Gurudeva! Of which god did you have darshan at the temple?'

'Why would you have such a doubt? Narayana murti, who else?'

'But I've heard that there is a lingam inside the Rameshwaram temple. Isn't that why those Shaivite bhattars swarmed around me?'

'Pillaai![12] Is it not true that you have taken on the name of Adiyaarkadiyaan—the servant of the servant[13]—in honour of our Sadagopar who manifested himself in Tirunagar?'

'Surely there is no need for doubt on this account?'

'Stir your memory up for Nammazhvar's divine words. And if you've forgotten them, let me remind you:

Lingathitta puranateerum
Samanarum saakyarum
Valindu vaadu seiveergalum matru nun
Deivamumagi nindrane!

You who speak of the Lingapuranam
And you who follow Jainism,
And you who follow Buddhism,
And you who discuss theology, know that
My God stands as your God too.

'When Sadagopar himself has seen fit to recite these words, is it wrong that I saw Narayana in a Shiva lingam?'

'Aha! One can't do better than Sadagopar for words. Look, he has lumped Shaivites together with Jains and Buddhists!'

'Appane! I wonder whether your twisted mind with its penchant for sarcasm will ever set itself straight. Here's another one from our Sadagopar:

Neerai nilanaai theeyaai kaalaai neduvaanai
Seeraar sudargal irandaai Shivanaai Ayanaai
Ullavan Sri Narayana Murtiye

As water, land, fire, air, and space,
As the radiant sun and moon,
As the antaryami of Shiva and Brahma,
It is our Sri Narayana Murti who transforms.

'And there's more, more for you to hear, Tirumalai, to get rid of the filth in your heart:

Muniye naanmugane mukkannappa
En pollaak kanivaai thamaraikan karumaanikkame!
En kalva! Thaniyen aaruyire enthalai misaiyaai vandittu

Ascetic with four faces and three eyes
With a mouth like sweet fruit and lotus eyes
A black gem, my black gem, my Lord!
The very life of the person that I am,
You have honoured me by entering my mind.[14]

'You hear this, Tirumalai? Sadagopar says "Mukkannappa", and asks the Three-Eyed Lord to enter his mind. And you're resentful of my having gone to a Shiva temple!'

'Gurudeva! Please forgive me. Pardon my blasphemy. Not knowing every pasuram that Nammazhvar has written has made me waste my days in pointless argument and prompted me to suspect you. You must grace me by granting me this wish.'

'Perhaps if I knew what this wish was, I could consider granting it.'

'I wish to go to Tirukkurugoor and stay there. I will collect all the songs Sadagopar has sung, every one of the thousand, and then travel from town to town spreading his word ...'

'And why has this desire taken root in you?'

'On my way back from Vadavengadam, I stopped at the Veeranarayana Perumaal Sannidhi and sang some Azhvar pasurams. Eeshwara Bhattar, the temple archaka, shed tears of joy when he heard those songs ...'

'Eeshwara Bhattar is a great devotee. A good shishya.'

'A young son of his was standing by, just a child. As he heard the words, his cherubic face began to glow like the full moon. He came up to me and asked with a mouth that had barely lost the scent of breastmilk, "Do you know other songs too?" I was embarrassed to admit that I didn't. I wondered at the time why I shouldn't dedicate myself to the service of the Azhvars and search out their songs. And now, I find that thought turning into a resolve.'

'Tirumalai, hasn't the Gitacharyar[15] said that each man must practise swadharma, the fulfilment of his particular duty?'

'Yes, Gurudeva!'

'There will be men, lots of them, to collect the pasurams of the Azhvars and spread the word. And there will be others to distil the Vedic philosophy contained in the songs of the Azhvars, collate them and translate them into the languages of the North in order to take them to those regions too. You and I have chosen royal service for our swadharma. Have you forgotten that we took oath to dedicate ourselves in mind, body and spirit to the service of the Chozha Chakravarti?'

'I haven't, Guruve! But I've been wondering whether that was the best course of action. This dilemma has been gnawing at my heart. Particularly, when I hear the things that are being said about you in some quarters ...'

'What are they saying?'

'That because the emperor has gifted you ten velis of land and had an inscription to that effect etched, you have cast aside the Vaishnava samprudaya. Some say you have cast aside the rules and restrictions of religion and creed, and crossed the seas although that would entail losing your caste status ...'

'There is no need for you to pay any heed to the ramblings of jealous tongues. They believe our caste requires us to be frogs in the well. It is true that the emperor has gifted me ten velis of land. And he has had that inscribed as well. But you do know that I became minister to the emperor four years before this gift was given, don't you?

Azhvarkadiyaan stayed silent.

'Do you, at the very least, know when my friendship with the emperor began? We were under the tutelage of the same teacher in our youth. We learnt Tamil and Sanskrit, along with mathematics, astronomy, astrology, theology, philosophy, grammar and everything else. No one could have dreamt at the time that Sundara Chozhar would be crowned king one day. Not he, not I. Who ever imagined that Rajadityar and Kandaradityar would pass away before their time, and that Arinjayar would ascend to the throne? When he was named the heir, Sundara Chozhar was worried that this could lead to several problems in future. He said he would only accept the title if I promised to stay by his side. He would reject it otherwise. I promised then that I would help him with matters of governance. And I am keeping that promise even now. Do you not know all this, Tirumalai?'

'I do, Gurudeva! But what is the point of my knowing all this? The public doesn't. The gossip-mongers don't.'

'There is no need for you to worry yourself about gossip-mongers. I myself have done some soul-searching about my decision to leave behind my heritage of service to the temple and accept a role in governance and in the overseeing of royal matters. But the last two days have dispelled the last remnants of my dilemma. Tirumalai! You do know that I didn't come here to pray at the shrine, but because it is the most convenient point for travel to and from Mathottam, yes?'

'I inferred as much, Gurudeva.'

'You inferred right. Mathottam is exactly as described by Sambandar and Sundaramurti long ago, nestled on the shores of the Paalaavi river.

Vandupannseiyum maamalar pozhil
Manjai nadamidumaathottam
Thondar naadorunthuthiseyya
Arulsei Ketheechura madhudaane!

Mathottam, where the white peacock dances,
Among bowers of flowers where the bees make music,
As devotees flock daily and sing praise
Of the lord of the Ketheeswara[16] *temple.*

'Could Sambandar have written these lines without having seen Mathottam for himself? Those frogs in the well claim he came to Rameshwaram and saw Mathottam from these shores. Why would you give any credence to what people like them say about anything?'

'Swami! Was it to admire the wonders of nature that you went to Mathottam?'

'No, I mentioned those wonders since I intend to send you there. It was to meet Prince Arulmozhi Varmar that I went to Mathottam.'

'You met the prince, Gurudeva?' Azhvarkadiyaan asked. It was only now that one could detect a note of enthusiasm, even eagerness, in his voice.

'Aha! So even you are interested in knowing about the prince, are you? Yes, Tirumalai. I met the prince and spoke to him. And I learnt for myself just how true the bizarre news we've been getting from Lanka is. Listen to me, appane! The Lankan king Mahinda had a huge army. Now, that army is gone. Do you know what happened? It simply evaporated like dew in the heat of the sun. Mahinda's army had many soldiers from the Pandiya and Chera kingdoms. The moment they learnt that our prince was leading the army, they laid their weapons on the ground and surrendered. Every last one of them asked to join our army. How, then, can Mahinda wage war? He disappeared. He's hiding somewhere in the Rohana Naadu, which is surrounded by hills. So, there are no enemies there now for our army to fight.'

'So why doesn't our prince come back with the army? What is the point of staying on there, with all this fuss about sending food from here to feed our men?'

'He *could* say there are no enemies and come back here. But the prince doesn't want to do that, and I don't think he should either. Once the prince and the army come back, Mahinda will come out of hiding. And then the same old war will start again. What is the point of that? Either the king and people of Lanka should become our friends and allies. Or, they should surrender to our rule, so the Tiger Flag will fly forever from that land. The prince is working towards both these possibilities. Do you know what our soldiers are doing in Lanka now? The city of Anuradhapura has been destroyed by all the old wars. The ancient Buddha Viharas, temples and Thathu Garbha gopurams are in ruins. As per the prince's order, our men are engaged in their renovation.'

'Wonderful. So, it appears our prince will shove both Shaivism and Vaishnavism aside and embrace Buddhism. Will you back him up on that too?'

'Whether you and I back him up or not is immaterial. Our "yes" and "no" mean the same thing. People like us can fight over the superiority of our respective religions. But the ruler of a land must encourage and promote every religion that his subjects follow. And the prince has realised this without anyone having to spell it out for him. And the moment an opportunity presents itself, he puts thought into action. Tirumalai, listen to this. They say, and you must have heard too, that our prince's hands have the sangu-chakram, the conch and discus, as birth marks. I haven't asked him to hold out his hands so I may examine the palms, but I can tell you this for sure. Whether he has the sangu-chakram or not, if there is one man who can bring the entire world under his rule, it is Prince Arulmozhi Varmar alone. Some time ago, a group of influential traders and then the generals of the Kaikkola Army came to see me. You must have heard them speak, yes? You see how these traders—men whose only concern is money—turn into philanthropists when it comes to the prince?

'A while ago, I saw a yogi meditating on the summit of the Podhigai hill. He is a clairvoyant. Do you know what he told me? *Yaanaikku oru kaalam vandhaal, poonaikku oru kaalam varum*. If the elephant has his day, so will the cat. The time has come for the

Southern lands to ascend to power. For aeons, it was in the Northern lands of this hallowed Bharatabhoomi that great emperors and valorous warriors and sublime poets and incredible intellectuals were born. But the Northern lands will soon be eclipsed. People from a savage creed will attack from the beyond the Himalayas and decimate those kingdoms. They will demolish temples and idols. Sanatana Dharma will be in great danger. At that time, our religion, Vedas, temples, ways of worship will all be safeguarded by the lands of the South. Emperors who are the bravest and most skilled of warriors will be born in these lands and conquer kingdoms in all four directions. Intellectuals, pandits and devotees of the gods will be born in these lands. These were the words of the Shiva yogi on the Podhigai hill. I am now confident that his prophecy will come true, Tirumalai.'

'Swami! You're building all sorts of castles in the air. But elsewhere, there are conspirators who intend to wreck the foundations of this empire, Gurudeva! If you had seen all that I have seen and heard all that I have heard, you could not possibly sound as cheerful as you do. You would be shaken by the threat that the Chozha empire now faces ...'

'Tirumalai, yes, I quite forgot. Enthusiasm and inspiration have clouded my mind. I haven't asked what you learnt on your way here. Tell me now, I'm all ears. However terrible the news, don't hesitate.'

'Swami, are you asking me to tell you all of that

right here? If Vayu Bhagwan were to hear the words I must utter, he will tremble. If Samudra Raja were to hear them, he would be stunned into stillness. If birds were to hear them, they would lose the power of flight and collapse. Akashavani and Bhoomadevi would sob. And you would have me speak of such matters in this place?' Azhvarkadiyaan asked.

'In that case, come with me. There is a cave on this island into which even the wind cannot sneak. Come there, and tell me what you have to say in detail,' said Aniruddha Bharmarayar.

13

PONNIYIN SELVAN

As Vandiyadevan was making his way to Mathottam from Naga Theevu, as Aniruddha Brahmarayar was talking to Azhvarkadiyaan about the state of the empire, Kundavai Devi and the Kodumbalur Princess Vanathi were seated inside the howdah atop their elephant, on their way to Thanjavur.

For some time now, Ilaiya Piraatti had avoided going to Thanjavur. There were various reasons for this.

For one, the Thanjai Fort did not have enough palaces within to accommodate the women in a separate building. They were compelled to stay in the emperor's large palace. The other palaces were monopolised by the Pazhuvettaraiyars and various important officials. In Pazhaiyarai, the women had the luxury of independence. They could go out as they pleased, and return when it suited them. If they were to stay at the Thanjai Fort, they would be bound by the rules the Pazhuvettaraiyars imposed. It would be impossible to make their entrances into and exits from their assigned palace, let alone the fort, at their whim. Ilaiya Piraatti did not like such conditions and restrictions.

Besides, the Pazhuvoor Ilaiya Rani's arrogance and sense of self-importance got on Kundavai Devi's nerves.

The emperor, too, preferred that the ladies of the royal household remain in the Pazhaiyarai Palace.

So, Kundavai Piraatti stayed back in Pazhaiyarai, stifling her instincts to be by her father's side and nurse him back to health.

But since Vandiyadevan's visit, Ilaiya Piraatti had had a change of heart. How could she possibly justify going on boating trips in the waters of the Pazhaiyarai palace, and dancing and singing in the gardens, when Thanjavur was teeming with traitors and conspirators? Her older brother was in Thondai Naadu, and her younger brother in Eezha Naadu. In their absence, did it not fall to her to sort out such matters? Aditya Karikalan had asked her to keep him abreast of what was happening in the capital through secret messengers. How would she know what was happening in Thanjai if she lived in Pazhaiyarai?

The news Vandiyadevan had brought had frightened her out of her wits. Before this, she had been irritated by the Pazhuvettaraiyars' propensity to overstep their bounds. But now it appeared they had designs on the throne itself. And they had drawn that poor, gullible Madhurantakan into their scheming. They had contrived to rope in several of Chozha Naadu's vassal kings and influential men, too. There was no way to predict what would happen and when it would happen. Who knew how far their aspirations and greed and cunning might reach? They could even pose a threat to the emperor's life. If he were to collapse when both his sons were away, it would become an easy matter to crown Madhurantakan the new king. There was no telling what the Pazhuvettaraiyar brothers might stoop to. And even if they were at a loss as to how to go about achieving this end, that rakshashi Nandini would come up with something. She would tell them what to do and if they hesitated, she would goad them into doing it.

It was imperative that Kundavai be by her father's side now. She would be able to keep her fingers on the pulse of this conspiracy. And she would ensure that her beloved father came to no harm.

Why did they want to install Madhurantakan, of all people, on the throne? So that justice would be done? No, absolutely not. They would be his puppet masters, pulling the strings from behind the scenes. And once this was accomplished, Nandini's word would be law. All of Chozha Naadu would have to bow to her authority. All the other women in the royal household would have to pay her obeisance. Chhi, chhi! Could Kundavai allow such a thing to come to pass? *No, not on my watch*, she thought. *Let me see just how smart and capable she is.*

Her stay in Thanjavur would be plagued by a host of inconveniences. Her parents would ask why she had chosen to leave the comforts of the Pazhaiyarai Palace behind and move here. She would have to give up all hope of independence. Someone or the other would bring up the subject of her marriage every time she made an appearance. There was little that annoyed her more. And she would inevitably run into Nandini, whose air of authority would grate on her, every now and again. But Kundavai couldn't allow such qualms to dictate her actions now. The kingdom was in great danger. Her father's very life could be in great danger. Under such circumstances, wasn't her place in Thanjai?

Besides all these considerations, there was another important reason—her desire to learn if there had been any news of Vandiydevan. She had heard he'd made for Kodikkarai, and that the Pazhuvettaraiyar brothers had sent men to capture him.

Would that street-smart young man evade capture? If he failed to do so, they would bring him straight to Thanjavur. In that case, it was imperative that she be in the current capital. They couldn't do as they pleased with Aditya Karikalan's messenger without consequences. They would have to fabricate an excuse, accuse him of a crime. They had laid the ground by claiming he had stabbed Sambuvarayar's son, Kandamaaran, in the back. It was, no doubt, a false charge. But she would have to prove it was false. It might be a good idea to talk to Kandamaaran and find out how reliable he was.

As Kundavai's mind was turning wheels within wheels and rearranging cogs and controls, her friend and companion for the journey had only one thing on her own mind—Vanathi's pristine heart, pure as milk, clear as marble, had dedicated itself to the question of when Prince Arulmozhi Varmar would return from Lanka.

'Akka, you said you'd sent an olai asking him to come home right away. If he does as you ask, will he make for Pazhaiyarai or Thanjavur?' Vanathi asked. What if he went to Pazhaiyarai while they were in Thanjavur?

Kundavai, who was lost in her own thoughts, turned to Vanathi and asked, 'Huh? Whom were you asking about? Ponniyin Selvan, was it?'

'Yes, Akka, I was asking about him. Akka, you've referred to the prince as "Ponniyin Selvan" several times, but you haven't yet told me why. You keep putting it off, saying you'll explain later. Can't you tell me, at least now? The Thanjavur Fort is some distance away. The elephant is walking at the pace of a tortoise.'

'If the elephant goes any faster than this, we won't be able to maintain our balance. We'll be on the ground, howdah and all,' Kundavai said, 'Adiyei! Do you know what happened at the Battle of Takkolam?'

'Akka! Tell me how the name "Ponniyin Selvan" came to be.'

'Adi kalli! You won't let go, will you? Fine, I'll tell you,' Kundavai Piraatti said, and began the story.

Sundara Chozha Chakravarti had just been crowned king, and his domestic life was an idyll. It was his wont to go boating with his family on the river Ponni. These outings were boisterous affairs, with the strains of the veena, the refrain of women singing, the antics of the children and the laughter of those who witnessed these antics mingling with the bubbling and gurgling of the waters. Sometimes, the children were sent off to play elsewhere on the boat while the adults conferred among themselves. At other times, everyone sat together.

Once, as the emperor, his queens and the children were on just such a pleasure trip, a panicked voice rose, asking, 'Where is the baby? Where is Baby Arulmozhi?'

The voice was Kundavai's. At the time, Arulmozhi was five years old, and Kundavai seven. Arulmozhi was the apple of every eye. But of everyone in the palace, it was his sister Kundavai who held him most dear. It was she who first noticed that he was not on the boat, and raised an alarm. Everyone was startled. They rushed about the decks, searching for the child. But even a royal boat is only so big. They looked and looked, in the same places, over and over again. There was no sign of the child.

Kundavai and Adityan broke into screams, the queens into tears and the maids into lament. Some of the boatmen jumped into the river and scoured the waters for the child. Sundara Chozhar dove in too. But where could one look? Who knew how far or in which direction the current had carried him? Who even knew when the child had fallen off the boat? There was no method to the madness with which they searched for him. The men went swimming in all four directions in pursuit of the prince. There was no sign of him. By this time, several of the women on the boat had lost consciousness. There was no one to tend to them. Those who retained their consciousness had lost all sense and sensation but pain. Their cries of 'Aiyo!' overwhelmed the omkara of the river, and scared the birds roosting on the trees by the shore into silence.

And then, there was a vision. It appeared in the swirl of the waters, some distance from the boat. A woman, bearing a child in her arms. The river rose to her hips, and only her face, chest and arms could be seen. The child's form hid most of her upper body.

Like everyone else, Sundara Chozhar, too, stared at this vision.

Then, he sluiced into the river and made for the woman. He held out his arms for the child. The boatmen steered the craft towards him. Sundara Chozhar had barely taken his son into his arms before the attendants reached down to hoist the prince, and then the king, up on the boat. Sundara Chozhar collapsed in a faint the moment his feet touched the deck. Everyone was preoccupied with reviving the royals, and no one knew what had become of the lady who had saved the child. Who was she? How did she look? No one seemed to have noticed. She never came forward either, to claim a prize for the service she had rendered.

And so, everyone decided as one that the river Kaveri had taken the form of a woman and saved the child. Goddess Kaveri was the baby's saviour. An annual puja was instituted on the anniversary of Arulmozhi's rescue. The darling of the palace was now Ponni's darling, Ponniyin Selvan. The members of the royal family, who had witnessed the miracle for themselves, largely referred to Arulmozhi Varman as 'Ponniyin Selvan'.

14

TWO FULL MOONS

Thanjai was in a tizzy that day. The entire town was brimming with excitement. The princess who had refused to visit for such a very long time had had a change of heart, and was finally about to grace their city. Could any resident of that place feel anything but exhilarated? Every living soul in Chozha Naadu had heard tell of the princess's beauty, intelligence, charm, compassion and generosity. Not a day went by without someone speaking of her in some context or the other, under some pretext or the other. Her very name brought them joy. A rumour had already done the rounds that the princess would be at the palace for the Navaratri[1] festival, and the residents of the city could not wait to find out whether it was true. When they learnt she was on her way, people thronged the streets, turning the city into an ocean of eager bodies. Just as the sea waters rise and jostle against each other in anticipation of the full moon, this sea of people all but bubbled over waiting for their own full moon.

Finally, the full moon did rise. Why, two beautiful moons rose at the very same time. Even as Kundavai Devi reached the outer walls of the city with her entourage, the doors of the fort were thrown open. The palace entourage made its way out to greet the princess and usher her inside. At its head were the Pazhuvettaraiyar brothers. And what's more, right behind them was an ivory palanquin studded with gems. When the silk curtains of the palanquin parted, the Pazhuvoor Ilaiya Rani Nandini Devi's lovely face appeared.

Kundavai dismounted the elephant. Nandini stepped out of the palanquin. Nandini hurried forward and greeted Kundavai with all the ceremony due to a princess. This pleased the latter, who acknowledged her welcome with a smile.

As they saw these two legendary beauties of Chozha Naadu together, the enthusiasm of the crowd was as a river that had breached its banks. Nandini's skin glowed as gold, while Kundavai's was infused with a lotus-pink tinge. Nandini had a round face that brought to mind the full moon. Kundavai Devi's face was the oval of a stunning statue, with contours crafted by celestial sculptors. Nandini's large black eyes were so dark it was as if they drew everything into them, leaving the whites laced with red blood vessels, the much-desired sevvari effect. They were wide-set with long lashes, and each looked like a honeybee with its wings abuzz. Kundavai's blue-black eyes unfolded like the petals of the neelotpalam flower, reaching nearly up to her ears. Nandini's nose could have been crafted from ivory, so fine it barely peeked out of her face. Kundavai's aquiline nose was the shape of a panneer flower bud. Nandini had full, soft lips, the red of coral glistening with nectar. Kundavai's lips were delicate and thin, like a pomegranate blossom just about to bloom, carrying all the promise of its honeyed juice. Nandini had arranged her hair into a bun, and ornamented each strand with flowers. As if to announce she was the queen of beauty, Kundavai's hair was in an updo, its layers bejewelled to resemble a crown.

We can't say the assembled crowd dissected and analysed the features of each of these two women as we have, but everyone was agreed that they were both unparalleled beauties, each with her own taste in ornamentation and her own regal bearing, vastly different from the other.

Until that day, the townspeople had looked at Nandini askance, not particularly pleased with her mien. Kundavai was a goddess to them. But as they saw the Pazhuvoor Ilaiya Rani honour the princess by receiving her personally at the gate of the fort, they found themselves marvelling at her graciousness and humility.

Even as the ocean of bodies around them swirled in delight, the dialogue between Nandini and Kundavai could have passed for a clash of thunderbolts, lightning striking lightning.

'Devi! Varuga, varuga ... welcome! We thought you had forgotten all about us. We now realise that Ilaiya Piraatti's compassion is boundless,' Nandini said.

'How do you say that, Rani? Is living far away tantamount to forgetting all about someone? Should I take your failure to visit Pazhaiyarai as evidence of your having forgotten me?' Kundavai asked.

'A flower in full bloom will draw honeybees without the need for an invitation. Anyone would visit a place as lovely as Pazhaiyarai. But for you to deign to set foot in this graceless, ugly Thanjai is evidence of the extent of your compassion, isn't it?'

'How can you speak as you have? Can one call Thanjai graceless and ugly when beauty itself has been imprisoned here?' Ilaiya Piraatti said.

'I've heard this, too, that the emperor has been imprisoned here. But there is no reason for us to worry on that account any longer. You have arrived to release him and give him his freedom, haven't you?' Nandini said, her eyes flashing.

'The things you say! Why, even Indra and his army of devas cannot imprison Sundara Chozha Chakravarti. How can lowly mortals aspire to this? I wasn't referring to that. I was speaking of Nandini Devi, who is the very epitome of beauty ...'

'Yes, you can say that again, Devi. Say it out loud. Say it so it reaches his ears. The King of Pazhuvoor has cosseted me away as if in prison. If only you could intercede and …'

'What could my intercession achieve? The prison in which he has cosseted you is no ordinary one. It is the prison we call love, isn't it? And that too …'

'Yes, Devi! And that too, an old man's love. There is no escape from such a prison, is there? I've heard tell of a dungeon here. People locked away in there can dream of release. Whereas …'

'Yes, Rani! Whereas, when our shackles have been worn of our own volition, when we have searched out a prison for ourselves, release is a complicated affair. And women who model themselves on Sita, Kannagi, Nalayini and Savitri[2] won't long for release, either … oh! What is that commotion over there?' Ilaiya Piraatti interrupted herself.

From some distance off, where a group of women had assembled a fair bit away from the entrance to the fort, there appeared to be an intense uproar. Kundavai and Nandini approached them, but with everyone talking all at once, they couldn't figure out what it was that the women wanted. Eventually, they realised the women were saying they wished to pay their respects to Ilaiya Piraatti as often as they could for the duration of her stay in Thanjavur, and to that end, they wanted the restrictions that governed entry into the fort suspended for the Navaratri period.

'Rani! Please speak to your husband or brother-in-law and have them grant these women's wish. Of all people, do these ladies pose a threat to the empire? Why fear them? Doesn't the Pazhuvoor brothers' influence spread in all four directions, right up to the seashore?' Kundavai asked.

'Why stop with the seashore? Their influence extends well beyond the seas. Their word is law on the other side of the ocean too. And there will soon be evidence of this,' Nandini said, with a smile that made Kundavai's blood freeze. *What could this wretch mean by those words?* she wondered. *They seem to be loaded with hidden connotations.*

By this time, Nandini had signalled discreetly for her husband to come up to them and told him of the women's request and Ilaiya Piraatti's wish.

'How can one possibly counter Ilaiya Piraatti's command?' Pazhuvettaraiyar said.

The entourage then entered the fort, to the deafening cheers of the assembled crowd.

From that day on, Thanjavur and its surrounds were in a delirium of bliss. Kundavai Devi's visit coincided with the Navaratri celebrations. Pazhuvettaraiyar, for his part, kept his word. There were no restrictions on entry and exit from the fort through those ten days. The doors of the fort were kept wide open all through, and people could come and go as they pleased. Within the fort, in the palaces and outside on the streets, there were events and programmes as part of the festivities. The people thronged the audience, and often, the two full moons could be spotted among them. The sight of those two beautiful women, seated side by side, thrilled the onlookers. But even as the air around them sparkled with cheer, each woman's heart was on fire. Why, they were veritable volcanoes, spewing lava that coagulated within the chambers the eruption had burned into those hearts. Pazhuvoor Ilaiya Rani and Pazhaiyarai Ilaiya Piraatti were engaged in constant battle. They had words for arrows and glares for spears. As their sharp swords clashed with each other, sparks flew. Spears with poison-laced edges burst into flame. Bolts of lightning flew into one another, both destroying themselves in the process. Tigresses lunged at each other and melted into a fatal embrace, the sharp claws of each drawing blood from the other's back. Two beautiful serpents reared their hoods and wound their forked tongues together, each trying to swallow the other whole.

This strange battle left them feeling exhilarated and devastated at the very same time.

And then there was another soul, suffering in silence, unable to join the festivities, unable to understand the cold war in which these two beauties were engaged. The Kodumbalur princess Vanathi barely found the time to speak to Ilaiya Piraatti. She accompanied her Akka everywhere. But she was lost to the world. She created an inner world for herself, of which she was the sole inhabitant.

15

A PRIMAL SCREAM AT NIGHT

It was a period when classical dance and music flourished in Chozha Naadu, as did drama. Several stalwarts of dance and artistes of the stage found their calling in Thanjavur. The Shiva devotee Karuvur Devar, who lived in that era, has mentioned 'Inji[1] soozh Thanjai'—Thanjai, which is girded by high walls—in several of his songs. One goes:

> *Minnedum puruvathu ilamayilanaiyaar*
> *Vilangal seya naadaga saalai*
> *Innadam payilum inji soozh Thanjai*
>
> *For young women, beautiful as peacocks,*
> *With eyebrows that move like bolts of lightning,*
> *To dance in formation are grand auditoriums;*
> *They learn this dance at 'Inji Soozh' Thanjai.*

As evidence that the art of theatre found great patronage in Thanjai, there were several prosceniums where plays could be staged. Of all these, the greatest and grandest was in the emperor's palace.

Several playwrights and dramatists who created and choreographed new plays had made their homes in Thanjai. Earlier, troupes would stage stories from the epics and folklore, over and over again. But for some time now, the artistes of Thanjai had succeeded in creating a new genre of theatre—plays that celebrated the lives of real heroes from history. These included kings from the era just preceding their own. And which dynasty had produced heroes as illustrious as the Chozhas? So, Karikaal Valavar, Vijayalaya Chozhar, Parantaka Devar and other Chozha emperors became subjects of these plays.

During the Navaratri celebrations, three days were dedicated to theatre that brought alive the stories of the Chozha kings. Thousands of people assembled in the courtyard of the palace, from where they had a view of that hallowed stage, a work of art in itself.

A special seating area had been created for the royal women. The awning was of blue silk, and supported by pillars studded with pearls and decorated with paintings and engravings. The queens, princesses and their companion maidens watched the plays from this platform.

Nandini made a habit of sitting right by Kundavai Devi's side. Although the other women didn't like it, they were forced to keep their peace. Who would dare cross Periya Pazhuvettaraiyar and Pazhuvoor

Ilaiya Rani? When Ilaiya Piraatti herself accorded that arrogant woman respect and welcomed her presence, what could anyone else say or do to object to her temerity?

The third play on the Chozha kings was based on Parantaka Devar. It had been highly anticipated and was a triumph of theatre. There was a buzz in the air even as the audience settled down to watch.

Of all the rulers that the Chozha dynasty had produced thus far, Sundara Chozhar's grandfather Ko Parakesari Parantakar was most famous for his valour. His reign had lasted about forty-six years. The Chozha empire expanded greatly under his rule, and extended from Eezha Naadu to the river Tunghabhadra. He led the army in numerous battles and won grand victories.

He was accorded the title *Maduraiyum Eezhamum Konda Ko Parakesari Varmar*—The Lion of the Clan Who Conquered Madurai and Eezham. He also won praise for the golden roof he built for the Chitrambalam at Thillai Chidambaram. Towards the end of his life, he found himself on the losing side at battle after battle, and his empire began to shrink. Not so his legend. His last war was waged at Takkolam against King Kannara Devan, who set off with a formidable army from Irattai Madalam in the North. His eldest son Rajadityar proved himself a warrior the like of whom Bharatam had never seen. It was Rajadityar who led the vanguard. He decimated Kannara Devan's army and ascended to the heavens while riding his elephant.

The arrow-riddled body of this great warrior was brought home to the king's palace. Parantaka Chakravarti and his queens welled up at the sight of their cherished son who had protected the empire by sacrificing his life.

As the play ended with this final scene, a purportedly celestial voice shouted from the wings, 'Do not worry, do not grieve. Prince Rajadityar is not dead. He lives on in the heart of each and every subject of Chozha Naadu!'

The audience brimmed with appreciation for this play, based on events just one generation removed from the current ruler's.

The reason there had been a buzz in the sabha was this—throughout Parantaka Devar's rule, two of his suzerain kings had been of great help to him. One of them was the king of Kodumbalur. The other was the king of Pazhuvoor. Both these houses were bound by marriage to the Chozha clan. Chozha princesses had married into these families, and the princesses of these families had married Chozha princes and kings. They were as Parantaka Devar's two hands. One couldn't quite say who the right-hand man was. Parantaka Chozhar praised and rewarded both kings, and saw them as his two eyes. We can't quite say one eye is superior to the other, can we now? It was the uncle of the Pazhuvettaraiyar brothers—their father's elder brother—who had ruled Pazhuvoor in Parantakar's time. His name was Kandan Amudanar. The king of

Kodumbalur at the time was the father of Kodumbalur Siriya Velaar, who had died in battle in Lanka—Vanathi's grandfather, in other words.

The troupe was careful not to prioritise one house over the other. They had rehearsed the play fastidiously, ensuring that the greatness of both the Pazhuvettaraiyar and Kodumbalur clan received equal attention. They even had a scene showing that Parantaka Devar rewarded both kings with exactly the same tokens of his affection and gratitude.

However, it was evident early on that the audience had no intention of forgoing a show of partisanship. Some members were in favour of the Kodumbalur clan, and some were supporters of the Pazhuvoor clan. A section of the audience cheered raucously when the valorous deeds of the king of Kodumbalur were portrayed on stage, while another section cheered every appearance of the Pazhuvoor king. At first, the competition was conducted in good spirit. Every now and again, someone would shout 'Naavalo Naaval!'[2] and others would echo it.

Kundavai Devi enjoyed the expression of rivalry between the two sides. Every time the Kodumbalur faction rose to cheer, she would turn to her friend and say, 'Look, Vanathi, your side has the upper hand now!' The guileless Vanathi would delight in this and express her own joy. When the Pazhuvoor faction got excited, Kundavai would turn to Nandini and say, 'Look, Rani! Now your side is on top!' But it was evident that this gave Nandini no pleasure. She was chafing at the fact that the two were even considered rivals, and that Ilaiya Piraatti was fanning the flames, drawing her and that nincompoop from Kodumbalur into the competition, as if they were equals. She was often tempted to stomp off in a huff. But she ground her teeth and sat through it—to walk away would be to admit defeat, and to magnify the importance of this trivial contest.

Her reaction did not escape Kundavai Devi's notice. Nandini's face was a giveaway. But there was something else that struck Ilaiya Piraatti as strange. She couldn't quite solve this mystery—every time the Pandiya king appeared, losing in battle and then surrendering to the Lankan king, beseeching him only to be turned away sans his bejewelled crown and a set of necklaces studded with precious stones, and fleeing to Chera Naadu, the audience cheered as one; but Nandini's expression was one of overwhelming sorrow. Ilaiya Piraatti wondered at this. What reason could the Pazhuvoor Ilaiya Rani have for such a reaction? Perhaps she could probe her by drawing her into conversation?

'What a pity the Chakravarti isn't able to sit with us and watch this play,' Kundavai said. 'Why, he's achieved the very same thing his grandfather did during his own reign! If only Appa would recover ...'

'Why, the body will mend itself. And now his dear daughter is here too. Soon enough, the medicinal herbs from Lanka will be here, and then the emperor will certainly recover,' Nandini said.

'Medicinal herbs from Lanka? What's that?' Kundavai asked.

'You're asking me as if you have no clue! Apparently, the royal physician at Pazhaiyarai has sent someone to Lanka to fetch medicinal herbs from there. And I heard that it was you who found a volunteer for the task? Is that incorrect?'

Kundavai bit her lip. Pretty as her teeth were, even and flawless as jasmine buds, her lips did hurt from the bite. Thankfully, a tremendous cheer of 'Naavalo Naaval!' rose at that very moment, and put an end to the exchange.

The play ended with the chant:

Sundara Chozharin vanmaiyum vanappum
Aayulum arasum vaazhga

May Sundara Chozhar's benevolence and beauty
His life, health and reign last forever more!

The members of the audience made their joyous ways home. The spouses of the suzerain kings left with their entourages. Then, Chakravartini Vaanamahadevi and the other women of the royal household left for the temple of Durgai Amman, who was the chief deity of the Chozha clan.

Malayaman's daughter Vaanamahadevi had undertaken various penances in prayer for the emperor's return to health. She would make frequent trips to the Durgai Amman temple. On each night of the Navaratri festival, special pujas were held for Durgai Amman. Animal sacrifices were made as offerings for Sundara Chozhar's well-being. The queen was in attendance at each of these pujas, and only returned after the final one of the day. Many of the older women accompanied her.

Young women were typically not encouraged to go to the Durgai Amman temple. Sometimes, the priests would get into a trance and dance as if possessed by spirits. They would tell terrible stories and speak of fearsome curses. These fits could frighten young women, and so it was customary to leave them behind when the married women visited the temple. But who dared tell Kundavai Devi she would be scared? And so, Kundavai Devi accompanied the matrons to the Durgai Amman temple on each day of the festival. Vanathi was left to her own devices at the palace.

On the day the play about Parantaka Devar was staged, Vanathi was infused with a restless energy. It had thrilled her to watch the heroic deeds of her ancestors played out on stage. But memories of Lanka and the losses she had suffered through the war haunted her. Thoughts of her father who had died in battle on those shores alternated with thoughts of the prince who had sworn revenge for his death and led an army there. Sleep eluded her. Her eyelids stubbornly refused to close. Perhaps she would feel more relaxed once she discussed the play and the emotions it had triggered with Ilaiya Piraatti.

Rather than toss and turn in bed until the women returned from the temple, it would be a better idea to get some air on one of the palace's upper balconies. The vista that would greet her there—all of Thanjavur spread out before her, lit by lamps and flares—would be a sight too. She might even be able to see the Durgai Amman temple. Vanathi got up from bed. She didn't foresee any difficulty finding her way to the terrace. The lamplit corridors with their ornate pillars would lead her straight there.

But the corridors seemed to go round and round. The paths that had been so bright during the evening were now dim. Most of the lamps had gone out. Smoke from their spent wicks spiralled misty curls in the air. The few remaining ones were running out of oil. Servants lay sprawled and sleeping in corners. Vanathi did not have the heart to wake them to ask the way. She went on and on, figuring that she would eventually find a terrace. But the path seemed endless.

Suddenly, she heard a scream, a voice heavy with grief. Vanathi's skin broke into gooseflesh. Her body trembled. Her legs froze.

Again, a scream and that horrific voice:

'Will no one save me?'

Aha! That sounded like the emperor's voice! What danger was he in? Had his illness precipitated an emergency? Or was it something else? The queen and her entourage were away at the temple at this time, but could the emperor truly have been left all alone in his chambers? Surely not! Perhaps she should check on him anyway?

Vanathi forced her shivering legs to move forward, one step at a time. She had only gone a few feet, when the voice sounded again. It seemed to be coming from down below. The path finally came to an end. She peeped over the parapet and saw an expansive hall on the floor below. This must be the emperor's bedchamber, then. Yes, she could spot his supine form. He was, indeed, all alone. And he was muttering to himself. What was he saying?

'Adi paavi! You wretch. Yes, it is true, it is all true. It is true that I have killed you. That wasn't my intention. But I'm the reason you're dead. What do you want me to do about that now? A quarter century has passed since. Why do you still haunt me? Why won't you let me go? Will your soul never rest in peace? And won't you allow me to live in peace? Tell me what penance I must observe, and I will! But leave me alone, please! Let me go! ... Aiyo! Is there no one who can save me from this woman's cruelty? Everyone wants to find a cure for my physical ailment. But who will cure my mind? ... Go! Go! Go away! No, don't go! Stay! But don't stay silent and torment me like this! Speak! Say something, say anything, before you go!'

The words poured like molten lead into Vanathi's ears. She began to quake from the top of her head to the tips of her toes. She peered into the bedchamber, hardly aware of what she was doing. She looked in each direction, as far as her eyes could see.

At some distance from the king, right in the line of his sight, was a figure. Rather, half a figure. It was a woman ... from what she could see, it seemed to be ... aha! Wasn't this the Pazhuvoor Ilaiya Rani? Was this a dream? A hallucination? No, no, this was indeed reality. And who was that, hiding behind a pillar? Wasn't it Periya Pazhuvettaraiyar? No, there was no doubt. It was that very couple. Was it the sight of the Pazhuvoor Ilaiya Rani that had prompted the king's rant?

It is true that I have killed you.

What did he mean by this?

All of a sudden, Vanathi felt faint. Her head began to spin. No. The palace itself began to spin. Chhi chhi! She couldn't be found unconscious here. No, no, she must keep herself alert. She must get away from here. She forced herself to trace back her path. But she had no idea where she was, or how she was to get back to her own quarters. She went some distance. No. She could go no further than this. She couldn't stop here either.

When Kundavai Devi returned from the temple, she found Vanathi some distance from their room, lying like a fallen log across the corridor.

16

THE HALLUCINATIONS OF SUNDARA CHOZHAR

The next morning, Sundara Chozha Chakravarti sent for his beloved daughter. He ordered the servants, helpers, physicians and everyone else attending on him to keep their distance, and bade Kundavai sit close to him. He stroked her back affectionately. She intuited that he was aching to tell her something, but was struggling to put it into words.

'Appa ... are you angry with me?' she asked.

Sundara Chozhar's eyes brimmed with tears.

'Why would I be angry with you, amma?' he asked.

'Why else? For flouting your orders and coming to Thanjai!'

'Yes. You ought not to have flouted my orders and come here. The Thanjavur palace is no place for young women. You must have deduced this already from last night's incident.'

'To which incident are you referring, Appa?'

'I'm speaking about that girl from Kodumbalur having a fainting fit. How is she doing now?'

'There's nothing the matter with her today, Appa. She was given to fainting fits in Pazhaiyarai too. She always recovers shortly after.'

'Did you speak to her, amma? Didn't she tell you anything about what she might have seen or heard in the palace last night?'

Kundavai thought for some time and said, 'Yes, Appa. When the rest of us were away at the Durga temple, she had tried to go to the terrace all by herself. On her way, she apparently heard someone lamenting pitifully. She says it frightened her out of her wits.'

'I thought as much. Do you see at least now, my child? This palace is haunted. A ghost wanders through it. Please don't stay here. You young girls should all leave!' Sundara Chozhar said.

Kundavai noticed that he was trembling. His eyes, burning and bloodshot, stared into nothingness.

'Appa, why must *you* stay on, then? Why must Amma stay here? Let us all return to Pazhaiyarai. Your move here seems to have done nothing for your health. You haven't recovered,' Kundavai said.

The emperor said, with a bitter laugh, 'Where is the question of my recovering anymore? I have absolutely no hope of it. I've given up.'

'Appa! Why must you be so forlorn? The chief physician at Pazhaiyarai is confident he can cure you.'

'Yes, I heard that you believed him and sent someone to Lanka to fetch herbs. My daughter! This is evidence of your deep affection for me.'

'Is it wrong for a daughter to nurse deep affection for her father, Appa?'

'No, of course not. It is my great fortune that I have a daughter capable of such love. It wasn't wrong for you to have sent someone to Lanka to fetch the herbs, either. But whether you bring me herbs from Lanka or Savagam Island[1], or even nectar from Devalokam itself, this body will not heal in this birth ...'

'Aiyayo! Don't say such things.'

'You've come here, even flouting my orders, amma ... this truly fills my heart with joy. I'd been wanting to sit you down one day and tell you everything, to make a clean breast of it all. The opportunity has arisen now. Listen to me! Ailments of the body might be cured by medicinal herbs. But mine is an ailment of the mind. Which herb can tackle that?'

'Appa, what could ail the mind of the emperor who rules the three worlds?'

'You, too, have imbibed the hyperbolic imagination of the poets, my child! I'm not the ruler of the three worlds. I'm not the ruler of even one whole world. My kingdom is a little patch of land in one corner of one world. I'm barely able to bear the burden of even this ...'

'Why must you bear the burden, Appa? Is there

no one you deem worthy of bearing the burden of governance? You have two gems for sons. Each was born a lion cub, each is a warrior among warriors, each is capable of bearing the heaviest burden one could place on ...'

'My daughter, it is this which makes my heart stop. Both your brothers are heroes without parallel. I've raised them as I have raised you, dearer to me than my two eyes. But I wonder whether I would be doing the right thing in handing over the kingdom to them. Would you say it would be right to bequeath a kingdom along with a curse to my sons?'

'What sort of curse could this kingdom carry? Our ancestors include Sibi, who gave of his own flesh to save the life of a dove,[2] and Manuneeti Chozhar, who sacrificed his son as penance for a calf.[3] Karikaal Valavar and Perunarkilli have ruled this very kingdom. Vijayalaya Chozhar, who bore six and ninety battle scars on his body, has sat on this very throne. Aditya Chozhar, who erected a hundred and eight temples along the banks of the Kaveri, and Parantakar, who donated a golden roof to the Chitrambalam, have expanded the realm. Kandaradityar, whose motto was "Anbe Shivam"[4] and who embodied both love and divinity, has ruled this land. What sort of curse could such a kingdom carry? Appa! You're labouring under some sort of delusion. If only you would leave this Thanjavur fort and ...'

'If I were to leave this place ... oh my dear girl,

you don't know what hell would break loose the next moment! Do you think I have traded the beauty of Pazhaiyarai for this gilded cage, this Thanjai prison, for my own pleasure? Kundavai, my presence here is simply to stop the Chozha empire from breaking into pieces. Think back to what happened when the play was being staged yesterday. I was observing it all from the nilamaadam[5]. I even wondered whether I should put a stop to it in the middle ...'

'Appa! What are you talking about? The play was quite wonderful. My heart was bursting with pride, thinking of the greatness of the Chozha clan! Why did you want to stop it in the middle? Which part of the play did you find unsavoury?'

'The play was wonderful, yes, my child. I saw no flaw in it. I'm speaking about the audience's reaction to the play. Did you not notice the undercurrents of rivalry between the Kodumbalur faction and the Pazhuvoor faction flowing through the audience?'

'I did, Appa!'

'If this was how they behaved when I was right here, think what would happen if I were to leave Thanjavur. The very next moment, war would break out between the two factions. There would be a massacre like that which broke out in the clan of Krishna Paramatma,[6] and our empire would be destroyed even as they destroy each other ...'

'Appa! You are the emperor. Your word is law. The Pazhuvettaraiyars and Kodumbalur Velir are both bound to your every whim and wish. If they cross a line, they're essentially asking for their own destruction and nothing else. Why must it worry you?'

'My daughter, over the last century, these two clans have rendered invaluable service to the Chozha empire. Would we have expanded as we have without their help? Wouldn't their destruction be the death knell for the empire too?'

'Appa ... if you were to come to know that one of those two factions comprises traitors who are conspiring against you ...?'

Sundara Chozhar stared at Kundavai in surprise and said, 'What are you saying, my girl? A conspiracy against me? Who is hatching such a plot?'

'Appa, people who are pretending to be your faithful allies are secretly plotting against you. They're scheming to deny your sons the title, and hand the kingdom over to someone else ...'

'To whom? To whom, my daughter? Whom are they going to crown king instead of your brothers?' Sundara Chozha Chakravarti asked almost eagerly.

Kundavai said softly, 'Chithappa[7] Madurantakan, Appa! Even as you lie in your sickbed, these people have been plotting such a betrayal.'

Sundara Chozhar sat up to the extent he could, and said, 'Aha! If only their efforts were to bear fruit, how wonderful it would be!'

Kundavai nearly jumped out of her skin.

'Appa! What is this! You speak like an enemy of the very sons you have birthed!'

'No, I'm no enemy of theirs. I wish to do them good and nothing else. Let this cursed kingdom not go to them. If only Madurantakan would consent ...'

'If only Chithappa would consent, you say! He has consented with all his heart. He is ready to be crowned king right away. Is this what you're going to do? Don't you need my older brother's consent? The heir's consent?'

'Yes. I'll have to ask Aditya Karikalan. And not just him. Your Periya Paatti[8] must consent too ...'

'Would a mother refuse to consent to her son inheriting a kingdom?'

'Why ever not? Don't you know your Periya Paatti even after all these years? I sat on the throne at Sembiyan Mahadevi's behest. It was she who persuaded me to become king, and later to make Aditya Karikalan the official crown prince. Kundavai, your Periya Paatti loves you very much. You must speak to her and persuade her to let Madurantakan become my heir.'

Kundavai was stunned into silence.

'After that, you must go to Kanchi. Go speak to your brother Aditya Karikalan and convince him to say he doesn't want this accursed kingdom. We will crown Madurantakan king. And then we will be able to live in peace, freed from this curse,' the emperor said.

'Appa, you speak of a curse over and over again. What is this curse?' Kundavai asked.

'My daughter, do you believe in the idea of rebirth? They say memories of our previous births can persist in our current births. Do you think this could be true?'

'Appa! What do I know of these things? They are grand philosophical conundrums.'

'They speak of the ten avatars of Mahavishnu. They say the Buddha took on many avatars before his last one. There are some quite beautiful stories about each of those births …'

'I've heard those, Appa.'

'If the gods and holy men are subject to rebirth, can ordinary mortals be exempt?'

'Maybe not, Appa.'

'Sometimes, I am visited by memories from my previous births, my daughter. I haven't spoken of them to a single soul. Even if I did, no one would believe me. They wouldn't understand, either. They will say I've lost my mind along with my body. As if it weren't enough to harass me with physicians, they would throw tantriks and mantravadis at me too.'

'Oh, yes, Appa! There are already those who say this—your ailments will not be cured by physicians. It is tantriks who must be called …'

'You see? You won't think this too, will you? You won't laugh at me when you hear what I have you say, will you?' the emperor said.

'Need you ask, Appa? Don't I know just how heavy your heart is? Would I think to laugh at you?' Kundavai said. Her eyes were bright with tears.

'I know, my daughter. That is why I'm trusting you with that which I have not told anyone else.

Let me tell you my memories from another birth. Listen ...' Sundara Chozhar said.

On a beautiful island surrounded by the ocean on all its sides grew lush green trees. In the few spaces that didn't sprout trees, bushes and shrubs flourished. In one such shrub by the seashore, a young man sat hidden, staring into the ocean at a ship with its sails unfurled. He didn't look away until the ship had disappeared. Then, he sighed and said, 'Appa! I've escaped!'

The young man had been born into a royal clan. But he was not in line for the throne. He had little wish to rule a kingdom. His father had three older brothers, and so he had never so much as dreamt of being king.[9] *He had never desired it either. He had gone with the army that had crossed the seas to battle on foreign lands. He had been given charge of a small battalion. His army had lost the war. Countless bodies had fallen on the battlefield. That young man had been all prepared to martyr himself in war, and wrought all sorts of daring feats. Yet, death was yet to claim him.*

The survivors of the vanquished army had made their way to the port, ready to return to their homeland. The young man alone did not wish to go. Having lost all the men whom he had led into war, it seemed wrong for him to return home. Songs had been composed in praise of the courage and heroism of the men of his clan. He did not wish to be a blot on this name. And so, as the ship was setting sail, the young man slipped into the waters and made for a lovely little island he had spotted from the deck. He swam to the island. He waited in a shrub until the ship disappeared from view, before looking about himself to take in his surroundings.

He was enraptured by the island. It appeared to be uninhabited, by humans at least. Not to its detriment, he thought. He felt energised and inspired. He swung himself on to a branch, leaned against the tree trunk and dreamt of his future.

Suddenly, a human scream—that, too, in a woman's voice—tore through the silence. He whipped around to see a young woman running as she shouted. She was being chased by a bear of terrifying proportions. The animal was gaining on her even as the young man looked. He had no time to think. He jumped off the branch, took up the spear he had left leaning against the tree and ran forward.

The bear had gone close enough to pin the woman down and was just about to dig its horrific claws into her neck, when the man aimed the spear. The spear struck the bear, who let out a wail that shuddered its way through the seven worlds, and then turned. The woman was safe, but the young man was now the target. The wounded bear lunged at him. Man and bear faced off in a long-drawn battle that ended in victory for the young man.

The jubilant young man's eyes now scanned all four directions. At first, he himself wasn't sure what they were searching for. And then it struck him—the woman his eyes sought was leaning against the crooked trunk of a coconut tree. Her eyes showed surprise, her face glowed with joy. She was a forest dweller. Her appearance and clothes revealed that she had had little contact with civilisation. But her loveliness was ethereal—it defied description, incomparable to anyone or anything in this world or in any other. As she stood by the coconut tree, it was as if an artist's masterpiece had come to life. Even if she were a woman of flesh and blood, she couldn't be of this world, the young man thought.

He approached her, expecting her to vanish into thin air, a mirage or a hallucination. But she did not disappear. However, she did do the unexpected—she turned and ran. He followed her at first, only to give up in some time. He was too exhausted to run. Moreover, it struck him as unseemly to chase a woman.

She lived on this little island, after all. He was bound to run into her some other time. He returned to the seashore, lay on the pristine sand and gave in to his exhaustion. His hopes did not go in vain. Soon enough, the woman returned. This time, she was accompanied by an elderly man. He was of the 'Karaiyar' caste, a community that made its living from fishing off the Lankan shore.

The young man came to know a crucial truth from this fisherman—that the woman had saved his own life in the nick of time. As he had been perched on the tree branch, staring at the ocean, he hadn't noticed a bear slink up behind him. He had been oblivious to the bear, even as the latter had begun to climb the tree. The woman had seen all this. She had screamed in order to distract the bear and alert the young man. The bear had then jumped off the tree and started chasing her instead.

Does one need to explain what emotions this stirred in the young man? He thanked the woman who had saved his life. But she made no reply. The elderly man spoke on her behalf, responding to everything the young man said. At first, this surprised the young man. But once he learnt the truth, it all made sense. The woman was mute. When he was told she couldn't hear either, his heart melted. His affection for her grew manifold.

The circumstances were conducive to the nurturing of this affection. Her lack of hearing and speech did not strike the young man as flaws. Her eyes were enough. Grand truths and hidden secrets that couldn't be put into words spilled out of them. What language could the world offer that could compete with the language of the eyes? And her sense of smell made up for her hearing. Her nose could break through the dense forest and long distances and tell which animal stood hidden where.

But what need did they have of these senses? Once two hearts fuse into one, who cares about eyes and noses and mouths and ears? To the young man, that island was Heaven itself. Days, months, years passed. He lost count of time.

However, the young man's halcyon existence was brought to a sudden end. One day, a ship dropped anchor close to the island. Several men descended from the ship onto boats and rafts. The young man went to see who they were. He realised they had come in search of him. A series of unexpected events had occurred in his homeland. Two of his father's older brothers had died prematurely. The third had no progeny. And so, a vast empire awaited him.

His heart was mightily conflicted. He could not bring himself to leave that beautiful island and the woman who had turned it into his personal paradise. And yet, he was besieged by a yearning to see his family, friends and future subjects. He learnt that the land of his birth was surrounded by danger, with enemies lurking across every border. From very, very far away, the sound of war drums beat a tattoo on his head. This helped him make a decision.

'I will come back. I will fulfil my duties and return,' he promised the woman a thousand times before he left. This child of the forest had no intention of making her appearance before the envoys who had come looking for him. As the young man waded into the sea and got on a boat, she sat on the same old crooked trunk of the coconut tree and watched. When the young man turned back, her eyes appeared to him as oceans of tears. Yet, he steeled his heart, stayed on the boat and reached the waiting ship ...

'Kundavai! The sight of that girl standing there and staring after me often greets my mind's eye. Try as I might, I cannot forget it. And another vision appears before me often, a sight even sadder, one that makes me shudder. It chases me in dreams and memories, when I'm asleep and awake, it torments and tortures me. Shall I tell you that story too?' Sundara Chozhar looked at his beloved daughter and asked.

In a voice made husky with the emotion, barely able to speak from the sorrow and sympathy her father had stirred in her, Kundavai said, 'Tell me, Appa.'

17

DO THE DEAD COME BACK TO LIFE?

Thus far, Sundara Chozhar had been speaking as if he was narrating the story of someone else. Now, he switched to the first person, as if this were an episode from his own life:

'My darling daughter! No father should have to tell his own child the sort of thing I'm going to tell you today. What I'm about to speak of, I've never yet disclosed to anyone. But today, I will open my heart to you. No one in this world knows anything about this except for my friend Aniruddhan. And even he doesn't know the entire story. He doesn't know of the war that rages in my heart at this very moment. But I'm going to tell you everything now. Someone in our family has to know about this. I cannot tell your mother. I've been wanting to tell you for a while. Only you. The opportunity has finally arisen today. You won't laugh at my predicament. You will try to heal the wound that gnaws at my heart. And you'll help me get things done as I will and wish. It is with this faith and hope that I confide in you ...

'I left from that island on a wooden ship and reached Kodikkarai. I learnt that my grandfather Parantaka Chakravarti was staying in this very same Thanjai palace, and came straight here.

'When I arrived, Parantaka Chakravarti was on his last legs. He was forlorn, his mind and heart exhausted. The empire he had built over forty years was now disintegrating. The man who should have been king after him, Rajadityar, had been killed in Takkolam. My own father, Arinjayar, had been badly wounded in that very battle and no one could tell whether he would survive. Kannara Devan's armies had captured Thondai Mandalam and were advancing upon us. The Pandiyas had reared their heads to the South. In Lanka, the Chozha army had lost. And in all these wars, some of our greatest heroes and soldiers had died. As bad news followed bad news to the ears of Parantaka Devar, it seemed he was doomed to spend his final days in a sea of despair and suffering and pain. When he saw me, alive and healthy, his face glowed. I had been a great favourite of his even as a child. He had kept me by his side in the palace for years, never letting me go anywhere out of his sight, let alone to war. I'd had to put up a grand fight and it was my stubbornness which finally saw me lead an army to war in Eezham. When he didn't find me among the survivors who returned from the island, my grandfather's heart broke into pieces. But no one had seen me fall on the battlefield. He refused to give up unless he had confirmed news of my death, and sent search party after search party to the island, hoping they would find me.

'At long last, one of these groups did manage to find me. Once I reached Thanjai, his besieged heart knew some measure of peace. He was, for some reason, certain that the Chozha empire would expand under my leadership, that we would regain all that we had lost and then conquer lands we hadn't even attempted to conquer thus far. The astrologers fanned his belief. As if to provide evidence, circumstances had ensured that although he had four sons, I was his lone grandson.

'The moment he saw me, he ushered me to his side, kissed the top of my head and began to well up, as he said, "Appane! Your uncle Kandaradityar will be crowned king after me. And you will inherit the throne from him. This empire will expand under you." He said this over and over again, and then reiterated that I must make it my life's goal to ensure that Chozha Naadu became the most powerful kingdom in these parts. He made me swear an oath too.

'His love for me was equalled by my adoration of him. His wish was my command. His every word was worthy of worship. And so, I took it upon myself to fulfil the promise I'd made him. But my own mind knew no peace. What was the fate of that Karaiyar girl who had saved me from the bear on that remote island? Could a deaf-mute woman of low birth be my queen and sit by my side on the Chozha throne? Could she even feel at home in the palace? Would a royal life suit her? Wouldn't I become the laughingstock of the kingdom if I were to marry her? Such thoughts often tormented me.

'And there was something else too. My uncle Kandaradityar had recently married for a second time. The woman who had the honour of becoming his wife was from the Mazhavarayar clan, as you know. His first marriage had produced no heirs, but how could one be sure that the second wouldn't either? And if he had a son, what claim could I have on the throne? There were murmurs about this even back in the day, and those fell on my ears too. But that mahatma, my uncle, wanted to ensure that such doubts did not arise. Once Parantaka Devar passed away, the coronation ceremony, the Raja Pattabhishekam, of Kandaraditya Devar was held. And he announced that my Yuvaraja Pattabhishekam, my anointment as the crown prince, would happen simultaneously.

'My beloved daughter! You see how the people of this land fall over themselves for your brother Arulmozhi now? How much they love him and adore him? How devoted they are to him? I was just as popular back in my day. When my anointment was being held inside the palace, a crowd of thousands thronged the streets outside, waiting for my appearance on the terrace. The subjects wanted the newly-crowned king and the crown prince to give them a darshan together. We did as they wished. When we looked over the railings, all we could see was a heaving ocean of people, joyous faces turned up to us. The moment they caught sight of us, they cheered and jumped, so it was like the sea was bubbling with waves. I thought at the time, when thousands upon thousands of my well-wishers have come all this way to see me wear a crown and cheer at the sight, how could I obsess over some woman living in some forest tucked away in some faraway island? Wasn't the joy of all these people, my future subjects, important? Or was a solitary deaf-mute woman more important?

'As these thoughts ran through my head, I scanned the faces below me. There were men and women, old people and youngsters, little girls and little boys. Everyone was rejoicing. But all of a sudden, there was a face ... a woman's face ... a face overcome with sadness ... a face that looked at me through tear-filled eyes. A pitiable face. I don't know how that lone face caught my sight and my attention in that sea of faces. But once I saw that face, I was transfixed. My eyes wouldn't move, my attention wouldn't budge. That face became bigger and bigger. I felt like it came close to me. In the end, that enormous crowd disappeared, everyone standing by my side disappeared, the entrance to the royal palace disappeared, why, even the Thanjai fort disappeared, the firmament and the earth disappeared, and only that face remained, like the Vishwaroopam of Devi Parameshwari[1]. I felt dizzy. The strength seeped out of my legs. The ground fell away beneath my feet. I lost consciousness.

'I would learn later that I had fainted. Everyone assumed the ceremonies of the Pattabhishekam had taken a toll on me. They decided the darshan had gone on long enough. Those gathered around me held me up so I didn't fall, and ushered me inside the palace. Once I'd regained consciousness, I sent for my friend Aniruddhan and told him what I had seen.

'I described that oomai[2] girl in detail. I ordered that search parties be sent out right away and not return until she was found. Aniruddhan came back to report that there was no sign of her, in spite of every nook and cranny of Thanjai having been searched and scoured. Perhaps I had imagined it all, he said. I snapped at him. "What kind of friend are you, if you cannot do even this much for me?" I demanded. I asked him to send search parties beyond the fort, including along the various paths leading to the seashore. Groups went in search of her, fanning out in various directions. The people who were sent to Kodikkarai reported that they had found an oomai woman in the house of the lighthouse keeper there. She appeared to be quite mad, they said. Every attempt at communicating with her through action and expression failed. When she finally understood that they were asking her to accompany them to Thanjai, she refused point-blank. Nothing could persuade her. I didn't know what to do. I was in a state of nervous tension for two whole days. My heart was in turmoil such as it had never known before.

'However much I tried, I simply couldn't forget her. Day and night, she was the only thing on my mind. I couldn't sleep a wink at night. Then, I set off for Kodikkarai with Aniruddhan. We drove the horses as fast as they could go. The turmoil grew, even as we ate the miles between here and Kodikkarai. If I were to find that oomai girl there, what did I intend to do? I had no idea. Should I take her to Thanjai or Pazhaiyarai and announce that she was my queen? The very thought made my mind and body shrivel up into themselves.

'My dear daughter, back then I had the unwelcome reputation of having unparalleled good looks. I did not consider this praise. I did not even think it was an asset. But everyone else would go on and on about it. Although I'd been named "Parantakan" after my grandfather, the epithet "Sundara Chozhan" was bestowed upon me and replaced my given name so entirely that it was simply forgotten. It struck me that it would be ridiculous for me, with this title and reputation, to take a woman who had no idea what civilisation was to the palace. Yet, what else could I do with the woman I loved? All this was playing on my mind as I reached Kodikkarai.

'That maharasi³ had ensured that I was put to no trouble. The news that was waiting for me at Kodikkarai left me stupefied. The day after my search party had left, that girl had climbed to the top of the lighthouse. That was Amaavasai, New Moon Day. The waves were enormous, and the sea had made inroads into the beach, surrounding the lighthouse. The girl had stood there for a while, looking at the waves as they broke against the bottom of the building. It was her wont to stand and stare at the waves from that perch, so no one had thought much of it. Suddenly, there was a whooshing sound that made itself heard over the din of the waves. And she herself was nowhere to be seen. A couple of people swore they had seen a woman dive headfirst into the water. Boatmen went out searching for her, but all the boats returned without completing a rescue. The sea must have swallowed her up whole.

'When I heard the story, it was as if my heart had been speared and the wound would not stop bleeding. But not long after, I knew a strange sense of peace. There was no dilemma anymore. I didn't have to worry about what I would do with her. And there was no point in brooding over it.

'I returned to Thanjai, reeling from the simultaneous assault of pain and relief, and turned my thoughts to governance. I led armies to war. I married your mother. I had strapping boys, sons who would fit right into my shoes as soldiers. And I had the rare fortune of becoming your father, my little girl …

'And yet ... I am simply not able to forget that paavi[4] who died. At times, that horrible sight—the sight I never saw—would haunt me in my dreams. In those dreams and in my imagination, I saw a woman fall headfirst into the sea. So very often, I've woken from sleep screaming. Everyone who heard me would rush to my side and ask what was wrong. At times, I would dismiss it as nothing. At others, I would recount terrible scenes from the battles I had fought and claim I had woken from a nightmare.

'Over time, thanks to the compassion of Kaladeva[5], that awful sight faded from my imagination. And she faded from my memory. Or so I thought, until recently. But now, it seems the dead are more cruel than the living. My daughter! That oomai's spirit will not leave me alone. It has been haunting me for some time, tormenting me. My dear girl, do you believe the dead can come back to life?'

And with those words, Sundara Chozhar turned to stare into empty space, his expression one of abject horror. She followed his eyes. There was nothing there. And yet, his body was trembling. She felt overwhelmed by pity for her father. Her eyes brimmed with tears. She buried her face in her father's chest and began to sob. It seemed to her that the tremors coursing through his body abated slightly as his arms received her.

She then looked at Sundara Chozhar and said, 'Appa! You've carried this unbearable grief in your chest for so long, keeping it all to yourself. That is why your body has broken. Now that you've told me, you'll know relief. Your body will recover too.'

The king responded with a joyless laugh that betrayed his complete loss of hope.

'Kundavai,' he said, 'You don't believe ... You don't believe the dead return to life. And yet, there, by that pillar you see, behind the kuthuvilakku[6], the ghost of that paavi appeared in the middle of the night. Last night. I saw it with my very own eyes. How can one not believe what one sees for oneself? If I was hallucinating, how would you explain your friend's reaction? She saw or heard something that terrified her so much she lost consciousness, isn't it? Bring her to me, Kundavai. I want to hear for myself what she saw.' He spoke in a frenzy, his words falling over one another.

'Appa! Vanathi is scared of her own shadow. I've no clue how she was born into the Kodumbalur dynasty, so famous for its courageous warriors. She is quite capable of taking fright and fainting if she were to encounter an ordinary pillar in the dark. There is little point in asking her what she saw or heard. She would have seen and heard nothing.'

'Is that what you think? Well, that's as may be. But listen to the rest of what I have to say. I didn't believe myself, for the longest time, that the dead could come back to life. Every time I saw her, I figured it must be a figment of my imagination, or a hallucination.

You remember when we went boating on the Kaveri, and baby Arulmozhi suddenly went missing? And as we were screaming and tearing about, scouring the boat and the waves for him, this queen among women appeared carrying the child? And she disappeared the moment she had handed him over. All of you said it was the Goddess Kaveri herself who had saved the prince. But do you know whom I saw? That oomai. It was that girl from the island who handed us the baby. Do you remember that I lost consciousness that day? Everyone thought it was the horror of losing the baby and then the relief of retrieving him that had made me faint. But that was not the case; I tell you after all these years. It was because I saw that the form carrying my son was the ghost of that woman.

'My daughter, do you remember the day your elder brother was named crown prince? After the Yuvaraja Pattabhishekam, Aditya Karikalan went to the antapuram to receive the blessings of the royal ladies, and I went with him too. And the ghost of that oomai was there, among the women, staring at Aditya Karikalan with such malice that I fell to the floor in a faint. But when I thought back to the incident, it made little sense. Why would she look at him so maliciously? What could she have against Aditya Karikalan? That must have been another hallucination, I thought. But once I moved to Thanjai ... I realised I'd been right all along. There was no doubt at all. There was a time, long ago, when she was alive ... a time when I could look at her face and discern her thoughts, when the gentle movements of her lips would prompt me to hear what she wanted to say. Now, those powers have come back to me, Kundavai. She's appeared four or five times before me, always in the dark of midnight, to give me a warning.

'"You killed me, didn't you? You killed me!" she says. "And I have forgiven you for it. But don't commit another sin. Don't give away the throne that is the birthright of one man to another!" I understood her clearly, I heard her say the words just as I would have if she'd spoken them out loud, if she'd gained the power of speech along with her return to life. My darling daughter, you must help me do as she has asked. This cursed empire, this benighted Chozha throne, must not go to my sons. Let us give it all to Madurantakan.'

Kundavai interjected at this point. 'Appa! What are you saying? What need do you see to reverse a decision that has been accepted across the empire? And even if you were to change your mind, will everyone else agree with you that it is the right thing to do?'

'What difference does it make whether they agree with me or not? It is my duty to know what is right and do as dharma dictates. Even when I accepted the title of crown prince and then of the chakravarti of the Chozha empire, my mind knew no peace. My conscience troubled me. How was it right for me, the son of a younger brother, to sit on the throne when the son of the elder brother was alive? I'm paying for that sin now. Why should I foist the same sin upon my sons? Adityan must not rule this empire. Neither must Arulmozhi. They must not be haunted by the curse that hangs over this empire. Let us crown Madurantakan king while I'm still alive. I'll hand over the sceptre to him, and then go to the golden palace Adityan has built in Kanchi, and spend the rest of my days there in peace ...'

'Appa! Don't you need Periya Piraatti's consent for this?'

'My dear daughter, that is why I seek your help. Find a way to make my Periamma[7] come here, concocting some reason or the other. Aha! That enlightened soul, who knows everything about everything, somehow failed to see that justice was done in this case. Why did she instigate me to commit this sin? What could she have against her own son? Why is she so adamant to do something that goes against a mother's very nature? It might have been justified for as long as Madurantakan wanted to become a sanyasi and immerse himself in the worship of Lord Shiva. But how could one possibly justify it now, when he has the desire to rule the empire? How can anyone else be crowned king in his stead?'

'Appa, he might have the desire to rule this empire. But doesn't one need qualifications for such an undertaking?'

'Why is he not qualified? How could a son born

to such a great soul as Kandaradityar and such a wise woman as the daughter of Mazhavarayar fail to qualify?'

'Let's put the question of qualification aside then. Shouldn't the subjects of the land he rules accept him as their king?'

'If we were to ask the subjects what they wanted, they would tell me to crown your younger brother king right away. Is that fair? And would Arulmozhi agree to it? All this discussion is pointless. You'll have to find a way to bring Periya Piraatti here. Tell her I'm fighting for my life. I'm locked in one last battle with Yama. If she wants to see me alive, she'll have to come here right away …'

'There will be no need for me to say such a thing, Appa. Periya Piraatti has been wanting to render some service to the Thanjai Thalikulaththaar temple. I'll use that as a reason to ask her here. Please don't work yourself up like this, Appa. Be patient until she comes.'

And with that, Kundavai took her leave from her father and made for her quarters. She ran into her mother Vaanamahadevi on the way. She stopped and said, 'Amma, don't leave Appa's side for even a single moment. Let the others go and do whatever puja has to be done.'

The formless doubts that had been sneaking into Kundavai's mind for some time had now solidified into shapes. Light was beginning to fall on corners that had been dark all this while. She understood that a grand conspiracy had been hatched against her father and brothers. But she wasn't able to gauge what form it would take, how it would play out and to what extent it had already been set in motion. However, it was clear that the Chozha empire was facing a grave threat. As was her brothers' claim to the throne of that empire. And she believed that the responsibility of saving them from this danger rested on her slender shoulders.

18

WHICH IS THE WORST FORM OF TREACHERY?

Those who are familiar with the history of ancient Tamizhagam must be aware that many women have occupied places of importance, and stood at the forefront of society. Royal women were held in great esteem. The women who were born into or married into the Chozha clan had a right to property of their own. Each of them was allocated villages which paid a tribute, nanjai nilam (wet lands) and punjai nilam (dry lands) as well as a separate allowance for regular expenses.

We must pay some attention to how they put their incomes to use. Many undertook various devotional services at temples. The royal women set aside money for the lighting of the tiruvilakku—the holy lamp—and the weaving of garlands that would be used on the deities, as well as the making of tiru amudu, the prasadam from milk, for pilgrims and devotees.

They had these decrees engraved on copper plates or otherwise inscribed for eternity.

While it was customary for queens and princesses to use their possessions for devotional work, Sundara Chozhar's beloved daughter Kundavai Piraatti rendered an entirely different kind of service. Perhaps because she had been so affected by her father's infirmity, it was her dream to establish hospices and treatment centres across the land. We already know she had started the Parantakar Aadurasalai in Pazhaiyarai. She had also made preparations for the inception of one in Thanjai that would be named after her father. It was all set for a grand opening on Vijayadashami, the tenth day of Navaratri, and commemorative plates were to be issued.

The spot she had chosen was the Garuda Mandapam opposite the Perumaal temple on the outskirts of Thanjai. Tirumaal was considered the guardian deity of all beings[1] and Garudazhvar[2] was the bringer of nectar[3]; and therefore, Kundavai Piraatti thought it fitting that the aadurasalai should be established there.

The residents of Thanjai as well as hordes of people from neighbouring villages had crowded into the temple for the ceremony that would mark the opening of the aadurasalai. Men, women and children dressed in their best clothes and accessories, and made a celebration of it all. The ministers of the court, the kings who governed small and large lands within Chozha Naadu, governors of various territories, sculptors who would inscribe the details of the occasion on stone and engravers who would etch them onto copper plates were all there. The Velakkaara Army turned up too, playing the thaarai[4] and thappattai[5] with such gusto that all eight directions reverberated from the beats. The guards of the Thanjai fort came swinging their swords and spears, with a 'danaar-danaar'. The Pazhuvettaraiyar brothers made a regal entry, each seated on an elephant. Prince Madurantaka Devar followed on a white horse he didn't know how to sit on, his face a picture of terror and torment, blanched to nearly the same colour as the horse. Princess Kundavai Piraatti, her friends and the elder women of the palace arrived in palanquins. The Pazhuvoor Ilaiya Rani's ivory palanquin with its palm leaf insignia made its way to the temple from a different direction.

All the royal women, including Kundavai Devi and the Pazhuvoor Rani, sat in the area that had been prepared for them, with its awning of blue silk.

The ceremonies began with a signal from Periya Pazhuvettaraiyar. Two oduvaars—devotees appointed to recite hymns and sing songs in praise of the temple deity—began the festivities with the padigam[6] 'Mantramaavadu Neeru' from the Devaram, accompanied by the music of the yazh[7] and maddalam[8]. The audience was so entranced that there was absolute silence except for the music.

But two soft voices could be discerned from the spot dedicated to the royal women.

The Pazhuvoor Ilaiya Rani Nandini seated herself close to Kundavai Piraatti and said, 'Devi! Once upon a time, Tirugnanasambandar cured the Pandiya king by singing this very verse and anointing him with consecrated water, isn't it? Why is it that the same lines don't have those powers now? And the consecrated water is ineffective too! We can't get by without medicines and herbs and physicians and treatment centres today. Why is it so?'

'True, Rani. Back in the day, the world was ruled by dharma. That is why mantras and consecrated water wielded such power. This is a world ruled by sin. There are traitors in this land who are conspiring against the emperor. Has one heard of such a thing happening in any bygone era? That is why the mantras have lost their power and we are forced to resort to medicine,' Ilaiya Piraatti replied, fixing the Pazhuvoor Ilaiya Rani with a penetrating stare, and observing her face carefully.

The Ilaiya Rani's countenance didn't betray the slightest change.

'Really? Traitors who are conspiring against the emperor? In this land? Who are they?' she asked innocently.

'I'm yet to find out for myself,' Kundavai Devi said. 'Some people say it's *this* person, some others say it's *that* person. I'm planning to extend my stay so I can get to the bottom of it. When I'm away in Pazhaiyarai, I have no clue what is happening in the world outside.'

'You've made the right decision. If you were to ask me, I'd say you should simply stay here for good. Or the empire will splinter. I'll help you all I can. We have a guest at home. He will be able to help you too,' she said.

'Who is this guest?' Kundavai asked.

'The son of Kadambur Sambuvarayar, Kandamaaran. Have you met him? He is as tall as a coconut tree and built like an ox. He's been blathering on, mumbling "spy" and "traitor". You spoke some time back about treason, didn't you? Can you tell me which the worst form of treachery is, worse even than treason?'

'Yes, I can, quite easily. A woman betraying her lawfully-wedded husband is a worse form of treachery than treason,' Kundavai Devi replied, and studied Nandini's face.

But the Pazhuvoor Ilaiya Rani was unfazed. Her lovely smile continued to light up her features.

'Yes, you're absolutely right. But Kandamaaran wouldn't agree with you. He would say the worst form of treachery is the betrayal of a dear friend. Not only did a man he considered his closest friend and ally turn out to be a spy, he also stabbed Kandamaaran in the back and ran away. Since then, Kandamaaran can only speak these two words.'

'Who is this? Which man would do such a lowly thing?'

'Apparently, he goes by the name Vandiyadevan. He claims to be from the Vaanar clan, which ruled from the town of Tiruvallam in Thondai Naadu. Have you heard of him?'

Kundavai bit down on her coral-red lips with her pearl-like teeth and said, 'Sounds vaguely familiar. What happened after?'

'What else? The *friend* ran away after stabbing Kandamaaran in the back. I've heard that my brother-in-law has sent men to scour the land for the spy.'

'How are you so sure he is a spy?'

'How could I be sure? I'm just telling you what Sambuvarayar's son has said. You can meet him yourself if you would like, and ask him whatever you want to know.'

'Yes. I must meet Sambuvarayar's son. I've heard that his surviving the wound was such a miracle, it must be considered a rebirth. Has he been staying in the Pazhuvoor palace since?'

'Yes. They dumped him at our palace the day after he was wounded. And the responsibility of tending to his wounds and nursing him back to health was dumped on me. He held on to his life with great difficulty, and is just about regaining his strength. His wound hasn't yet healed fully.'

'How strange that the wound hasn't healed in spite of your constant tending to him! Well, that's as may be. I will certainly visit him. The Sambuvarayar clan belongs to a house of great standing and long lineage, going back to the time of Parantaka Chakravarti, isn't it?'

'That is why I suggested it. Our lowly palace will be graced by your presence under the pretext of your visiting Kandamaaran, at the very least,' Nandini said.

By this time, the recitation of the Devaram had ended, and the Daanasaasana Vaasippu—the reading out of the endowments to charity made by the various royals—had begun. First, the royal order issued by Sundara Chozha Chakravarti was read out.

'In our elation over our daughter Kundavai Piraatti endowing her entire income, from the Nalloor Mangalam village that we had bestowed upon her, to the aadurasalai at the outskirts of Thanjai, we have decided to declare all the nanjai lands of that town "Iraiyili land"[9],' said the scroll from the emperor.

Once the royal scribe had read this out, he handed the scroll over to the Dhanadhikari Periya Pazhuvettaraiyar, who received it with both hands as a mark of respect and humility before the emperor, touched the scroll to his eyes in a show of worship and then passed it on to the accountant, asking him to note the details down.

Then, it was Kundavai Piraatti's turn. The list of endowments she had made was read out. The lands she had been given in the village named above had been distributed among the farmers of that village. They were to send two hundred kalams[10] of grains a year to the physician who supervised the Sundara Chozhar Aadurasalai, and fifty padis[11] of cow's milk, five padis of goat's milk and a hundred coconuts containing tender coconut water per day for the patients of the aadurasalai. This had been carved into granite, along with the names of the inscriber and the officials who had supervised the inscription.

Once it was read out, the granite slab was handed over to the heads of the Nalloor Mangalam village. They received the slab with great decorum, touched it to their eyes reverentially and then mounted it on an elephant standing nearby.

A cry of *Maduraikonda Ko Rajakesari Sundara Chozha Chakravarti Vaazhga*—Long live the lion of the royal clan, Emperor Sundara Chozhar who conquered Madurai—was taken up by the thousands of voices in the assembly, and its reverberations tore through the eight directions. As if to compete with those voices, a hundred drums sounded all at once and the very sky shook.

Then, the following cries rose in turn:

Ilaiya Piraatti Kundavai Devi Vaazhga!

Long live Ilaiya Piraatti Kundavai Devi!

Veerapandiyan Thalaikonda Veeradi Veerar Aditya Karikalar Vaazhga!

Long live the vanquisher of Veerapandiyan, Aditya Karikalar, hero among heroes!

Eezhangonda Ilavarasar Arulmozhi Varmar Vaazhga!

Long live the conqueror of Eezham, Prince Arulmozhi Varmar!

Sivagnana Kandaradityarin Tava Pudalvar Madurantaka Devar Vaazhga!

Long live Madurantaka Devar, the blessed son and the fruit of the prayers of the great Shiva devotee Kandaradityar!

By the time the final cries, 'Long live the Dhanadhikari, the Head of the Treasury and Chief of the Granaries, the Lord Who Determines the Taxes, Periya Pazhuvettaraiyar!' and 'Long live the Head of the Thanjai Fort Chinna Pazhuvettaraiyar Kalantaka Kandar!' rose, the number of voices in the chorus had greatly reduced. The members of that chorus were chiefly the soldiers of Pazhuvoor, and there was little enthusiasm from the commonfolk.

Although Kundavai Piraatti tried to catch a glimpse of the Pazhuvoor Ilaiya Rani's expression at this time, she was unsuccessful. If she had only managed to see Nandini's face as the assembly had cheered Aditya Karikalan, Ilaiya Piraatti—whose heart was strong as iron—would have been struck by terror.

19

'THE SPY HAS BEEN CAUGHT!'

The events of that day had infuriated Periya Pazhuvettaraiyar. The inauguration ceremony had been reduced to an opportunity for the subjects of the empire to fawn over Sundara Chozhar and his family, and express their trust in the emperor.

'People, they call themselves, *people*! They've got all the brains of a herd of cattle. Cows and goats! Four people head one way, and four thousand will follow them without thought. How many of them are capable of using their heads?' he huffed to himself. 'Before the emperor ascends to the heavens, he'll ensure he has ruined the empire. "Exempt this town from paying tax," he says. "Declare that village Iraiyili land." Soon, there won't be a single village left that pays tax! But then, God forbid that we fail to send money and grain to the battlefront for our brave soldiers! How am I supposed to provide all that if the treasury is empty?' he hollered, frightening the servants who heard his tirade.

'Anna! What is the point of shouting yourself hoarse? One must bide one's time and let one's actions speak,' Chinna Pazhuvettaraiyar advised him.

His elder brother's fury crossed all bounds when he heard that Kundavai would be visiting his palace.

Periya Pazhuvettaraiyar marched up to Nandini and demanded, 'What is this I hear? Why must that rakshashi come to our palace? I believe you have invited her? Have you forgotten the ignominy to which she subjected you?'

'I never forget a good turn. Neither do I forget malevolence. Have you not understood this about me yet?' Nandini said.

'Then why is she coming here?'

'Because she wants to. Because she feels entitled to, as the emperor's daughter.'

'And why did you invite her?'

'I didn't invite her. She invited herself. She said, "I hear Sambuvarayar's son is in your house. I must meet him." What could I say, "You're not welcome"? A time will come, a time when I can actually say that. But until then, I must endure the various humiliations she visits upon me.'

'I cannot endure this. I cannot be at the palace when she visits. I have some business to attend to at Mazhapadi. I'll head there.'

'That's exactly what you must do, Naadha! I was going to suggest it myself. Leave that poisonous snake to me. I know how to drain out her poison. If you should happen to hear some quite astounding news when you return, please don't be surprised.'

'What kind of astounding news?'

'That Kundavai Piraatti is going to marry Kandamaaran, or that Aditya Karikalan is going to marry Kandamaaran's sister ...'

'Aiyayo! What is this now? If those things were to happen, what will become of our plans?'

'Does talk of something guarantee that it will happen? You've gone and told all your friends that the next king will be Madurantaka Devar. Is that really what is going to happen? Is it to seat Madurantakan, with his woman's gait and coy mannerisms, on the throne that we're putting ourselves to so much trouble?' Nandini said, and looked deep into her husband's eyes. The old man was not able to withstand the gaze from those black orbs. He bent down, took her hands and raised them to his eyes in a gesture of devotion.

'Kanne! The day is not far away that will see you ascend to the throne of the Chozha empire as Chakravartini.'

~*~

Kandamaaran had been beside himself with excitement right from the moment he'd heard that Kundavai Devi was going to visit him. Her brains and beauty were legendary. It was a matter of great pride, wasn't it, that Ilaiya Piraatti herself was coming to meet him?

He would have taken several more stabs and faced far graver illnesses for this honour. Adadaa! If only he'd been wounded in battle! If only he'd been wounded in the chest and was recovering, a brave soldier who had taken on an enemy face-to-face? How wonderful it would have been if Kundavai were visiting under those circumstances! Now, he wouldn't have a grand story of his great exploits to tell her. He would have to sing the same song he had already sung to scores of people, of his friend's treachery.

Every now and again, it struck him that he was involved in a conspiracy against this very lady's family, and his conscience troubled him. Kandamaaran was a principled young man. He wasn't one for wiles and schemes. Even when he had been intoxicated by Nandini's ethereal beauty, he'd reminded himself that she was another man's wife, and had held his mind and heart on a tight leash.

But Kundavai Piraatti was a maiden. How was he to conduct himself with her? What manner should he adopt while talking to her? Could one speak pleasantly to someone against whom one was working in secret? Or, would her beauty have such an effect on him that he would go back on his word? No, no, he could not allow that. He must never allow place for such a sentiment. Why was the princess coming to see him anyway? Well, let her come, and he would say something snappy or impertinent and ensure she never wanted to see him again!

However, this resolution of Kandamaaran's dissolved and disappeared the moment he laid eyes on Kundavai Piraatti. Her lovely appearance, her glowing face, her generosity of spirit, her composed mien and the sincerity with which she spoke words of compassion rendered him helpless.

His imagination took flight. He feigned great reluctance while telling her of his war wounds and bravery on the battlefield. He showed her the scars on his shoulders and chest as if embarrassed by them.

'It would have been all right if that traitor of a friend Vandiyadevan had knifed me in the chest and killed me. But the fact that he stabbed me in the back ... this is what compels me to speak of his treachery. Or, I would be mistaken for a coward who ran from the battlefield and turned his back in flight. I could have forgiven him if he had attacked me face-to-face, and got me in the shoulder or chest,' Kandamaaran said, in a voice heavy with emotion that seemed quite genuine to Kundavai.

She wondered whether Vandiyadevan was truly capable of such an act. Had she been mistaken in her reading of him? She asked Kandamaaran to recount what had happened in detail. He obliged, and his imagination broke all barriers, surprising Nandini herself.

'You see, Devi, he tricked me the very day he stayed in Kadambur. He didn't tell me why he was coming to Thanjavur. He got into the fort on a pretext, using a fake ring. He went and met the emperor himself. He lied that he was carrying a scroll from Aditya Karikalar. But was that all? No. He used your name, and claimed he was carrying a scroll for you too. This aroused the Thalapathi's suspicions. He thought it likely this man might be a spy, and placed him under guard so he wouldn't escape. But Vandiyadevan managed to give them the slip. One has to hand it to him, I don't know how he did it.

'When all this news came to me, I found myself unable to believe my friend was an enemy spy. It is true that he is a bit of an odd character, a loose cannon and of an impulsive nature. I thought he might have got himself into this fix trying to do something foolish. I promised the Thalapathi I would find him and bring him here one way or another, on the condition that he would be forgiven for his transgressions.

'I was walking by the banks of the Vadavaaru, which loops around the fort, late at night. I didn't want company because I did not want to subject my friend to humiliation. No one should witness our confrontation, I thought. I figured that anyone who escaped the fort would have to jump over the wall to get out. Even if he had already managed to scale the wall, he would have to hide in the forest nearby until it was safe for him to carry on with his journey. So, I walked along the river bank.

'I could see someone working his way down the wall, in the dim light of the moon. I went right up to him. Once he got down, I said, "My friend! What have you got yourself into?" That sandaalan[1] punched me in the chest. This is a chest that has withstood elephants ramming into it. What could his fist do to it? But I was stunned that he had punched me, *me*—his friend who had approached him with the best of intentions. So, I punched him right back. We got into a fistfight. Within half a naazhigai, he was drained. As he panted for breath, entirely spent, I said, "Tell me the truth about your mission. I'll forgive you and help you get out of this mess."

'He told me he was exhausted and needed to sit. He would tell me everything once he had got his breath back. I agreed and escorted him to a resting spot. I was leading the way. Suddenly, that paavi plunged a knife into my back. Half the blade was embedded in my body. I felt dizzy. I collapsed to the ground. And that traitor escaped. When I came to, I realised I was in the mute woman's home.'

Nandini laughed to herself as Kandamaaran made all this up. Kundavai wasn't sure how much of it to believe.

'How did you reach the mute woman's house? Who carried you there?' she asked.

'Yes, I find myself wondering about that too. I have no idea. That oomai doesn't know anything. And even if she did, she wouldn't be able to tell me. Apparently, she has a son. He, too, has been missing since that day. No one knows how he disappeared. If he returns, we could ask. If not, we'll just have to wait until the soldiers of Pazhuvoor capture my friend.'

'Do you think he will be caught?'

'How can he avoid capture? He can't grow wings and fly away, can he? I'm only waiting for him to get caught, so I can meet him. Or I would have returned home. I'm still hopeful I can intercede on his behalf with the Pazhuvoor kings.'

'Aiya, you are the very embodiment of generosity,' Ilaiya Piraatti said. Her heart said, *Vandiyadevan must never be caught. So what if he is a traitor? That's all right.*

Just then, one of the servants ran in and cried, 'Amma! The spy has been caught! They've captured him and are bringing him here!'

Nandini's and Kundavai's faces both betrayed their dismay. Nandini quickly disguised her expression. Kundavai couldn't.

20

A CLASH OF TIGRESSES

The servant girl's announcement that the spy was being marched through the streets to the palace had sent all three people in the room into a tizzy. Kundavai's heart nearly burst out of her chest.

'Devi! Shall we go and see how this clever spy looks?' Nandini asked.

'Why should we bother with him?' Kundavai said, after some hesitation.

'Oh, well, if that's how you feel,' Nandini shrugged.

'I'll go and see,' Kandamaaran said, struggling to his feet.

'No, no, you can't walk steadily yet. You'll fall,' Nandini said.

As if she had had a sudden change of heart, Kundavai said, 'Perhaps we should also see what his wonderful friend looks like. Will we have a view of the street from the upper terrace of the palace?'

'Yes, a perfect view. Please come with me,' Nandini said, getting up.

'Devi! If he turns out to be my friend, would you please intercede on my behalf and get me permission to speak with him?' Kandamaaran asked.

'How would we be able to tell whether he is indeed your friend?' Nandini asked.

'In that case, I must be there,' Kandamaaran said, and struggled to his feet again.

The three of them made their way to the balcony of the palace's uppermost terrace. They could see a group of horses, seven or eight of them, approaching from some distance. The riders carried spears. A man was being marched along in the middle of this phalanx, his hands bound behind his back with rope. Each end of the rope was held by a soldier on either side of him.

Not far behind the group, a crowd had gathered to watch the drama unfold.

The face of the man was not immediately visible from the balcony. There was absolute silence among its three occupants, as they waited for the horsemen to come closer.

Kundavai's anxious eyes were fixed on the procession.

Nandini's eyes alternated between two targets, the road and Kundavai's expression.

It was Kandamaaran who broke the silence.

'No, he is not Vandiyadevan!' he declared.

Kundavai's face was suffused with joy.

By this time, the strange procession had reached directly below the balcony. The man who was being marched forward looked up. Kundavai recognised him as the son of the physician.

Holding her relief in check, she said, 'What madness is this? Why have they captured this man? He is the son of the chief physician at Pazhaiyarai!'

The man opened his mouth as if to say something. But he was yanked forward by the rope before he could act on his intentions.

'Oh! Is that so? My brother-in-law's men have made a habit of this. They let the actual criminal slip, and bring some other poor fool in his stead and put everyone to trouble,' Nandini sighed.

'Would Vandiyadevan get caught quite so easily?' Kandamaaran said. 'My friend is no less than Indrajit[1]. He managed to con me. Will he allow these men to trap him?'

'You still call him your friend!' Nandini said.

'Well, yes, he turned out to be a traitor. But the affection I hold in my heart for him hasn't changed,' Kandamaaran said.

'Perhaps they have killed your wonderful friend. I heard these soldiers pursued two spies to Kodikkarai,' Nandini said, and turned to take in Kundavai's face.

It was evident that the word 'killed' had struck terror in Kundavai's heart. *Ha, you arrogant fool, you've given me just the right weapon to avenge myself. If I don't use it to every advantage, I'm not worthy of being the Pazhuvoor*

Rani. Just you wait, just you wait, Nandini said silently.

Kundavai channelled her turmoil to rage and said, 'Spies, they say, *spies*! What nonsense! These two old men seem to have let go of their senses completely. They suspect everyone they see. It was I who sent the physician's son to Kodikkarai to fetch herbs! What have they captured him for? I'm going to demand an explanation from your brother-in-law right away!'

'Oho! So, he's *your* man, is he? Devi! You spoke of suspicion. Now, I have a suspicion myself. Did you send him alone to fetch herbs? Or did you send another man along?' Nandini asked.

'I did send another man along. I asked that one of them go to Lanka.'

'Aha! Now it's all clear to me. It is just as I suspected!'

'I don't understand a thing. What did you suspect? What has happened as you suspected?'

'There is no doubt anymore. I'm certain of it, Devi. The man you sent with him, is he someone you knew from before? Or a stranger, a new face?' Nandini asked.

After a pause, Kundavai said, 'New face, old face, who cares? He brought a scroll from Kanchipuram. My elder brother had sent him.'

'It is he, it is indeed he!'

'Indeed who?'

'He *is* the spy! Apparently, he claimed he had brought a scroll for the emperor too!'

'But whatever made them suspect he is a spy?'

'What do I know about such things? These are men's matters. But if you ask me, the spy did behave in a suspicious manner. If his intentions were innocent, why should he make an escape by night? And why should he stab this poor gentleman?'

'I don't believe it was he who stabbed this gentleman. If he had, why would he carry him to that oomai's house and deposit him safely?'

'You speak as though you witnessed it all for yourself, Devi! You seem to have formed quite an attachment towards this spy, for some reason. He must have magical powers. Why, this gentleman still refers to him as his friend. But nothing can bring back a life that has been taken away, can it? If these men have killed him ...'

Kundavai broke into a sweat. Her eyes turned red. There was a catch in her throat. Her heart beat a tattoo against her chest. *It cannot be, it can never be*, she said to herself.

'If that spy is as clever as this gentleman claims ...' she began.

'Yes, Princess! Vandiyadevan will never let these men catch him!' Kandamaaran said.

'If he isn't caught today, he'll be caught tomorrow,' Nandini said.

Kundavai ground her teeth and said, 'Who knows what will happen tomorrow?' Then, she added angrily, 'The emperor is ill, and the administration of the empire has been turned on its head! Who gave these people the authority to go capture the men I had sent to fetch herbs? I'm going to go speak to my father right away!'

'Devi! Why trouble the emperor in his sickbed about such minor matters? Let's ask my brother-in-law instead. Perhaps he doesn't know that you are involved in this. All you have to do is tell him your wishes, and he will act in accordance with them. Who in all of Chozha Naadu would dare flout the orders of Ilaiya Piraatti?' Nandini said.

It was she who had triumphed in this round of battle between the tigresses. Kundavai's heart had borne several wounds, and it took the princess an enormous effort to keep those hidden.

21

THE DUNGEON

There is nothing quite as strange as this earthly life we lead. Who can tell where our comforts and our problems, our joys and our sorrows come from? The skies could be bright and clear for what seems like eternity, only for clouds to gather within moments and darken the entire world, turning day into night. And then there are great claps of thunder, tearing through the eight directions, and flashes of lightning as the rain pours down on the earth. At times, one feels the world has come to an absolute standstill, with no hint of a breeze. The leaves on the trees are frozen as in a painting. And then, all of a sudden, there is a whirlwind that births a hurricane that whooshes through the forest, uprooting trees as tall as palaces. Groves that were a sight for a sore eyes, lush and green, could transform within an instant into the Ashokavanam[1] after Hanuman had destroyed it.

Just such a whirlwind was sweeping through

Kundavai's life at this very moment. Until recently, she had never known anxiety. Her life had been an uninterrupted joyride. Every endeavour of hers was encouraged, love was lavished upon her as a birthright. She had spent her days singing and dancing, painting and reading, trying on clothes and jewellery, running about without a care through gardens and riding boats to explore the various waterways around the palace. Her father and his consorts, her brothers, the ministers of the court, her teachers, friends, companions, servants and subjects treated her not so much as the apple of their eye as the very pupil of their eye. Grief was what came to other people, and she had only encountered it through the characters who populated epics and plays.

And when misfortune finally arrived at the door of someone who had been so lucky all her life, it came as a cluster of troubles, one after the other, crowding her and assaulting her from all sides. Her father's health was cause enough for worry. At the same time, the empire was facing its toughest test yet. Both her brothers were fighting wars in faraway countries. Astrologers and clairvoyants spoke mysteriously of some unutterably horrific calamity that was waiting to strike the Chozha clan. There were conspirators across the land, meeting secretly in their various corners. The common folk seemed stricken by a fear they couldn't quite place.

Kundavai, born into a clan of war heroes with

hearts as strong as diamond, had the fortitude to face all these challenges. She was certain that she could overcome any obstacle and defeat any danger that crept up on their dynasty or empire, by putting her sharp mind to use. But a little wrinkle in her life, an unexpected encounter, had caused her diamond-like heart to melt and her fortitude to wilt.

The moment she had met Vandiyadevan was when her heart had flowered, a bud unfolding its petals in the glow of love.

And yet, how unfortunate it was that even as the flower blossomed, a dark worm had crept into its whorls and begun to inject its poison into the delicate petals! Ammamma! How worrying it all was, how anxious she felt by the thought that the scion of the Vaanar clan might have been imprisoned! The cruel words she had heard, the possibility that he might have been killed, had torn her heart asunder. How hard it had been to subdue the emotions those words had evoked, and hide the effect they had had on her! She had parents and relatives, siblings and friends who loved and cherished her, and yet, why did her heart ache for this one man whom she had run into by chance a couple of times, a man who was simply passing through the land?

Well, there was no time to think about all this and analyse her feelings and then arrive at a conclusion. There was no time to wait for an auspicious hour, or study portents and omens. She would simply have to conduct her enquiry as expeditiously as she could, and do what had to be done as efficiently as possible.

And so, she sent word that she would be visiting Chinna Pazhuvettaraiyar's palace that very afternoon. The women of the antapuram welcomed Ilaiya Piraatti warmly, showing her every respect that was due to a princess and all the affection that was due to Kundavai on her own merit. She made some obligatory conversation with them and then went straight to the Chitra Mandapam. Chinna Pazhuvettaraiyar was waiting to welcome Ilaiya Piraatti. He escorted her through the hall, telling her the story behind each of the paintings that adorned it. Kundavai looked at them intently, and listened to everything he said.

As they came to the last one, Kundavai turned to Kalantaka Kandar and said, 'Aiya! The Pazhuvettaraiyar clan has rendered the Chozha dynasty unparalleled service, generation after generation.'

'Ammaiye! That is our great fortune,' Kalantaka Kandar replied.

'There is no doubt that the just reward for such service would be the Chozha empire itself ...'

'Thaaye! What sort of talk is this?'

'But surely you can wait until the emperor's time on this earth has ended and he has found his place in Kailash before you grab the reins? Must you be in such a hurry to run the empire?'

These words struck Chinna Pazhuvettaraiyar Kalantaka Kandar's heart as piercing arrows. His face was a picture of pain. Drops of perspiration appeared on his forehead. His moustache quivered. His arms and legs trembled.

Kalantaka Kandar wiped his brow and then said, 'Ammaiye! Why such rage? Do you intend to send me to Yamalokam with your words for fatal arrows?'

'Aiya! You know I have no such powers. Yama himself wouldn't dare approach Kalantakar. What could I, after all a helpless, clueless woman, do?'

'Ammani! It would have been kinder to pour molten lead into my ears than to hurl such words at me! What crime have I committed to evoke such fury in Devi's heart?'

'Who am I to speak of your crimes? It is you who must tell me of which crime I am guilty. Was it a crime to send a man to fetch herbs to cure my father's illness?'

'No, Ammani, that could never be a crime.'

'Do you know that I had sent the son of the chief physician of Pazhaiyarai to fetch herbs from Kodikkarai?'

'Yes, I do know, Ammani.'

'Just today, that very physician's son was marched through the streets by your horsemen. He was pulled along by rope. Was it not you who gave the order? And did you not do this knowing that it was I who had sent him?'

'Yes, Piraatti. But you might have sent him on his mission without being aware that he was a spy, isn't it?'

'The son of the Pazhaiyarai physician, a spy? Do you expect me to believe this story?'

'Thaaye! Surely you must believe it if he confesses to it?'

The princess was rattled. She asked, with some effort, 'He confessed to it? How? To what exactly did he confess?'

'He confessed that his companion was a spy. That his companion was not really headed for Lanka to fetch herbs, but to deliver a scroll to someone in Lanka.'

'He is a moron, the biggest fool I ever met. He must have blabbered some nonsense in his fright. It was I who sent his companion to Lanka. You're aware of that, aren't you?'

'Yes, thaaye! But I'm aware that he has tricked you too. That young man who goes by the name Vandiyadevan is truly a spy.'

'No, most certainly not. He brought a scroll from my brother in Kanchipuram.'

'Princess! He brought the emperor himself a scroll from the prince. Why is that of any significance? Spies must find some pretext or the other to go about their work, isn't it?'

'Aiya! What evidence do you have that Vandiyadevan is a spy?'

'If he is not a spy, why would use a ruse to enter the fort? Why would he go to the astrologer of Kudandai and ask about the emperor's horoscope?'

'I myself have asked the astrologer of Kudandai

about the emperor's horoscope. What does that imply?'

'It is one thing for the emperor's beloved daughter to ask about his future. And quite another for a stranger who has no stake in the matter to ask. The only reason he could have for making such an enquiry would be that he is a spy working for an enemy king.'

'This is your hypothesis. Is there any other reason for such a charge?'

'He could have sought my permission openly and entered the fort. Why should he choose to show me the Pazhuvoor signet ring instead and lie his way inside by claiming that it was Periya Pazhuvettaraiyar who gave him the ring?'

'But who else could have given him the ring, then?'

'I don't know yet. We must find out.'

'And what have your men been doing, if they haven't managed to find this out?'

'Ammani, my men are not mantravadis. We can only find out by capturing and interrogating the spy, isn't it?'

'And what is the guarantee that he will tell the truth?'

'There are ways of making one tell the truth. Thaaye! That is what the dungeon is for. The spy had figured this out. That is why he ran away in the dark of the night, stabbing Sambuvarayar's son on his way too!'

'And what proof do you have that it was he who stabbed Sambuvarayar's son?'

'The fact that Kandamaaran said so.'

'That is not enough. I say he did not stab Kandamaaran.'

'Thaaye! Did you witness this from close quarters?'

'No. But I can determine from a man's face whether he is a criminal or not.'

'That damned spy is a fortunate man. He has contrived to get into your good books. I, alas, have not had that honour.'

'Aiya, why do you refer to him as a spy yet again?'

'Thaaye! If he were not a spy, why would he join a drama troupe and wear a mask to enter Pazhaiyarai? Why would he go to the Kodikkarai seashore in disguise? And why would he hide the entire day in Kodikkarai after seeing my men there? And why would he set off for Lanka in the dark of the night? Unless he is a spy?'

'Oh, so he has set off on a boat and escaped? Your men were not able to catch him?'

'Yes, thaaye. That spy seems to be a sorcerer too. He managed to give my men the slip yet again. These fools have let him go and brought the physician's son here instead.'

'Aiya, let's leave the spy aside for now. The physician's son was sent forth on my express orders. I know for a fact that he is innocent. You must release him right away.'

'Ammani! He may not be a spy, but he has aided and abetted one. He has told my men all sorts of stories to try and trick them. He has helped the spy hide and eventually escape on the boat.'

'Whatever the case may be, the physician's son must be released right away.'

'I'm not ready to take that responsibility. There are dangers cropping up in every corner of the land. We are surrounded by enemies, who are simply waiting for the right moment to gather their armies and march on us. Veerapandian's Aabathuththavi Army has vowed to destroy the Chozha clan. Conspiracies are being plotted across the empire as we speak.'

'Aiya, if you were to throw everyone who is part of a conspiracy into the dungeon, you would run out of space.'

'We can arrest them for as long as there is space, can't we?'

'Let us keep some space aside for the real conspirators. Aiya, please release the physician's son right away.'

'I cannot take that responsibility, thaaye.'

'Will you do it if the order comes from the emperor? Or will you cast his order aside too?'

'Ammani, there is no need for the emperor to give the order. The entire world knows that Ilaiya Piraatti's wishes are as scripture to the emperor. Here, I hand over the keys of the dungeon to you. You may go yourself and let him out of the prison. If you wish to release anyone else while you're at it, please feel free to do so. All that follows, any consequence whether good or bad, is entirely your responsibility.'

With those words, Kalantaka Kandar handed over an enormous key to Kundavai Piraatti.

Kundavai controlled her fury and said as she received the key, 'As you say, aiya. I take full responsibility for all that follows, good or bad.'

'If the Chozha empire is brought down by some evil, it will be entirely because of two women,' said the Thalapathi of the fort.

'I am one. Who is the other?'

'The Pazhuvoor Ilaiya Rani Nandini Devi herself.'

Kundavai smiled and said, 'Why, you're equating me with the highest authority of the Chozha empire. If this were to fall on Periya Pazhuvettaraiyar's ears, he would banish you from the empire.'

'That would be an excellent outcome. I'm waiting for the day,' Chinna Pazhuvettaraiyar said.

22

SENTHAN AMUDAN IN THE DUNGEON

The goldsmith's workshop, where the empire's gold coins were minted, was within a smaller fortress-like structure inside the Thanjai fort. The security arrangements to enter this fortress were quite as rigorous as those at the entrance of the main fort.

When Kundavai and Vanathi arrived at the mint, it was the time of evening when the workers were leaving. The guards were readying themselves to search the workers before they went home. The latter were assembled at the entrance.

The royal chariot approached the mint even as this was happening. Kundavai and Vanathi stepped down.

The guards and workers forgot themselves the moment they saw the princesses and chorused, 'Vaazhga Ilaiya Piraatti! Long live Ilaiya Piraatti!'

The head of the mint ran out of the fortress to receive them.

He escorted the princesses inside and eagerly showed them around, pointing out the kiln where the coins were forged, the press where the designs for the coins were prepared and the finished coins fresh from the mint.

The coins that had been produced that day were kept in a separate heap. They shone so brightly that the princesses had to shield their eyes from the glare. On one side of each coin was the emblem of a tiger, and on the other the image of a ship.

'Look, Vanathi! For aeons, gold has been coming to Chozha Naadu from all over the world, through land and sea both. Thus far, carrying all that gold was the burden of the women of the clan. The gold was shaped into jewellery that we had to wear, our bodies bent by the weight of it all. For some time now, though, that burden has been lessened. The dhanadhikari Periya Pazhuvettaraiyar has arranged for the gold to be minted into coins,' Kundavai said.

'Akka, how does this help?' Vanathi asked. 'Of what use is it to anyone?'

'Of what use is it, you ask? You're so clueless about everything! If gold is minted into coins, one doesn't have to check for weight every time. We can simply count out the coins. It is easier for households to pay their taxes. When traders cross the seas to ply their wares, they can do away with the barter system and use gold as currency. This is why traders hold the dhanadhikari Periya Pazhuvettaraiyar in such high esteem,' Kundavai said. She then lowered her voice to add, 'And let me tell you something else. These coins are of even more use to the conspirators who are plotting against the emperor and his family. The most noble of men can be persuaded into treachery with the help of this mesmerising gold, you see.'

The head of the mint, who was standing close by, heard most of Kundavai's last sentence, softly though she spoke.

'True, thaaye,' he said. 'We hear such terrible rumours these days. That is why the security of the mint has been bolstered of late. And the number of people entering and exiting the dungeon below this floor has increased too.'

'I know people enter. But do people exit?' Kundavai asked.

'Why not? Just this morning, they brought a man. About a naazhigai ago, they took him away,' her interlocutor replied.

'Who could that man be?' Kundavai wondered, rather surprised.

They had a tour of the mint, and then went to the far end, where a door stood before them. They opened the door, and found themselves in a dim space with a low ceiling. All around them rose a hair-raising hum, as if the walls were reverberating with growls. A servant held up a flare.

Under its light, they saw that they were surrounded by cages, each with a tiger inside, gleaming golden with black stripes. Some were lying down, and others were stomping up and down their cages. Their eyes glowed like balls of fire in the shadows of the hall.

Kundavai gripped Vanathi's hand tightly and said, 'Adiyei! Are you scared? Don't go and faint now!'

Vanathi said, with a little laugh, 'Why must one be scared of tigers, Akka? They are the guardians of our clan, aren't they? They are here to guard us.'

'Well, sometimes guards can cross over to the enemy's side. And that makes them the most dangerous of beings, doesn't it?'

'No, Akka, human guards might be capable of such treachery. But these tigers would never do such a thing.'

'How can one be so sure? These tigers have grown fat on the flesh of traitors. What if the blood of those men has seeped into the animals' veins and influenced their behaviour?'

Now, Vanathi, who had just declared that she had no reason to be afraid, felt a tremor run through her body.

'Akka! What are you saying? They feed people alive to these tigers?' Vanathi asked in horror.

'No, they don't. But I told you there is a dungeon below the mint, didn't I? There is only one path there, which serves as both entrance and exit. And that path winds through this mandapam of tigers. If anyone were to try and escape the dungeon, he would have to pass through this mandapam. And he will become the tigers' prey.'

'Shiva-Shivaa! How cruel!'

'That is how empires are run. Kindness and cruelty cohabit in the minds of rulers. Vanathi, who can tell? They might throw me into the dungeon one day. If only you had heard how Chinna Pazhuvettaraiyar spoke to me today ...'

'What a notion! There is no one in the seven worlds above or the seven worlds below who would dare throw you in the dungeon. Why, if someone were to try, the very earth would yawn open and swallow this city of Thanjavur whole! I'm not worried about such an occurrence. What I *am* worried about is the fate of the physician's son. That poor, soft-spoken boy wouldn't have attempted an escape, would he?'

'Soft-spoken indeed. But who knows in what ways one might change?'

The growls of the tigers were louder now.

'The tigers seem terribly angry!' Kundavai said, turning to the guard.

'No, thaaye! They are simply welcoming the empire's divine daughter with cheers,' the guard quipped in response.

'Some welcome!' Kundavai said.

'And it's time for their feed too. They're growling in anticipation of their dinner.'

'Then perhaps it's best we get out of here quickly. Where is the entrance to the dungeon?'

They had reached the far end of the hall. The guards moved a tiger cage to one side, and they spotted a trapdoor on the floor below. Two men bent down and pulled it open. Stairs led downwards.

The visitors climbed down the steps in single file. The flares held by two servants lit their way. The path was suffocatingly narrow.

If the growls of tigers had given them gooseflesh upstairs, here it was human groans, moans and howls that echoed through the walls. No one could listen to those sorrowful wails without one's heart pounding and body trembling.

Yet, in the midst of those terrible sounds, was—wonder of wonders—a melodious voice singing:

Ponnaar meniyane
Pulitholai araikasaithu
Minnaar senjadaimel
Milir konrai anindavane!

He of the golden skin,
Who wears a tiger's skin at his waist,
He of the lightning-like locks,
Ornamented with a garland of konrai flowers!

The cells within the dungeon were not arranged in neat rows. They were jaggedly placed, along crooked corridors. The guards went up to each cell in turn, and held up the flares. Some held a single prisoner, and some two. In some, the prisoners were shackled to the walls with heavy, iron chains. In some, they were unrestrained.

Kundavai Devi examined each face and shook her head. The party made its way back towards the stairs.

'What is this terrible fate?' Vanathi blurted, suddenly. 'Why have they shut them all up like this? Is there no such thing as an inquiry? No such thing as an investigation so justice may be served?'

'Inquiries and investigations are held for ordinary crimes. But people who conspire against the king, spies from foreign lands and those who have been allies to these spies are the ones who populate this dungeon. If they get the truth out of their captives, they let them go. But in some cases, they never do. How can one tell a truth that doesn't exist? Confess to a crime one hasn't committed? The fate of such people is, indeed, terrible,' Kundavai said.

Suddenly, lines from the song *Ponnaar meniyane* sounded from close quarters.

When the guards went up to the cell and shone their light, a young man's face appeared. This is a face we know—that of Senthan Amudan.

The princesses were intrigued by his innocent expression.

'Is it you who has been singing?' Kundavai asked.

'Yes, thaaye,' he replied.

'You seem to be in high spirits?'

'Why would one not be, amma? The omnipresent lord is in here with me too.'

'You speak like a true gnani, a realised soul. Who are you? What was your vocation before you were captured?'

'I am no gnani, true or false, amma. Before I was captured, I was weaving garlands of flowers to offer the lord. Now, I draw joy from offering garlands of song.'

'You're not just a gnani, but a poet too, it appears. Is this the only song you know? Or are there many others?'

'I do know some others. But this is the only one I've been singing since I came in here.'

'Why is that?'

'I passed through the workshop where gold is minted on my way here. I saw pure gold for the first time in my life, the gold known as "paththarai maatru pasumpon". It reminded me of the divine form of our golden-skinned lord, and I began to sing *Ponnaar meniyane.*'

'You're a lucky man. Gold would induce greed in most people. It induces faith in you. Do you have no near and dear ones, appa, no friends or family?'

'Just my mother. She lives by the lotus pond outside the Thanjai fort.'

'What is her name?'

'Vani Ammai.'

'I'll go meet her, and tell her that you're in high spirits in here.'

'That would be pointless, amma. My mother can neither hear nor speak.'

'Oho! Is your name Senthan Amudan?' Ilaiya Piraatti asked, in some surprise.

'Yes, amma. How do you know the name of as ordinary a man as I?'

'For which crime have they brought you to this dungeon?'

'I had no idea until yesterday. I came to learn of it today.'

'And what did you learn?'

'I learnt that I have been apprehended for aiding and abetting a spy.'

'What! Which spy did you aid and abet?'

'Just outside the Thanjai fort, I ran into a man who was journeying from elsewhere. He said he wanted a place to stay for the night. I took him home. But I didn't dream that he could be a spy.'

'Do you know his name?'

'He said his name was Vallavarayan Vandiyadevan, and that he belonged to the Vaanar clan of ancient glory.'

Kundavai and Vanathi glanced at each other in silent communication.

Vanathi turned to Senthan Amudan and said, 'Tell us the whole story.'

Senthan Amudan did as she asked, telling them everything that had happened from the moment he had first encountered Vandiyadevan to when he had been arrested by the soldiers of Pazhuvoor at the riverbank.

'Why did you go so much out of your way to help a stranger of whom you knew nothing at all?' Vanathi asked.

'Thaaye! There are some people to whom one is instinctively drawn. One feels one could even lay down one's life for that person. How can I tell you why? There are others the very sight of whom induces fear or rage. One wants to kill them right away. They had thrown another person in here with me today. I felt such a surge of fury when I saw him. Thankfully, the Pazhuvoor Ilaiya Rani's men came some time ago to release him.'

'Is that so?' Kundavai asked, biting her lower lip. Her eyebrows knit themselves into a frown. She felt sighs of anger escape from her. She asked, 'Who is this man who was released in such a hurry? Do you know?'

'Of course. Apparently the son of some physician from Pazhaiyarai.'

'What did he say or do to evoke such fury in you? You said you wanted to kill him?'

'My uncle's daughter Poonguzhali lives in Kodikkarai. He said things about her that he shouldn't have. That is why I was so furious. But he also brought me some good news, and so I let him be.'

'What good news was this, that melted away such fury?'

'He had gone to Kodikkarai with my friend Vandiyadevan. He then tried to betray my friend to the Pazhuvoor soldiers and get him caught. He failed in that attempt.'

'He failed? So the spy escaped?' Vanathi and Kundavai chorused.

Wasn't it to hear just this that they had entered the dungeon?

'Yes, Ammani. My friend gave them the slip and made his escape. Poonguzhali took him by boat to Lanka in the dark of night. Both this wretch and the soldiers were tricked.'

The two women looked at each other, their faces glowing in silent joy.

Kundavai looked at Senthan Amudan and said, 'Appane! You are so delighted at the news that a spy escaped. You do deserve to be imprisoned!'

'Thaaye! If I deserve to be imprisoned for that crime, the two of you ought to be in here with me,' he said. 'In the very next cell.'

The women laughed. The sound of laughter was as much at odds with the gloom of the dungeon as the strains of Senthan Amudan's song had been.

'You're a clever man and a cheeky one. If we leave you here, you will spoil everyone else inside with your song. I must ask the Thalapathi to release you before I do anything else,' Kundavai said.

'Thaaye! Please don't. There is a man in the next cell. He has promised a hundred times that if I teach him a song, he will tell me the location of the secret place where the Pandiya crown and the chain of precious stones are hidden in Lanka. Please ask them to let me stay until I learn that secret,' Senthan Amudan said.

'Poor thing. You want to stay on until you go as

mad as he is? Then what will become of your mother Vani Ammai?' Ilaiya Piraatti said as a parting shot, before heading for the stairs. The others followed her.

Within half a naazhigai, guards were at Senthan Amudan's cell to release him and escort him outside the Thanjai fort.

23

NANDINI'S LETTER

The evening found Nandini leaning against the side of her hamsatulika settee in the lata mandapam, writing a letter.

The letter contained only a few lines. As she wrote, Nandini's entire body trembled like a delicate flower stem in the throes of a whirlwind. A heavy sigh escaped her lips every now and again. Even though a servant was standing by, trying to cool her with a peacock-feather fan, beads of perspiration appeared on her porcelain-like forehead.

These are the contents of the letter she wrote:

O Young Prince[1]!

It is after having overcome my great hesitation and much trepidation that I sit down to pen this letter to you. One hears all sorts of things about the state of the empire. You don't seem to pay any attention to any of it. In spite of your father, made frail by ill health, asking you to come to Thanjai ever so often, you haven't visited. I am tormented by the thought that I might be the reason for your boycott of our city.

If I could meet you just once, I could dispel all these doubts. Would you be so gracious as to grant me this? If you do not wish to come to Thanjai, we can meet at the palace of Kadambur Sambuvarayar.

Today, I am as a grandmother to you. What objection could anyone have to our meeting each other? The young man who brings you this letter, the son of Sambuvarayar, may be trusted implicitly. You may tell him anything at all in response.

Thus signed,

The unfortunate soul born at a most inauspicious hour and carrying only ill luck,

Nandini

Once she had finished the above letter, with just as much hesitation and trepidation as she had claimed to have overcome, she sat back. Then, she turned to the servant and said, 'Po di! Go fetch the Kadambur prince right away.'

The servant did as asked, and stood some distance away from Kandamaaran and Nandini.

Kandamaaran could barely bring himself to meet Nandini's eyes. To look upon her beauty was to look upon the sun—it hurt one's eyes. He stood nearby, staring at the garden instead.

'Aiya! Do sit down,' Nandini said, with a tremor in her voice.

The tremor startled Kandamaaran into looking up to stare at her face.

'It comes as no surprise that eyes that have rested on Kundavai Devi should baulk to rest on me,' Nandini said, with a smile.

Those words tore Kandamaaran's heart to shreds. Her smile drove all thought from his head.

'A thousand Kundavais could never be the equal of one Nandini Devi!' he stammered.

'And yet, all Ilaiya Piraatti has to do is point, and you'll go all the way to Devalokam and bring back Indra's throne for her. While here I am, begging you to sit, and you won't oblige even this little request.'

Kandamaaran sat on a bench opposite her right away and said, 'Why, I would go to Brahmalokam and bring back Brahma's head for you if you so wished!'

Nandini trembled. Without looking at Kandamaaran, she said, 'Brahma has four heads after Shiva relieved him of one. You could lop off another, and he would yet survive.'

'Devi! You can tell me anything at all—but there's just one thing I ask, and it is that you don't speak in praise of Kundavai Devi to me. To think of how she defended that traitor of a friend, Vandiyadevan … why, it makes my blood boil!'

'And yet, this morning your imagination was in full flow. With what creativity you described this long, hard fight in which you and your friend clashed!' Nandini said.

Her words left Kandamaaran embarrassed. 'I had to give her some explanation for how I met and spoke to him, didn't I? That was why I had to resort to that. But it *is* true that he stabbed me in the back, isn't it?'

'Aiya! Don't you think it would be a good idea to revisit what exactly happened that day and make sure you've got your facts right?'

'Do you, too, suspect that my words may not be true?'

'No, I don't. But you've forgotten a couple of things. Some day they will arrest Vandiyadevan and bring him here. We must be able to prove then that he is guilty of the charge of which you accuse him, isn't it?'

'I am not in the least interested in doing that. I'm ready to forgive him.'

'Your generosity is, indeed, praiseworthy. But it is better we confirm the truth to ourselves, at least. Remind yourself of the events of that night. You came through the underground passage, and you met Periya Pazhuvettaraiyar and me. Do you remember this?'

'I remember all too well. For as long as there is breath in my body, I will never forget that encounter.'

'Do you remember what you said then?'

'No, I don't. I was lost the moment I set eyes on you. I barely knew where I was.'

'But I remember clearly. You said, "Aiya, I have heard so much about the legendary beauty of your kumari[2]. But none of that does justice to the truth," you said.'

'Aiyayo! Is that really what I said? So that's why his

face turned red with fury! He doesn't like me much even now ...'

Nandini laughed and said, 'It is of no consequence if he doesn't like you. *You* like *him,* don't you? That is enough!'

'Devi! I'll speak the truth. What is the point of hiding it from you? I don't like him either.'

'Well, that's of no consequence either! *I* like him, and that's enough. I must have done some great penance to be granted this boon of having him for a husband.'

Kandamaaran was bewildered by this. He didn't know how to respond, and so he stayed silent.

'Well, that's as may be. Let's not concern ourselves with all this anymore. What did you do after you met us in the subterranean passage?' Nandini asked.

'The guard who held the flare went ahead of me to light the way. I followed him, my head filled with thoughts of you. The guard opened the secret door and stepped aside. I went through. Right then, someone stabbed me in the back. That's all I remember. Vandiyadevan must have somehow learnt that I would be coming that way, and been lying in wait for me outside.'

'No, aiya! Your surmise is wrong. He wasn't lying in wait outside at all.'

'So you, too, have crossed over to his side, have you?'

'Why should I cross over to his side? What do I

stand to gain? And what does he stand to gain? It's just that I can see exactly what must have happened. I see clearly now how it all played out.'

'Do tell me, Devi! Tell me how it happened!'

'Vandiyadevan was not lying in wait outside.'

'Then who else was lying in wait?'

'Nobody else. I only said Vandiyadevan wasn't lying in wait *outside*. He was lying in wait *inside* the underground passage.'

'What? What? How could this be true, Devi?'

'He disappeared without a trace all of a sudden. How could he have disappeared? Think about it. He must have somehow found the subterranean passage, entered and discovered all its secrets. Then, he would have seen you and followed you to the exit. Once you opened the door, he stabbed you and got out himself. Then, perhaps his conscience pricked him, and he was moved to take you to the oomai's house for treatment.'

'Devi! You're right. This is exactly how it must have all played out. There is no doubt. All these days, it never occurred to me. And it didn't strike anyone else either. I'll tell anyone who asks that you have the sharpest brain in Chozha Naadu. There are those who are born with brains, and those who are born with beauty. It is rare to come across one with both in all of Brahma's creation. And you, you have both beauty and brains, Devi!' Kandamaaran gushed.

'Aiya! Are these words of yours sincere? Or are

these the regular words of flattery all men use on women?'

'No, they are not words of flattery. I swear they come from the heart.'

'In that case, will you place your trust in me? Do you have enough faith in me to do me a favour?'

'I am ready to do anything at all that is within my powers.'

'You will have to go to Kanchi for me.'

'Why, I would go to *Kashi* at your command.'

'There is no need to make such a long journey. I will give you a letter for Prince Aditya Karikalar in Kanchi. You must hand it over to him. And then invite him as a guest to your Kadambur palace.'

'Devi! What are you saying! Are the plans of your husband, my father and so many other leaders of Chozha Naadu, the arrangements they are making for the future of the crown, entirely unknown to you?'

'They are, indeed, known to me, as are several other things. Your family and mine and several others of prominence are standing at the very threshold of great danger. Do you know who is the cause of this danger?'

'Do tell me, Devi!'

'Why, your guest of this afternoon, that very paadagi[3]!'

'Aiyayo! You're referring to Ilaiya Piraatti!'

'Yes, that very snake. *Paambin kaal pambariyum*—it takes one to know one—and only snakes can sniff out each other's trails. It is only Nandini who can see through Kundavai's schemes. She has sent your friend Vandiyadevan to Lanka. Do you know why? It is a grand lie that he has been sent to fetch herbs. She's not putting herself to all this trouble so Sundara Chozhar survives. All she wants is that Madurantakar should not succeed him. Neither should Aditya Karikalar. Her darling little brother Arulmozhi Varman is the one she is plotting to seat on the Chozha throne. She has him wound around her little finger, and she will run the country as she pleases once he is the emperor. She will practically be the Chakravartini. And you know who the Chakravarti will be? Your friend Vandiyadevan!'

'Aha! Is that so? We'll have to put a stop to this somehow. We must tell my father and the Pazhuvettaraiyar brothers.'

'There is no point in telling them. They won't believe it. We must counter her schemes with schemes of our own. And we can only achieve this with your help.'

'I am at your service, Devi!'

'Here, take this scroll and guard it with your life until you personally hand it over to Aditya Karikalar at Kanchi. Will you?' Nandini asked, holding out the scroll and the tube into which it would go.

Kandamaaran, blinded by lust, grabbed hold of Nandini's hands instead of the scroll and the tube, and gasped, 'I will do anything for you!'

There was a 'sada-sada' at that very moment.

Periya Pazhuvettaraiyar was striding down the passage that connected the palace to the lata mandapam. The servant, startled by this unexpected arrival, hurried out of his way.

From one of the beams of the lata mandapam hung a triangular perch to which a large parrot had been chained.

As Pazhuvettaraiyar stormed into the mandapam, his hands wound themselves around the parrot. The rage in his heart found an outlet in his fingers. The parrot's wings fluttered, 'sada-sada'. Unable to bear Pazhuvettaraiyar's cruel grip, the parrot shrieked.

24

LIKE WAX IN A FLAME

The parrot's shriek and the servant's startled cry blended into a screech that made Nandini and Kandamaaran jump out of their skins. When Kandamaaran turned and saw Periya Pazhuvettaraiyar approaching, he got the shock of his life. It struck him that the man could have heard him say, moments earlier—'I don't like him either'. There was an even more frightening prospect—Periya Pazhuvettaraiyar might be nursing suspicions about Kandamaaran and Nandini. Men who married in their dotage were said to behave in bizarre ways. They were bound to be suspicious that their young, beautiful wives would be attracted to other men. Perhaps that was why he was storming down the corridor in such a fury? What would he do once he reached them? One couldn't quite say. He must be ready to face anything at all, Kandamaaran told himself.

All these thoughts flitted through Kandamaaran's

mind in the fraction of a second. But that day, he was destined for a revelation—he had the opportunity to witness something wondrous. Things unfolded in a manner quite contrary to his expectations.

Once Pazhuvettaraiyar had come close, Nandini turned to him with a glowing face and looked right into his eyes as she said, 'Naadha! I was afraid you would take a while to return. Thank god, you're back!'

The moment he saw her expression and heard the note of joy in her voice, Pazhuvettaraiyar lost every trace of anger. He melted like wax in a flame, and all but giggled as he said, 'Yes. The work I had to attend to was done early. And I've returned.' He then turned to Kandamaaran and asked, 'What is this boy doing here? Has he been composing a love poem for you?' And he laughed at his own joke.

Kandamaaran's face flushed.

But Nandini laughed even louder than her husband and said, 'He knows nothing of love and nothing of poetry either. All he knows is how to get wounded in a fight. Thankfully, the wound has healed. He was just saying he'd like to return home.'

'What can one say about the mettle of today's youngsters? I've fought twenty-four wars which gave me sixty-four scars. But not once have I taken to bed. This boy's wound has taken forever to heal. Of course, all my wounds were carved on my chest and shoulders and head and face. This boy has taken a wound to the back, hasn't he? That is why it needed so much time to heal. Fair enough!' Periya Pazhuvettaraiyar said, breaking into a mocking laugh.

Kandamaaran's blood boiled over, and he took a step forward. 'Aiya! You are as a father to me. And so, I've borne your jibes!'

'Why, what would you have done otherwise, boy?' Pazhuvettaraiyar asked, placing a hand on the dagger at his waist.

Nandini intervened at this moment. 'Naadha! He has not taken a wound simply to the back. He has taken a wound to the heart too. You know this, don't you? The fact that someone whom he thought of as a dear friend stabbed him in the back has hurt him deeply. The wound on his back may have healed, but the injury to his heart is still raw. We must not speak words that make this injury bleed, should we now? Don't you know what happened that night, the night he was wounded?' she said. There must have been some hidden meaning in the gaze with which she held her husband, for his expression changed right away.

'True. What you say is right. Poor boy, he is an innocent. And his father is a bosom friend of mine. I shouldn't take this boy's thoughtless outburst seriously. All right, let's leave this aside Nandini. I came here to speak of an important matter. It's something this boy should be told too. Apparently, they've caught someone in Mathottam in Lanka, on suspicion of being a spy. And he has a scroll for Prince

Arulmozhi Varmar. From the description I've got of the captive, it appears to be our Kandamaaran's dear friend. He must be quite something. Our men nearly had him here, but he managed to give them the slip and escape to Lanka!'

Neither of the two men present noticed the momentary change this announcement prompted in Nandini's expression.

'Ade! He's escaped? He's gone to Lanka?' Kandamaaran asked, sounding betrayed.

'Naadha! It comes as no surprise to me that he escaped. How many times I've told you your brother is not qualified to supervise the security of the fort! How do you expect his men to be any better?' Nandini said.

'All the times you've said this so far, I've refuted the charge. But after what has happened, I'm inclined to agree with you. Now, listen to yet another bizarre thing—apparently, the spy who was caught in Mathottam was carrying our Pazhuvoor insignia. He wouldn't say how he got hold of it.'

Nandini said with a sigh, 'What a strange turn this is! How did he get hold of the insignia? What does your brother say?'

'My brother? His theory will make you laugh. Kalantakan says the only person who could have given it to him is you!' Periya Pazhuvettaraiyar said, with a thunderous laugh that made the very foundations of the lata mandapam quake. The trees in the garden trembled at the sound.

Nandini joined him in laughter, saying, 'Not in all the seven worlds above and seven worlds below will you find my brother-in-law's equal in astuteness!'

'And do you know what else your brother-in-law says? What a joke! It makes me laugh even to think of it. He claims that this Inderjit of a spy met you as you were being ferried to the Thanjai Fort in your palanquin. And that he came to this very palace for a private audience after. And, therefore, it is you who gave him the signet ring with the Pazhuvoor emblem. If not, this mantravadi who comes to visit you all the time must have been the courier of the ring, he says! Kalantakan has let his imagination run wild in his attempt to cover up his foolishness,' Pazhuvettaraiyar said, and then bellowed another laugh, opening his mouth wide enough to display every one of his large teeth.

'I was mistaken about my brother-in-law's astuteness. There is no doubt that he is not simply unparalleled, but that he cannot possibly ever find parallel! Now, what comes as a surprise to me is that you heard him out as he said all this, without so much as a rebuke,' Nandini said.

Her expression changed yet again. Her eyes blazed with fury, and her face twitched in rage.

The great war hero, who had endured so much on the battlefield, could not endure the slightest anger on Nandini's face. His face and form wilted, and he said, 'Devi! Do you really think I let him get away with saying all this without so much as a rebuke? I spoke so savagely about his ineptitude that I reduced him to tears. If you had been there, you would have even felt sorry for him!'

Kandamaaran was greatly troubled by the scene he had just witnessed. He felt apprehensive of Nandini, and sorry for Pazhuvettaraiyar. His awe of the man had given way to a smidgen of derision for him. He didn't want to be caught in the domestic strife of this odd couple. Intending to make his escape, he cleared his throat and said, 'Aiya …'

'Oh! In all this discussion about my brother-in-law's efficiency, we've forgotten all about our guest. He wants to go back home. That's all right with you, isn't it?' Nandini asked.

'Of course. His father must be worried that he has been here for such a long time.'

'I wish to send a scroll through him. I may do so, yes?'

'A scroll? For whom?'

'For the prince in Kanchi.'

Pazhuvettaraiyar looked suspiciously at Nandini and Kandamaaran, and said, 'A scroll for the prince? That you have written? Why?'

'Ilaiya Piraatti has sent a scroll for her younger brother through this young man's friend. Why should the Pazhuvoor Ilaiya Rani not write a letter to the elder brother? Why should she not send it through this man?'

'The scroll that this boy's friend was carrying was written by Ilaiya Piraatti, you say? How do you know this?' Pazhuvettaraiyar asked.

'Why do you think the mantravadi comes here so often? I divined this through his magical powers. Do you see what your brother's men are made of? They reported that the Pazhuvoor signet ring was on this man, but they did not tell us that the scroll he was carrying was sent by Kundavai Devi.'

'It wasn't our men who told us about the signet ring. Aniruddha Brahmarayar has returned from Rameshwaram. It was he who brought this news.'

'Did that revered Brahmin tell you about Kundavai Devi's scroll?'

'No.'

'Naadha! Think about the warning I gave you. Didn't I say everyone in the court has got together to plot against you? Do you see that this is the case, at least now? I didn't rely on the mantravadi alone. I wanted to confirm his vision. So I had the men bring the physician's son, who had been apprehended at Kodikkarai, and interrogated him. He admitted that Ilaiya Piraatti had sent her brother a scroll,' Nandini said.

Pazhuvettaraiyar felt like he had been blindfolded and dumped in the middle of a forest. He looked at Kandamaaran with distaste. He didn't like it one bit that Nandini had spoken as she had, all in the presence of this boy.

Sensing this, Nandini said, 'Anyway, why should we delay this boy's journey by speaking of such matters?' She then turned to Kandamaaran and said, 'Aiya! You must personally hand over this scroll to the prince in Kanchi. If he writes a letter in response, you must have it delivered here with the utmost care. And please don't forget to invite him to your Kadambur palace!'

'What do I tell my father, though? May I tell him that this is by wish of the King of Pazhuvoor?' Kandamaaran asked, hesitantly.

'You certainly may. My wish is his wish. Naadha! I'm right, am I not?' Nandini said.

'Of course, of course,' Pazhuvettaraiyar said with a nod. He was entirely lost. His head was spinning. He wasn't able to contradict Nandini.

Once Kandamaaran had left, Nandini turned to her husband with her limpid eyes and said in a timorous voice, 'Naadha! It appears your faith in me is shaken. My brother-in-law's instigation has worked, it seems.'

'Never, Nandini! My faith in the spear I hold and the sword I carry may be shaken, but never will my faith in you falter,' Pazhuvettaiyar said. 'I might lose my faith in a heaven for war heroes. But never will I lose my faith in your words!'

'If this is true, why did you subject me to such a severe interrogation in the presence of that boy? What humiliation!' Nandini said, her eyes blurred by tears.

Pazhuvettaraiyar was tormented by the sight. 'No,

my kanne! Please don't punish me like this!' And he reached out to wipe the tears in her eyes and console her. After a pause, he said, 'But ... there are some things you do that I don't quite understand. Don't I have the right to ask what you have planned, and why?'

'You do have that right. And I have a right to answer. Who has ever denied this? All I asked was that you not cross-examine me in the presence of strangers. Ask me anything you want to know now, and I'll tell you,' Nandini said.

'Why are you sending a scroll to Aditya Karikalan? Why do you want him invited to the Kadambur palace? Isn't he our main enemy, the first obstacle to our reaching our goal?' Pazhuvettaraiyar asked.

'No, no! Aditya Karikalar is not our main enemy. That she-snake from Pazhaiyarai is. Why do you think I invited her to our palace? That is the very reason I'm asking that Aditya Karikalar be invited to the Kadambur palace. Naadha! I ask that you remind yourself of the words I've spoken every so often. I've said, haven't I, that Ilaiya Piraatti has some designs of her own? I've found out what they are now. She has decided to get everyone else out of the way and seat her younger brother on the throne of Thanjavur. We must counter her every scheme and ensure that her dream does not turn into reality. Do you see now why I sent a scroll to Kanchi?' Nandini said, looking straight at her husband.

Her gaze melted his heart and muddled his brain.

Although he still didn't understand a thing, the old war hero said, 'Yes, yes, I see.'

'Naadha! The Chozha empire has expanded only because of the heroic deeds you and your ancestors have wrought on the battlefield and the stellar service you have rendered to the crown. Until I see you seated on the throne of this very empire, my eyes will find no sleep, neither during day nor during night. And if you should nurse any suspicion against me before that happens, stab me with your dagger and kill me!' Nandini said.

'My kanne! Don't torture me with such cruel utterances!' Periya Pazhuvettaraiyar said.

25

THE CITY OF MATHOTTAM

It's been a long time since we last met our hero, Vandiyadevan. We've spent quite a while in Thanjai. It's only been a few days, but it does seem like an age. In these few days, Vandiyadevan has walked along the Eezham shore and reached the city of Mathottam which lies on the banks of the Paalaavi river. This city, which was right across the ocean from Rameshwaram, on the Eezham side, was as lush and green as it had been in the time of Tirugnanasambandar and Sundaramurti. Its orchards and groves remained a sight for sore eyes. The shore was rich with mango, jackfruit, coconut and palm trees, and fields of plantain and sugarcane stretched into the distance. Monkeys swung from branch to branch and played on the hanging roots of various trees. The air hummed with the buzzing of bees and tittered with the prattle of parrots.

The sea waves drummed out a 'sala-sala' as they crashed against the city walls. Sea vessels of all types and sizes stood anchored by the shore. The goods that had made their way to the city of Mathottam from these vessels had been heaped into mountains.

Although these sights were quite as they had been in the time of Sambandar and Sundarar, there were indeed some changes. The streets didn't see quite as much footfall of pilgrims to the Ketheeswara temple any longer. In the city squares and temple courtyards where devotees would sing hymns and lose themselves in the bliss of faith, one now saw soldiers standing guard, armed with swords and shields, daggers and spears.

For more than a century, the city had been all too frequently turned into a Yuddhakendra, a war zone. The armies that went from Tamizhagam to Eezham typically landed at the shores of Mathottam. The retreating armies, too, boarded their ships from this port. The city had changed hands many times. Sometimes, it was under the control of the Lankan king, and at other times under Pandiya rule. Since the time of Parantaka Chakravarti, the Chozhas had been in charge.

To get back to our story, Vandiyadevan arrived at the city wall. He told the sentries that he had to enter the city to meet the senapati of the Chozha army. The men refused to let him in. And so, he resorted to the same strategy he had used in Kadambur when faced with a similar situation. He tried to force his way in. The guards surrounded him, arrested him and marched him to the security chief of the fort. Vandiyadevan told him he had a crucial scroll for Prince Arulmozhi and that he would only speak to the senapati of the Chozha army about it. They searched him, and found a scroll addressed to 'Ponniyin Selva' along with a signet ring with the Pazhuvoor emblem on it.

The senapati of the Lankan wing of the Chozha army was Kodumbalur Periya Velaar Boothi Vikramakesari. The guards rushed to apprise him of the day's developments. At the time, Boothi Vikramakesari was in conference with Prime Minister Aniruddha Brahmarayar. The senapati had decided to accompany the prime minister to Rameshwaram, and so he instructed the guards to keep the prisoner in custody until he returned and was able to conduct an inquiry.

The guards then escorted Vandiyadevan to a room in a dilapidated palace, threw him inside and locked the door. They left a sentry behind. Vandiyadevan was exhausted from his long journey, and was relieved to have been imprisoned. Now, he could rest for a couple of days.

The first day, he did get the rest for which he had longed. But the second day brought an inconvenience with it.

Strange sounds entered his room. Someone was shouting at someone else, using bizarre phrases. 'Here!' 'Chhi, chhi!' 'Get lost!' 'Don't come near me!' 'One more step, and I'll kill you!' 'I'll twist your neck!' 'You've been warned!' 'Your life is no longer in your hands!' 'I will send you to Yamalokam!' 'I'll kick your life out of your body!' The speaker was in the cell next to his own, Vandiyadevan surmised. It wasn't clear who the speaker's interlocutor was. Vandiyadevan did not hear any response to the man's threats. Was his neighbour a soldier who had lost his mind, he wondered. If that was the case, there would be little chance of sleep that night. What a nuisance. All he had wanted was another good night's sleep, and now he wouldn't get it.

'So you won't listen? You won't get lost? Fine! Just you wait and see what I do to you!' came the voice again.

A moment later, something landed with a thump in his own cell. Vandiyadevan, who had been lying down to rest, jumped up in shock. He squinted into the darkness, trying to figure out what had fallen inside.

The moment he realised what it was, he broke into helpless laughter—for the interlocutor, it turned out, was a cat.

'Oho! So you can laugh, can you? Laugh, laugh, laugh all you want! All I ask is, don't come back here!' the man from the next cell called.

There was no doubt that the man was insane. Why else would he hold such a long argument with a cat? Or expect the cat to produce a human laugh? But strangest of all was Vandiyadevan's distinct sense of having heard this voice before. Somewhere, sometime, he had heard this voice. But where? And whose voice was it? He thought about it over and over again, but couldn't place it.

Well, whatever it was, it didn't matter anymore, Vandiyadevan decided and lay back down. He closed his eyes, and tried to drift off, but sleep eluded him. Something soft brushed against his foot. He opened his eyes and looked. The cat had chosen to lie down by his foot. Dear god. How was he to sleep with this creature sharing his bed? He kicked the cat away and closed his eyes again. Suddenly, something nudged his hand. He opened his eyes to see the cat cuddling close to him. He pushed the cat away and closed his eyes once more. Now, the cat sat by his head, gracing his forehead with tail strokes.

Our hero, who could face sword and spear without fear, found himself unable to handle the cat's tail. He got up, scruffed the cat and looked for an opening. He noticed that the wall between his cell and the neighbouring one had begun to fall apart in one spot. He pushed the cat through the gap.

This was followed by a grand ruckus from the next cell. The hisses and meows of the cat accompanied the screams and threats of a human voice. After a while, the human voice shouted, 'Go! Get lost!' For a while, the cat's fading meows could be discerned, growing ever fainter. And then there was silence.

Vandiyadevan closed his eyes. In a state of half-sleep, he found himself dreaming of something most pleasant—Ilaiya Piraatti Kundavai was sitting by his side and stroking his forehead. Aha, what a difference there was between the tail of a cat and the fingers of a princess!

Then, he woke again with a start. What a pity the dream had ended prematurely, he thought disconsolately.

Someone was knocking on the wall. It must be his insane neighbour.

'Who are you? Who is the person who threw the cat at me?' the man called.

Vandiyadevan did not respond. He stayed silent. Ah! What was this now? Was the cat scratching the wall again? No, no, someone was trying to climb the wall separating the two cells. Vandiyadevan remained on his back, listening carefully. His hand slipped down to his dagger.

He saw two hands appear at the hole in the wall. And then a turban. And then, beneath the turban, a face that peeked over the rim of the opening.

Ah! Surely, this was Azhvarkadiyaan? The turban had altered his appearance slightly. But there could be no doubt that it was the man himself. Why and how had he got to this place? He must have come here knowing that he would find Vandiyadevan in the cell. Was he going to help? Or cause more trouble?

Vandiyadevan sat up and said, 'O Veeravaishnavare! Welcome, welcome, militant Vaishnavite. Welcome to this pilgrimage centre for devotees of Shiva, Tiruketheeswaram!'

'Thambi! Is it really you? I thought as much. Who else could have sat in such absolute silence and stillness for so long?' Azhvarkadiyaan said, and jumped into Vandiyadevan's cell.

26

A DAGGER BAYING FOR BLOOD

Vandiyadevan was troubled by the appearance of the militant Vaishnavite. How had the man got here? And why? But he was careful to act unperturbed.

'How strange this is! I was thinking of you a short while ago. And here you are, jumping over a wall to appear before me. They say *Kodukkira deivam kooraiyai pichikkondu kodukkum*.[1] This is indeed the case.'

'Appane! You were thinking of me a short while ago, you say? What could have prompted you to think of this ordinary human being? You'd have been better off thinking of Shri Rama, wouldn't you?'

'Your tongue deserves a gift of sugar.[2] I did think of Shri Rama at first. I could see the temple gopuram of Rameshwaram on the other shore as I made my way here. I thought about how that was the place where Shri Rama had prayed to Lord Shiva as penance for the sin of having killed Ravana ...'

'Nillu, thambi, nillu!³ Stop, stop!'

'I can't, swamigale! I absolutely can't. Please don't command me to stand. I have walked and walked and stood and stood and my feet are begging me not to torment them further. Why don't you do me the honour of sitting down? So, I was telling you how I did indeed think of Shri Rama ... and then his devotee Hanuman the Monkey God came to mind. And once I thought of Hanuman, how could I help but think of you? And right on cue, you appeared before me. Did you simply leap over the wall, or did you leap over the seas like Hanuman did?'

'Where is that icon of devotion Hanuman, and where am I? How can you draw such a comparison? The moment Hanuman came to Lanka, he put every terrifying asura on the island in his place. And I can't put even a damned cat in its place. Look here now. See how the creature has mauled me. You see these claw marks on my legs?' Azhvarkadiyaan said, and began to show Vandiyadevan his wounds.

'Adada! What a terrible fate! But what prompted you to challenge a cat of all things to a duel?'

'I didn't challenge the cat to a duel. It was the cat that came here spoiling for a fight.'

'How is that, swami?'

'I came here in search of you. I tricked the guards and slipped in by jumping over a wall. That cat was lying in wait for me, its tail stuck out right at the spot where my feet would land. My feet just about grazed its tail. But that vengeful cat clawed me nearly to death. Thambi, take my word for it—you can fight a tiger if you wish, an elephant if you wish. But never, ever take on a cat!'

'Swamigale! I'm aware of the secret behind this.'

'Which secret? Behind what?'

'That cat came here, too, and visited me in my cell. It stroked my forehead. And then cuddled up to me. It didn't scratch me at all. It's singled you out for that honour. What could the reason be? Ah! It is a Veera Shaivite cat that cannot brook Vaishnavas!'

'Oho! Is that so? Why didn't this occur to me? If only I'd known that it was a Veera Shaivite cat, I'd have whacked some sense into it with my staff!'

'It's a good thing you don't have your staff on you. Because since the moment I first stepped on these sands, my veins have been bubbling and threatening to boil over with Veera Shaiva blood. The dagger at my waist has been baying for Veera Vaishnava blood. I've mollified it in the light of the great favour you've done me.'

'Appane! I have done you no favour at all.'

'Vaishnavare! You told me about your sister, the Pazhuvoor Ilaiya Rani, didn't you?'

'Yes, I did.'

'When the Pazhuvoor Ilaiya Rani was travelling in her closed palanquin near Kadambur, the screen parted, and you pointed her out to me, didn't you?'

'Yes, yes, so what?'

'I'm coming to that. The very same palanquin was on its way to the Thanjai fort. I chanced upon the entourage when it was nearing the fort. The palanquin bearers came and rammed against my horse on purpose. I ran to the palanquin and parted the curtains to demand justice.'

'And who was inside?'

'The Pazhuvoor Ilaiya Rani herself, Nandini Devi!'

'Oho! You're a lucky man. I tried my level best but failed to meet her. And you've had that great fortune.'

'Yes, when luck shines on one, it truly shines!'

'And then?'

'I mentioned you to her. And I said you had an important message for her.'

'In all my years in this world, I've seen many things. But I've never seen someone who lies as effortlessly as you.'

'Vaishnavare! My ancestors were most fond of poets. Some of them were, indeed, poets themselves.'

'And so?'

'I come from a lineage of poets. Their blood flows in my veins. And so, my imagination tends to take flight at times. But common folk like you choose to term this phenomenon a "lie".'

'Excellent. What happened after?'

'Nandini Devi was so stunned by the powers of my imagination that she gave me the Pazhuvoor signet ring and asked me to come see her at her palace.'

'And you went?'

'How would I not? I went right away. Having heard me speak of my great acts of courage, Nandini Devi gave me an important assignment.'

'And what is this assignment?'

'Apparently, the bejewelled crown and a necklace of precious stones belonging to the Pandiya dynasty is in Lanka. The royal family of Lanka is said to have hidden these treasures away somewhere in a kingdom in the hills. She asked me to bring back those gems at whatever cost. I didn't realise it would be quite so difficult.'

'They say the gems in Periya Pazhuvettaraiyar's treasury weigh a thousand donkeyloads. That's not enough for the Ilaiya Rani, it appears. Well, that's as may be. What did she say she would give you in return for your bringing those two precious items back?'

'She said she would seize the responsibility of protecting the Thanjai fort from Chinna Pazhuvettaraiyar and hand it over to me.'

'Thambi! Thambi! If you're in charge of the security of the Thanjai fort, I can come and go as I please, can't I?'

'Some chance of that happening. How am I going to get hold of that title, when I've been thrown into prison myself in this city?' Vandiyadevan asked in a dejected voice.

'Why have you been thrown into prison? Do you know why they've put you here?' Azhvarkadiyaan asked.

'I brought along the signet ring the Pazhuvoor Ilaiya Rani had given me. I thought its influence would hold good here too. My calculations were wrong.'

'Yes, they were, indeed they were! The Senapati here is Kodumbalur Periya Velaar, don't you know? The Pazhuvoor and Kodumbalur clans have always been at loggerheads! How can you not know this?'

'I didn't. And that's why I've got myself into this position. I don't know what to do.'

'Thambi! You needn't worry anymore.'

'How can I not worry?'

'I've come here to release you.'

'Oho!'

'Once upon a time, I asked you for a favour. You refused. And yet, I've come here to do you a good turn. Now, come with me. Let's get out of this prison right away.'

'Vaishnavare! You must leave this place immediately.'

'Why, appane?'

'The dagger at my waist has begun to get shrill now. It's screaming that it wants to drink the blood of a Veera Vaishnavite!'

'Oh, let it scream. There's enough blood in my body. If your dagger wants a taste, it's most welcome to a spoonful. You come with me now!'

'No. I can't.'

'Why?'

'I feel exhausted. I'm so sleepy I'm not able to

keep my eyes open. It's been a long time since I had a good night's sleep. I've decided to sleep well tonight. That is why I sent the cat away.'

'Thambi! What kind of talk is this? Is this any way of fulfilling the task you've undertaken for Kundavai Devi? Didn't you promise her you wouldn't rest day or night until you'd personally handed the scroll over to "Ponniyin Selvan"?' Azhvarkadiyaan said, brandishing the scroll and holding it out to Vandiyadevan.

Vandiyadevan took it eagerly. All this while, he had figured Azhvarkadiyaan had an agenda, that the Vaishnavite was trying to get him to let slip what exactly he was up to. Now, he saw the man in a different light.

'How did this scroll reach you?' he asked Azhvarkadiyaan.

'Senapati Vikramakesari gave it to me. And here—he asked me to return the Pazhuvoor signet ring to you too. And he said you could resume your journey whenever you pleased.'

'Vaishnavare! You have my heartfelt gratitude.'

'Yes, yes, keep all this in mind. You can repay me when the time comes.'

'Aiya! Do you know where the prince is now?'

'No one knows. He went from Anuradhapuram towards Malainaadu, the land of hills. We'll have to search for him. The senapati has ordered me to be your guide. If you wish it, I'll accompany you.'

A mild suspicion nagged at Vandiyadevan again.

'Swamigale! May I meet the senapati before we leave?' he asked.

'Certainly! Why, you absolutely must meet him before you resume your journey. Can you leave without telling him about Vanathi and how she is doing?' Azhvarkadiyaan said.

Vandiyadevan wondered whether the Vaishnavite truly had powers of divination.

27

THE FOREST PATH

The senapati, Kodumbalur Periya Velaar Boothi Vikramakesari, was a veteran of life and war. In all his years in the world, he had spent the most on the battlefield. He had close ties with the Chozha clan. His younger brother, Kodumbalur Siriya Velaar, had lost his life in Lanka some years earlier. The army that he had led into war—or rather, its remnants—had returned, decimated. It was to avenge this defeat that Boothi Vikrama Kesari had assumed charge of the Chozha army in Lanka, in spite of his advanced age.

We already know that the Pazhuvettaraiyar brothers had thrown obstacles in the way of the war in Lanka, by delaying or denying shipments that the army needed. The rivalry between the Pazhuvoor and Kodumbalur clans had soured into enmity. And so, Vandiyadevan's being in possession of the signet ring would not have gone down well with the senapati. It was a stroke of luck for our hero that the senapati had conferred with Aniruddha Brahmarayar about this—for it was the latter who had eventually learnt the truth about Vandiyadevan from Azhvarkadiyaan, and then dispatched the Vaishnavite to Lanka right away to enlighten Boothi Vikramakesari.

Something about the scion of the Vaanar clan must have appealed to the senapati when they finally met, for, having looked him up and down, Boothi Vikramakesari said warmly, 'Thambi! Were you comfortable here? Did the men look after you well? I hope you were given a place to stay and food to eat?'

'Yes, senapati! They ensured I lacked for nothing. There were always half a dozen men at the ready, waiting to carry out my commands. I certainly had a place to stay. They sent a cat to me for my dinner. I was all set to cook and eat it, when the creature got into a fight with this militant Vaishnavite, clawed him and ran away,' Vandiyadevan said.

'Oho! This boy likes his jokes, I see. Tirumalai! Does he speak the truth?' the senapati asked.

'Senapati! Apparently, he is descended from a clan of poets. And, therefore, he has inherited their powers of imagination. Most of what he says is true. A cat did scratch my arms and legs at the site of our meeting,' Azhvarkadiyaan said.

He displayed the wounds he had suffered at the cat's claws, which made the senapati fall over with laughter.

'A cat was able to reduce you to this state, I see,'

said Boothi Vikramakesari. 'It's a good thing you have a warrior by your side to escort you through the forest.'

'Senapati, I need no escort. My staff is more than enough. The problem was that I left it behind when I went to meet him.'

'Well, then I suppose *you* will be *his* escort. Feed him well before you leave. Thambi! You've come to Lanka at a time of severe food shortage. Mahinda's men have disrupted the water supply to farms by breaking the banks of the rivers and filling in the ponds, and so cultivation has suffered. There are no farmers here either. The people of this land are starving themselves, so how can they possibly spare food for our troops? And we don't get enough grain from our land either ...'

'Senapati! I'm aware of this. I was there when the women left behind in the army quarters of Pazhaiyarai spoke to Ilaiya Piraatti about it. They told her they had heard their husbands and sons were starving in Lanka.'

'Oh, so the news has reached them, has it? Well, that's good, that's good! How did Ilaiya Piraatti respond?'

'She consoled them by saying that as long as the senapati, Kodumbalur Periya Velaar, was in Lanka, he would never let the men go hungry. They need have no cause for worry, she said.'

'Aha! Did Ilaiya Piraatti really say this? There are so many royal women across so many clans who have earned universal fame and praise and respect. But not one is the equal of our Ilaiya Piraatti,' said the senapati.

'There is another princess who is nearly her equal senapati.'

'And who might that be thambi?'

'Why, the princess of Kodumbalur, Vanathi!'

'Aha! This boy is something! I might fall under the spell of his glib tongue and imaginative prowess myself,' laughed the senapati. He then asked, 'Thambi! So you saw the guiding light of our clan, our beacon of hope in Pazhaiyarai, did you?'

'Yes, aiya, I did. How could I miss seeing someone who never leaves Ilaiya Piraatti's side? They arrived together on an elephant to see me off from the physician's house. Just as light can never be separated from the lamp, nor fragrance from the flower, nor one's shadow from one's body, so can Vanathi Devi never be separated from Ilaiya Piraatti.'

'Adade! This boy ... his cleverness leaves me speechless. Tirumalai! Escort this young man to our treasury, and let him have all the clothes and ornaments he wants before you take him on his way.'

'Aiya! Let the treasury remain undisturbed for now. I'll take everything I need on my way back.'

'Thambi! Did Ilaiya Piraatti not send me a message? Did she ask you to convey nothing about our girl, our Vanathi?'

'Senapati, I don't wish to lie to you.'

'You must never lie to anyone, ever, thambi.'

'But you must exempt me from that obligation with this Veeravaishnavar alone, senapati. My head will burst if I tell him the truth.'

'Oh, no, that can never be. Well ... so, I suppose Ilaiya Piraatti has not sent any message for me, then ...'

'No, she hasn't sent a message for you. But ...'

'But ...? What ...? But what, thambi?'

'She *has* sent a message for whoever she must. She has asked me to personally tell the prince a couple of things about Vanathi Devi.'

'I have never seen a boy as clever as you!' Senapati Periya Velaar said, and embraced Vandiyadevan. 'Well, let's not waste time. You both must get started on your journey.'

'Aiya, is there no way around this Veeravaishnavar accompanying me? May I not go alone, without him?'

'What is your objection to his accompanying you?'

'It is not I who has an objection, but my dagger. You see, my dagger is a Veera Shaivite one. It's been baying for Veera Vaishnavite blood for a very long time now. I'm just concerned that his life may be in danger, for what if the dagger overcomes me and attacks him? It does have a mind of its own.'

'In that case, leave the dagger here and take another one with you. If Tirumalai doesn't accompany you, you won't be able to find the prince. No one knows where he is. Besides, he, too, is carrying an important letter for the prince. So, it's best the two of you go as a unit. Only, don't ruin everything by getting into a quarrel with each other en route.'

And with that, the senapati called Vandiyadevan closer as if for a parting embrace, and whispered in his ear as he held him, 'Thambi! You won't have any problems because of him. But, please do be careful nevertheless. Listen carefully to whatever he tells the prince, and report it to me when you return.'

Vandiyadevan had figured they were sending Azhvarkadiyaan along to spy on him. Now, he was being tasked with spying on the latter. He liked this turn of events.

~*~

That very night, Vandiyadevan and Azhvarkadiyaan left with two soldiers for their escort. They went eastwards for a couple of days. At first, they passed through urban settings, well-populated towns, which slowly gave way to more rural surrounds, eventually leading to forest and then to jungle. The shrubs grew into trees and then into ancient trunks, whose tops shot into the very skies. There was evidence of water bodies having punctuated the path, but their shores had been disfigured, forcing the water to run off. The beds were now dry. Then, they came across a flooded plain. The Paalaavi River's banks had been broken, so that the water had stagnated, unable to follow its rightful course.

As they observed the devastation the long years of conflict had visited on the land, Azhvarkadiyaan spoke about what a terrible thing war was. Vandiyadevan disagreed strongly, and the two of them inevitably got into a series of ferocious arguments.

After two days, they changed direction and headed southwards. The landscape began to change. Forest gave way to valley, and then to desert, and then to hilly regions. They could see enormous mountains on the horizon, their peaks blue in the distance. The jungle itself became denser and more menacing as they walked towards those mountains. The sweet chirps of birds had long dissolved into sinister calls.

The men began to speak about the threat wild animals posed. Foxes and jackals, various species of big cats, bears, elephants and other such creatures were known to inhabit these forests, Azhvarkadiyaan said.

'If the jackals attack in a pack, that would pose a danger, won't it?' Vandiyadevan asked. The nightmare he had had at the Kadambur palace came to his mind.

'There is more danger in the howl of a lone jackal than in their arrival as a pack,' Azhvarkadiyaan said.

'How is that?'

'In these forests, jackals and jaguars hunt in tandem. The big cats roam here and there, while the jackals run in chase of prey. Once they spot prey, be it man or deer or some other hapless creature, they let out a single howl. Then, the jaguar runs at full tilt, leaps on the unsuspecting victim and turns it into meat. These jackals which work as spies for big cats are called "ori", you know ...'

As they went on their way, exchanging such pleasantries, they heard a hum as if of sea waves.

'We left the shore behind a long time ago. Why do I hear water?' Vandiyadevan asked.

'Must be some pond or river nearby. I think it's a herd of elephants approaching for a drink of water,' Azhvarkadiyaan said.

'Aiyayo! What if we get caught in the middle of that?'

'Oh, you need have no fear of that. When elephants approach in a herd, they don't attack. As long as we step out of their path, the herd won't so much as throw a glance our way.'

One of the soldiers who had accompanied them now climbed a tree to do a recce of what lay ahead.

'Aiya! Aiya! A lone elephant! An elephant in musth! It's uprooting trees and charging!' he yelled.

'Aiyo! What is this peril! How do we escape?' Azhvarkadiyaan cried in fear and looked about himself.

'You said one need have no fear of a herd. Why does a single elephant scare you, then?' Vandiyadevan asked.

'Appane! A lone elephant in musth has the strength of a thousand ordinary elephants! No one can stand up to it!'

'The three of us have spears, and you have your staff.'

'A thousand spears are as nothing before an elephant in musth. There! You see that steep hill! If we make a run for it, we might get there in time!' Azhvarkadiyaan cried, dashing towards the hill even as he spoke.

The others followed.

But then they noticed a fissure in the ground before them, with a steep drop into what looked like a bottomless pit. There was no way to reach the hill they had spotted. They stood at the edge of the crevasse. The elephant was now visible, charging towards them at top speed. As the elephant raised its trunk and trumpeted, it was a wonder the entire universe didn't splinter from the sound. The four men raised their hands to their ears and took off, each in a different direction.

The elephant got closer. And still closer. It appeared to have set its sights on Azhvarkadiyaan, making straight for the place where the Vaishnavite stood. Only two strides of the pachyderm separated Azhvarkadiyaan from the afterlife. There was no place to run. The undergrowth was simply too thick.

Vandiyadevan aimed his spear. But the elephant was running so fast not even Indra's thunderbolt could have stopped it. The arm that was holding up the spear wilted in impotence.

Azhvarkadiyaan's reaction almost made Vandiyadevan laugh.

The Vaishnavite raised his staff and hollered, 'Stop, stop! Stop right where you are! One more step, and you're finished! I'll kill you and bury you in a pit. Careful!'

28

THE ROYAL PATH

Would an elephant in musth possibly be daunted by Azhvarkadiyaan's staff or his threats? The animal charged forward, using his trunk to uproot the trees in his way. In a moment, Azhvarkadiyaan would be history. The two soldiers who had accompanied the two royal envoys stood where they were, shouting 'Haiiii!' as if it would deter the elephant. Vandiyadevan reached for the spear that had slipped from his hands, and decided to make one last effort to save his friend.

But Azhvarkadiyaan had disappeared. His turban was flying in the air, and eventually got stuck on the branch of a tree. Before they could even contemplate what fate had befallen the man, something of still greater urgency occurred.

The elephant reached the spot where Azhvarkadiyaan had stood a moment ago.

The animal then bent his forelegs and lurched forward. And then there was a roar that echoed from every part of the forest, before the elephant's entire, enormous body disappeared from view. A cloud of dust rose from the fissure. It took Vandiyadevan some time to figure out that the dust was from the stones that the elephant had dislodged on his way down the crevasse, to a certain and horrific death.

As for Azhvarkadiyaan, it was all too evident what had happened—the force with which he had wielded his stick had made him lose balance. He had fallen into the pit to hell too. The elephant had simply followed him. The animal had tried to pull back, but having placed both forelegs on thin air, there was no way to stop the fall. In the case of both man and animal, the bulk of the body had proven to be a dire enemy. They had suffered the same fate at the same time.

When this realisation hit Vandiyadevan, his hair stood on end. His heart felt heavy with sorrow. The doubts he had once nursed about the Vaishnavite had dissolved and given way to affection through the course of their journey. Why had such an awful thing happened to Azhvarkadiyaan? It then occurred to Vandiyadevan that he would have to complete the task he had undertaken all on his own. He would have to do without Azhvarkadiyaan's assistance as well as his company. He approached the fissure that had devoured man and beast and peeped over the edge.

At first, all he could see was a fog of dust. Everything was lost in the mist the sand had raised. Once it settled, he could see the torn shrubs and dislodged stones that traced the path down which the elephant had fallen.

'Thambi! Do you intend to gawk at the scenery, or give me a helping hand?' called a voice.

Vandiyadevan jumped out of his skin.

He just about stopped himself from stumbling in shock, and gingerly approached the source of the voice he had just heard. Just off the path of the elephant's descent, hanging on to the branches of a tree that was growing perpendicular to the rock face, was Azhvarkadiyaan. Can you imagine how thrilled Vandiyadevan was? He found his sense of humour restored right away.

'Ohoho! Vaishnavare! You've ensured that Gajendra alone attained moksha[1] and got yourself stuck in Trishanku Swargam[2]?' Vandiyadevan called, even as he clapped to call the soldiers to the spot.

Vandiyadevan unwound his waistcloth, and bade the two men to hold on to one end tightly. He then lowered the other end down to Azhvarkadiyaan, who let go of the tree branch and held on to the cloth instead. The three men then pulled the hefty Vaishnavite to safety, not without a fair bit of effort.

For some time, Azhvarkadiyaan could only take in huge gulps of air and pant noisily. He looked about himself, dazed. The others surrounded him, trying to make him as comfortable as they could.

Suddenly, he got to his feet and said, 'Let us leave! We must reach the Rajpath, the royal path, before dusk falls. Where is my turban? And my staff?'

'There's no hurry. Rest for a while. We can leave after,' Vandiyadevan said.

Just then, they heard the howl of a jackal. Another one from its cohort lent its voice to the harmony after half a bar. There were growls and rustles in the undergrowth, even as hundreds of jackals sang together. The men didn't need to look below to sense the tigers and jaguars making their way to the spot where the elephant lay. In the sky above, eagles and kites whirled about.

'The death of an elephant is no ordinary affair. Animals and birds of prey will approach from every direction and traverse long distances to get to this meat. We'll be their dessert if we don't get out of here,' Azhvarkadiyaan said.

Vandiyadevan didn't argue. The four men made haste, going as fast as they could through the brush. They reached the Rajpath by sunset.

The road was teeming with people, animals and vehicles. They saw people riding elephants. Vandiyadevan marvelled at them, reflecting that it was one such animal that had created such a commotion in the forest.

'Where does the royal path lead? Where are we now, and where are we going?' he asked.

'We're on the road that leads from Anuradhapuram to Simhagiri. Half a kaadham from here is Thamballai. We'll be there by nightfall,' Azhvarkadiyaan said.

'We could have travelled comfortably on the royal path all through. Why did we take the forest route?' Vandiyadevan asked.

'If we'd taken the Rajpath, we'd have been stopped and searched at a hundred checkpoints. And they would have halted us at Anuradhapuram. I got to know that the person whom we are looking for is now in Simhagiri. That is why I took a shortcut. And even so, we don't know whether we'll find him or not. Let's hope he's not gone anywhere else!' Azhvarkadiyaan said.

They could see houses, paths leading to villages, markets and workshops of various kinds on either side of the wide road. The majority of those who lived and worked there appeared to be Sinhalas. Warriors from Tamizhagam were walking about on the royal path. But the Sinhalas went about their business with no hint of nervousness or fear.

'Who has control over these areas?' Vandiyadevan asked.

'The Chozha army has captured all the towns up to Thamballai. Beyond, the Simhagiri mountain and fort are still in Mahinda's control,' Azhvarkadiyaan said.

'And the people who live here?'

'Mostly Sinhala. Once Ponniyin Selvar arrived here, the way the war was conducted changed entirely. The fight is between the Chozha warriors and Mahinda's warriors. And that, too, on the battlefield. He declared that the people of the land should be free to go about their business unhindered and unafraid. The Buddhist monks are all enthralled because the prince has ordered that every one of the viharas that were destroyed or that have fallen to ruin and dilapidation be renovated or rebuilt. Has anyone heard of such a thing? Why would the monks not be delighted? When I meet the prince, I'm going to tell him to his face, "I don't like what you're doing one bit!"'

'Please do. Who does the prince think he is, doing things you don't like? Did he sprout kombu on his head or what?'³ Vandiyadevan demanded.

'No, he hasn't sprouted kombu, thambi, true enough. But he does have a certain power or pull. You could find a million faults with him behind his back, but the moment you look at his face, you are spellbound. No one is able to say a word against him. The superpower—the power to make the *prince* follow orders—rests with a single person.'

'Of course, of course! Who can be ignorant of Veera Vaishnava Azhvarkadiyaar's magical powers? What is a prince to one who has defeated an elephant in musth by wielding a wooden staff?'

'Thambi, you haven't understood the implication of what I just said. What is the stature of Ponniyin Selvar, and what is that of this poor Vaishnavite by comparison? I can oppose an elephant in musth with a staff in hand; I can take on tigers and bears and lions bare-handed. But the moment I stand face-to-face with Ponniyin Selvar, all my courage disappears. My heart melts as wax. My throat catches. It takes a mammoth effort to speak a single syllable.'

'Then who is the person you mentioned, who can make him follow orders?'

'Don't you know what the entire world knows? I was speaking of Ilaiya Piraatti. Kundavai Devi's word is as scripture to him.'

'Oho! You meant Pazhaiyarai Ilaiya Piraatti, did you? I thought you were talking about your sister, the Pazhuvoor Ilaiya Rani!'

'Oh, Nandini certainly does have her powers. But those are of a different kind.'

'How so? What is the difference?'

'If a man is about to fall into the fires of hell, Kundavai Devi will rescue him and carry him to the heavens. Now that's some power, isn't it? And do you know what Nandini would do? You could say she has a superior skill. She will swear hell is heaven, ensure this man believes it, and then entice him to jump joyfully into hellfire.'

Vandiyadevan's skin broke into gooseflesh. How well this Vaishnavite had sized up and articulated Nandini's powers of seduction and persuasion! Could it really be that she was his sister? Vandiyadevan was lost in his thoughts, and didn't ask any further questions.

His silence was broken by the sound of hooves. Horses were approaching them, from the opposite direction, it seemed. Within minutes, four horses came galloping their way, raising a cyclonic cloud of dust before crossing them at the speed of lightning. But even in that split second, Vandiyadevan recognised one of the horse-riders. Aha! Wasn't that Parthibendra Varman, the close friend and confidante of Prince Aditya Karikalar in Kanchi? And a man not particularly fond of Vandiyadevan? What was he doing here, and where was he headed? What was his business in Lanka? And when had he arrived?

Not long after the horses had crossed the travellers, an authoritative voice commanded, 'Stop!'

The horses stopped. Then, they turned and began to approach the travellers from behind. The man who appeared to be their leader edged his horse ahead of the others. As Vandiyadevan had surmised, this man was indeed Parthibendra Pallavan, whom we last met in Mamallapuram.

He stared at Vandiyadevan and asked, 'What is this! What brings *you* here? They said you'd disappeared all of a sudden in Thanjavur. I thought the Pazhuvettaraiyars had put paid to you.'

'You think it's that easy to put paid to me? Am I not of the ancient Vaanar clan?'

'Yes, yes, you certainly have no equal in escaping by the skin of your teeth.'

'Aiya, when the situation calls for escape, I escape. When the situation calls for sacrifice, I'm ready to lay down my life. And if I must die such a death, should it not be at the hands of a member of such an old and honourable clan as your Pallava dynasty, rather than the Pazhuvettaraiyar clan of all things?' Vandiyadevan said, as he pulled his sword out of its scabbard.

'Tchah, tchah, are you challenging me to a duel? And that, too, in this foreign land? No, thambi, let us do no such thing. I'm on an urgent mission. What happened to the task the prince assigned you?'

'I've accomplished it, aiya. I've personally handed over the olai he sent for the emperor as well as the one he sent for Ilaiya Piraatti to the intended recipients.'

'What brings you to Lanka?'

'I've wanted to see Lanka for the longest time. So I tagged along with this Vaishnavite.'

'Aha! Your companion looks familiar too ...'

'Yes, you have seen me before, Maharaja. I had come to meet Prince Adityar to ask if he knew anything about the fate of my sister. You were by his side then,' said Azhvarkadiyaan.

'And who is your sister?'

'The current Ilaiya Rani of Pazhuvoor, Nandini Devi!'

'Aha! When I think of the poison that has slipped into the soil of this country thanks to that snake ... you should be impaled on a spike for the crime of being her brother!'

'Maharaja! I've sworn I'll kill myself by impalement when the time comes. On that day, if you would be so kind as to carry out that task with your hallowed hands ...'

'Can I possibly carry you to the spike by myself? It would take a hundred men to do that. Well, that's as may be. Did you happen to hear any news of the prince on your way? Do you know whether he has reached Anuradhapuram?' Parthibendran asked.

'What do we know of such things, Maharaja? We took the forest route. Why, a crazed elephant chased me, and …'

'Enough with your stories. Who cares! One day, I just might fulfil your request and impale you with my own hands,' Parthibendran said, turning his horse around.

Azhvarkadiyaan had been observing Parthibendran's companions while he was speaking to the Pallava scion.

Once all the horsemen had gone on their way, he turned to Vandiyadevan and asked eagerly, 'Thambi! Did you see the other three men's faces? Did you recognise any?'

'No, I've never seen them before.'

'True, you couldn't have. I've seen two of them before. At midnight, in the Tiruppurambiyam pallipadai[4]. What a terrible oath they swore!' Azhvarkadiyaan said, his entire body quaking.

'What oath could be so terrible that it makes you shake and shiver like this?'

'That they would wipe out every single trace of the Chozha clan from this earth!'

'Aiyayo!'

'I don't know how they've contrived to get here

before us. They're cunning. They've managed to lure this hot-headed Pallava somehow,' Azhvarkadiyaan said, and then sank into silence.

Vandiyadevan suddenly remembered something he had learnt in Kodikkarai—that two men had arrived the day before him in a tearing hurry to get to Lanka, and that Poonguzhali's brother had rowed them across. Could those two men have been the conspirators Azhvarkadiyaan had mentioned? In that case, what was their connection to Parthibendran?

They were nearing Thamballai, one of the holiest sites of Buddhist pilgrimage.

29

THE MAHOUT

Two thousand years ago—a thousand years before the time in which our story is set—there lived a Sinhala king called Valahambahu. At this time, too, armies from Tamizhagam would regularly march on Lanka. Once, Valahambahu fled from his capital and hid in the caves of Thamballai's mountains. He eventually gathered an army and recaptured land up to Anuradhapuram. And he expressed his gratitude to the caves that had sheltered him by expanding them into a temple. He installed idols of Buddha of various sizes in different parts of this temple. The sculptors, who had carved hundreds of these Buddha idols, were yet not satisfied that they had done justice to their skill. And so they also sculpted ornate idols of Hindu gods, which were placed among the Buddhas. These incredible feats of artistic excellence can still be seen inside the cave temple of Thamballai.

When Vandiyadevan first entered this hallowed

place, he had the distinct sense of having stepped into another world. The fragrance of the fresh flowers that had been gathered for worship was intoxicating. In the street corners, heaps of lotus and shenbagham blooms were on display for purchase. The devotees bought these flowers and carried them in beautifully woven baskets to the temple as offerings. These men and women filled the streets leading to the temple. Saffron-clad Buddhist monks walked among them.

A loud cry of 'Sadhu! Sadhu!' rose from the crowd every now and again.

Vandiyadevan found these sights and sounds quite incredible. He turned to Azhvarkadiyaan and said, 'Here I was thinking we were at a Yuddha Kendram, a centre of war. Instead, we seem to have arrived at a Buddha Kendram.'

'Yes, appa, this is a Buddha Kshetram dating back a millennium,' Azhvarkadiyaan said.

'But you said this was within the control of the Chozha army.'

'Yes, it still is.'

'But I don't see any Chozha soldiers about.'

'The army camps have been set up outside the town. The prince has ordered that they remain there.'

'Which prince?'

'The very prince of whom we are in search.'

'I was going to ask you about this—Parthibendran has just searched unsuccessfully for the prince at this very spot and is returning the way he came. What is the point of us searching here?'

'Should we take the Pallavan's word for it? Does his inability to find the prince prove that Ponniyin Selvar is not here? I'll have to look myself before I give up. Hiranyakashipu denied the existence of Vishnu. Did Prahlada take him at his word?'

'By the way, Vaishnavare, you were spoiling for a fight with every Shaivite who was simply going about his business back in our land. This place is swarming with Buddhist monks. And you're walking along placidly. Why? Has the fact that you're outnumbered induced so much fear in you that you've conquered your zeal?'

'Thambi? What is fear? How does it look?'

'Black and monstrous and as large as an elephant. Have you not seen it?'

'No,' Azhvarkadiyaan said, and then left his side to walk towards two men who were standing at a street corner, watching the procession of devotees. They appeared to be Tamilians. Azhvarkadiyaan conferred with them for some time before returning to Vandiyadevan.

'Vaishnavare! What did you ask them? Whether Vishnu is greater or Buddha? You could pose that question to anyone in this land, and the answer would be that Buddha is greater. Do you see how enormous each Buddha statue here is?'

'Thambi, I've packed all my militant Vaishnavism into a bundle and left it behind in Rameshwaram. I'm here solely in the service of the crown, you understand?'

'Then, what did you ask those men? Did you inquire into the prince's whereabouts?'

'No, I asked what the festive occasion was.'

'And what did they say?'

'Apparently, two Chinese pilgrims are expected to arrive here today. There's a celebration at the Buddha vihara in honour of their visit That is why the town wears such an air of festivity.'

'Where are the Chinese travelling from?'

'They arrived here yesterday and then left for Simhagiri. They're now returning and are expected here shortly.'

'Where is Simhagiri?'

'About a kaadham from here. It is under the Sinhalas' control for now. You can see the town from here when it's light. There's an imposing fort on the Simhagiri mountain. And inside one of the caves are incredible murals that have withstood the vagaries of weather over aeons. The Chinese pilgrims must have gone there to look at those cave paintings. They would have had a tough time climbing up and down the mountain ... Oh, look!'

An elephant decorated with opulent finery was approaching from the direction in which Azhvarkadiyaan pointed. Two men sat in the howdah. Their clothing and facial features made it evident that they were the Chinese pilgrims in question. A mahout sat before them, an ankusha in his hand. An enormous crowd of people surrounded the elephant, shouting and cheering as the procession moved forward.

'You see?' Azhvarkadiyaan said.

'I saw, I saw. Amma! What a mammoth elephant! Should we look for a crevasse nearby?'

'No, there's no need for that. All we need to do is stand to one side of the road.'

As the elephant neared them, Azhvarkadiyaan and Vandiyadevan moved to one side of the road. The elephant passed them by, along with the throng of people cheering the visitors.

Vandiyadevan's eyes were entirely focused on the two Chinese men. He was astonished by their faith, which had brought them across seas and over land, crossing who-knew-how-many obstacles, all to visit a Buddhist shrine. They were certainly due the raucous welcome they had received in this land. But how bizarre it was that a pilgrimage could be arranged uninterrupted at a time of war! Prince Arulmozhi Varmar must have organised it. Only he could have been as thoughtful and generous. But where was he now? Would they be successful in finding him? Or would the arduous journey Vandiyadevan and Azhvarkadiyaan had undertaken end in failure?

'Thambi, did you see?' Azhvarkadiyaan asked.

'I did.'

'What did you see?'

'The Chinese pilgrims have flat noses and wear strange clothes.'

'I wasn't asking about them.'

'Who, then?'

'I asked whether you saw the mahout.'

'The mahout? No, I didn't pay him any attention.'

'Wonderful. Didn't you notice how his eyes lit up when they chanced upon us?'

'Why, did someone strike a match in his eyes? Why would they light up?'

'What a man you are! I'm not sure what astonishes me more, your absolute carelessness or Ilaiya Piraatti's judgement in choosing someone like you for such a critical task. Well, never mind. Come with me.'

The two men followed the elephant and the accompanying crowd.

The elephant stopped at the entrance to the Buddha vihara. The mahout whispered in the animal's ear, and the elephant knelt so the pilgrims could dismount. The two men got down, to be greeted by the Buddhist monks who were waiting outside the vihara. Temple bells clanged and conches were blown. Someone threw flowers down from the upper floor of the vihara.

'Buddham sharanam gachami!' the crowd chanted.

The Chinese pilgrims entered the vihara, followed by most of the crowd.

The mahout, who had got off the elephant before the pilgrims now nudged the animal to its feet and walked ahead. He approached four men who were waiting some distance away, and handed the elephant over to one of them. He then pointed towards Azhvarkadiyaan as he said something to another. After a while, he disappeared down an alley, accompanied by the two remaining men, as the man to whom he had spoken moved towards Azhvarkadiyaan and Vandiyadevan.

'Aiya, would you care to come with me?' he asked.

'We've been waiting for you to ask,' Azhvarkadiyaan said.

'Do you carry some form of identification?'

Azhvarkadiyaan proffered the ring the senapati had given them.

'Right, come with me,' the man said, and led them to the city gates.

Once they had crossed the town, a little path appeared through the forest. They followed this path until they reached an old ruin. Their escort asked them to wait there for a while. He climbed a tree and squinted down at the path they had taken.

'What is all this secrecy in honour of? I don't understand a thing that is going on,' Vandiyadevan said.

'You'll find out soon enough,' Azhvarkadiyaan said. 'Have some patience.'

Two horses had been tethered outside the ruin. The fact that there were only two troubled Vandiyadevan. What was this great mystery surrounding the mahout? He had only glanced at the man, before turning his attention to the Chinese pilgrims. Vandiyadevan tried to recall the mahout's face, to no avail.

'Vaishnavare! Who was the mahout? Can't you tell me?'

'Who could he have been? Give it some thought, thambi.'

'Was the mahout actually Ponniyin Selvar?'

'From the radiance in his eyes, it would appear so.'

'Wouldn't everyone else have recognised him, as you have?'

'No. Who would think the prince would serve as a mahout to the Chinese pilgrims? Besides, the people of this town have never set eyes on the prince.'

'You said the pilgrims were returning from Simhagiri.'

'Yes.'

'And you also said Simhagiri was still in the clutches of the Sinhalas.'

'I did.'

'So, the prince has gone right into the enemy's den and returned?'

'Forget Simhagiri, the prince has gone all the way up to Mahiyangana and Samandakoodam, which are deep within enemy territory, accompanying the Chinese pilgrims,' Azhvarkadiyaan said.

'Why is he taking such a risk?'

'Well, quite obviously because of his desire to see those holy sites and the remarkable sculptures and paintings there.'

'Excellent desire. Excellent prince. Is it this eccentric boy that the astrologer of Kudandai predicted would become an emperor to whom all kings bent their knees?'

'Did the astrologer of Kudandai say this, thambi?'

'Do you believe it too?'

'I don't believe in astrology. And I have no need to rely on it either.'

'Then?'

'I know for sure that the prince will become such an emperor, even without the aid of astrology.'

Suddenly, the sound of horses' hooves approached. The man who was playing sentry on the treetop began a hurried descent. He fetched the two tethered horses. He mounted one, and asked Azhvarkadiyaan to get on the other.

'In some time, a group of horsemen will come this way. We must join them,' the man told Azhvarkadiyaan.

'Where is my horse?' Vandiyadevan asked.

'I was ordered to bring him alone.'

'Ordered by whom?'

'I'm not authorised to tell you.'

'I must meet the prince right away. I carry crucial information for him.'

'I haven't been told anything about this, aiya.'

Azhvarkadiyaan turned to Vandiyadevan and said, 'Thambi, have some patience. I'll speak to the prince and arrange for them to bring you along too.'

'Vaishnavare! The information I carry must be conveyed with extreme urgency. Don't you know how critical it is?'

'Give me the scroll. I'll pass it on.'

'I cannot.'

'In that case, you'll just have to wait. There is no other option.'

'Is there really no other option?'

'None at all.'

Vandiyadevan was disheartened. There was no doubt Azhvarkadiyaan was being escorted into the presence of the prince. The senapati had asked him to listen in on what the Vaishnavite told the prince. That would be impossible now.

The horses came closer. They passed the group in a blur of manes and tails. Azhvarkadiyaan and their escort, already seated on their horses, took the reins and were about to urge them to follow, when something most unexpected occurred.

Vandiyadevan caught hold of their escort's leg and pulled him off the horse. The man fell to the ground, even as Vandiyadevan took his place on the horse. The horse flew at Vandiyadevan's touch. Azhvarkadiyaan's horse followed suit. The soldier who had been thrown off hollered and reached for his dagger. Vandiyadevan bent low, pressing himself against the horse's back. The dagger flew past him and wedged itself deep in the trunk of a tree.

The two horses galloped along, keeping the three that had passed before in sight, without getting too close or falling too far behind.

'You did well, thambi,' Azhvarkadiyaan said reassuringly.

But Vandiyadevan didn't reply. He was worried

about how this would all end. Why had he landed up in this place, so far from home, and taken such a risk? All for a woman? What a fix he was in now, he thought, even as the horses flew at the speed of wind, at the speed of thought.

30

THE DUEL

The horses seemed to be travelling along an endless path, to Vandiyadevan. Had this Vaishnavite tricked him into a trap? Was he going to deliver Vandiyadevan to the enemy now? There was dense forest on either side. Vandiyadevan tried to peek through the boughs of the trees, only to find a frightening darkness that seemed to suck the very light into itself. Who knew what dangers lurked in that darkness and what forms they assumed? Big cats of various stripes—and spots— along with bears, elephants, poisonous snakes and other wild animals must roam through its inky depths. The southernmost point under Chozha control was Thamballai. Had they not already crossed it? Where was Azhvarkadiyaan leading him now?

Thankfully, there was some moonlight. The rays of the moon grazed the tops of the trees that reached up into the sky. Sometimes, the rays playfully pulled at the leaves and tapped the branches, causing dappled shadows to dance across the path that the horses were taking. The three steeds galloping before Vandiyadevan sometimes appeared as silhouettes in the dark. The clip-clop of their hooves, though, was consistent.

All of a sudden, other sounds began to fall on his ears, sounds one wouldn't expect to hear in the middle of a forest. The sound of numerous excited human voices, of song and dance. Ah! There among the trees, one could see light. Aha! Who were the soldiers camped out in the jungle now? Where they Chozha men? Or enemies?

Vandiyadevan did not have a chance to dwell on this for long.

You see, he hadn't noticed that one of the three horses leading the way had swung round and begun to charge towards him. The horse approached his own, and the rider leaned over and punched Vandiyadevan square in the face. Stunned by the blow, Vandiyadevan was still coming to his senses, when the rider caught hold of his knee and pulled him off the horse. Vandiyadevan fell to the ground and his startled horse jumped out of the fray.

By this time, his assaulter had jumped off his own horse and marched up to Vandiyadevan. As our man struggled to get up, his opponent reached for the dagger at Vandiyadevan's waist, took it out of its sheath and threw it across the path.

Vandiyadevan was livid with rage. He jumped to his feet, drew both hands into fists and threw a punch that could have felled an elephant at the man who had attacked him. His rival remained standing, though, and gave it right back to him.

The two men engaged in a duel. And what duel it was! One would think Ghatotkacha and Hidimba were taking each other on in battle. When Lord Shiva wore the guise of a hunter and fought the Pandava prince Arjuna, they must have flown at each other and rolled about on the forest floor as these two men did. But, no, this was a duel of far larger scale. Imagine this scene—two of the Diggajas that keep the world in place leave their positions and then clash in a fight unto death. This was a duel of such magnitude.

As the two men fought, Azhvarkadiyaan and the soldiers who had accompanied our mystery warrior stood by the side of the path, watching in admiration as each tried his manoeuvres, in the strange moonlight that filtered through the canopy of trees.

Footsteps were heard soon enough. More men appeared, carrying flares. They stopped and stared in astonishment as the duellers fought on, matching move for move. The crowd of onlookers grew.

It was a long time before Vandiyadevan was finally pushed to the ground. His opponent sat on his chest and unwound the cloth Vandiyadevan had tied around his waist. He found the scroll in its tube and snatched it away, even as Vandiyadevan struggled to push him off his chest and retrieve it.

Once the man had secured the scroll, he leapt off

Vandiyadevan's chest and went to read it in the light of a flare. At a sign from him, two of his men ran up to Vandiyadevan and gripped his arms so he could not get off the ground.

Fuming with frustration and fury, Vandiyadevan called, 'Paavi Vaishnavane[1]! Who betrays a friend as you have? Go, grab the scroll from him!'

'Appane! You're asking me to do something I will never be able to,' Azhvarkadiyaan said.

'Chhi, chhi! I've never come across such a coward as you! What a fool I am for having trusted you to be my companion and guide!' Vandiyadevan snarled.

Azhvarkadiyaan casually slipped off his horse, approached Vandiyadevan and whispered in his ear, 'Ade asade[2]! The scroll has reached its intended recipient. Why are you whining so much?'

As the man had moved towards the light to read the scroll, his face had been revealed to the gathering, and a wave of excitement rippled through the men. One of them shouted:

Ponniyin Selvar Vaazhga! Long live Ponniyin Selvar!
And the other chorused:
Vaazhga!
Soon, other cheers followed:
Anniya mannarin Kaalan Vaazhga!
Long live the man who is Yama to our enemies!
Engal Ilango Vaazhga!
Long live our prince!
Chozhakula thondral Vaazhga!
Long live the scion and beacon of the Chozha dynasty!

The cries rang through the forest, and as if it were an echo, the birds roosting in the trees rose, flapped their wings and chirped so the air bubbled with their various cries.

Now, dozens of men from the camp broke through the undergrowth, running to see what the matter was.

Noting that there was a throng of people around them now, the prince said, 'All of you head back to the camp. Make arrangements for a meal, a feast. I'll be there shortly.'

The men disappeared as one at his bidding.

Vandiyadevan, bruised and bleeding, watched from the ground. He had forgotten all his pain and humiliation in the wonder of the discovery that his rival was the prince himself.

'Aha! So, this is Prince Arulmozhi Varmar! How much strength his arms wield! How fast he moves! They say, *kuttuppattaalum modhira kaiyaal kuttuppaduvendum*— if you must be punched in the head, let it be by a bejewelled fist. That the bejewelled fist should belong to this man! How fortunate I am. He has Arjuna's unmatched beauty and regal stature and Bhima's bodily strength. No wonder everyone sings his praises!'

It has so happened that the readers' introduction to the man who has given this series its title, the man who is unparalleled in the annals of Tamil history, the man who ensured the Chozha dynasty's fame would be indelibly etched into lore, Arulmozhi Varmar who would become Raja Rajar, has occurred under strange circumstances, at an inopportune moment when the prince wore no identifiers of his royal rank and when his face could barely be seen for the dark. It is but natural that some of our readers feel betrayed. However, what can one do? This is the first time the hero of our story, Vandiyadevan, has met him. We couldn't possibly have met Ponniyin Selvar ahead of our protagonist, now, could we?

Arulmozhi Devar now approached Vandiyadevan again. Our man sat up, nervous that he was going to be consigned to the role of punching bag yet again. But the prince's beaming face and welcoming smile put those anxieties to rest.

'Welcome, my friend, welcome to this beautiful island. You've crossed an entire sea and trekked through forest to join the Chozha forces here. I hope my welcome was befitting of your valour. Was it lacking in some way? Would you have preferred a more flamboyant reception?' the prince asked, smiling.

Vandiyadevan jumped to his feet and bowed low, bringing his hands together in greeting. 'Ilavarasare! The scroll your sister sent you has reached you, and with that my duties are over. I have no reason to protect my life any longer. If you so wish, we can resume our duel.'

'Aha! What can one say in reply to such an offer? You aren't worried about your very life. Well, let that worry be mine. I take full responsibility for your safety. How will I face Ilaiya Piraatti if I fail in this regard? My friend, I see that the scroll I read has been written by my sister herself. It is her own writing. Did she hand it over to you personally?' the prince asked.

'Yes, indeed, Ilavarasare. I had the great fortune of receiving this scroll from Ilaiya Piraatti's hallowed hands. And I came right here, journeying nonstop, through the day and through the night,' Vandiyadevan said.

'That's evident from the speed with which you got here. How could I possibly repay you for such a tremendous favour?' the prince said, and then pulled Vandiyadevan into a deep embrace.

As the prince threw his arms around his shoulders, Vandiyadevan felt the pain dissipate from his limbs. He was in Swargalokam.

The story continues in
BOOK 4
WIND STORM

An Extract

WHEN THE PAINTINGS SPOKE

The prince stopped his narration suddenly, and asked, 'Do you hear footsteps?'

The two friends, who had been listening intently to his story, shook their heads and said they hadn't.

Azhvarkadiyaan thought for some time and then said, 'It suddenly seems a little warmer where we're sitting, doesn't it?'

'I can smell smoke too,' Vandiyadevan said.

'Aiya? There is no danger here, is there?' Azhvarkadiyaan asked anxiously.

'If there is any danger at all, Kaveri Amman will warn us. There's no need for worry,' the prince said, and went on, '... so, we dismantled the camp and cleared out of that place right away. Even so, ten of our soldiers fell terribly ill. Ammamma! That is a devastating illness. It would turn the most courageous of men into snivelling cowards. Those, who stood strong and bore wounds on every inch of their bodies in the battlefield, would find themselves so demoralised and debilitated by a sickness that lasts three days that they would beg to be allowed to return home. I believed it was the Chozha clan deity, Durga Parameshwari, who arrived in the form of that mute woman and made us leave from that place.

'Even after that incident, the goddess continued to watch over me. She has followed me everywhere I have gone. Wild animals, poisonous snakes, hidden enemies ... she has saved me from them all. She disappears as quietly as she arrives. Within days, I learnt to communicate with her through facial expressions and bodily gestures. Sometimes, it is as though my heart perceives whatever is on her mind with no need for articulation. And that's not all. Even without seeing her, I can sense when she is around. Actually, at this very moment ... right, both of you head to bed right away. Even if you're not able to sleep, pretend you're asleep. Quick!' the prince said.

They did as he bade them do. They tried to close their eyes too. But such was their curiosity that their eyelids refused to obey them.

They watched as a figure approached the latticed window through which the moonlight filtered into the room. She was the same woman whom they had seen earlier on the street, by the mansion that had caved in. A barely audible hiss escaped her lips. Arulmozhi Varmar stood up and went to the window. The woman outside made a series of signs.

The prince pointed at the two of them, his friends who lay pretending to sleep. The woman responded with more gestures.

The prince walked up to them right away and asked them to come with him. The three men left the building, and followed the elderly woman.

They walked for a long time along a path flanked by tall trees that allowed little light in. All of a sudden, they arrived at a clearing and came upon a stunning sight. Several enormous elephants stood in a row, guarding a massive stupa.

Vandiyadevan's heart stopped.

The elderly woman showed no hesitation as she walked up to the herd.

Azhvarkadiyaan whispered, 'How life-like those statues look!'

It was only then that Vandiyadevan's fear abated. His wonder, however, did not.

As they came closer, they saw that the elephants had been sculpted in a phalanx, positioned as if they were bearing the weight of the stupa. Each of them had two massive tusks. There were hundreds of such elephants, across the length and breadth of the stupa. One alone appeared to have a broken tusk, and it was this elephant that the woman approached.

She moved a large stone lying by the feet of the elephant and they could see a stairway. She disappeared down the steps and they followed. They hadn't gone far when they came upon a mandapam lit by two oil lamps.

The woman teased the flame on one of the lamps to brighten it and then held it up. She signalled to the prince that he alone must follow her. The other two men found this worrying, at first. But once they saw that the woman was showing the prince a series of paintings on the walls of the mandapam, their anxiety for his safety lessened.

The paintings seemed to be sketches that illustrated the key incidents in a story. They were of the same style as the stories of the Buddha that decorated the walls of the various viharas. But there was no Buddha in these paintings. These seemed to tell the story of a woman, whose face was a younger version of that of the lady who now held a lamp to them. The prince realised she had illustrated her own life history on these walls.

The first vignette was of the young woman standing all alone on the shore of a little island, as her father brought back a catch of fish on his catamaran.

In the next picture, the woman walked through the forest.

Sitting on the branch of a tree was a young man, with the appearance of a prince. A bear was climbing the same tree, unnoticed by the young man, who was staring into the distance.

The woman screamed as she ran.

The bear began to chase the woman.

The young man jumped off the tree, aiming a spear.

He hurled the spear at the bear.

He then engaged in a duel with the bear.

The woman watched, leaning against a coconut tree.

At last, the bear collapsed in defeat.

The young man approached the woman.

He thanked her.

Unable to respond, the woman's eyes glistened with tears.

She ran to fetch her father.

The father arrived along with her to tell the young man that she was mute.

The prince looked sorrowful.

Then, his sorrow dissipated as the two of them became close friends.

The prince made a garland of wild flowers, which he gently placed around her neck as she smiled shyly.

The couple wandered the forest, holding hands.

One fine day, an enormous ship approached the island.

Several soldiers disembarked.

The soldiers found the prince and saluted him.

They asked him to accompany them on board the ship.

The prince went up to the young woman, reassured her and then left.

He boarded the ship.

The woman ached for him, and sobbed inconsolably in his absence.

Her father observed this.

He readied a boat, asked her to climb aboard and set sail.

They arrived at a lighthouse, where they were welcomed by a family.

The entire group boarded a bullock cart.

They went on a long journey.

They arrived at a city, with huge fortress walls guarding its entrance.

On one of the highest balconies was the prince, now wearing a crown as he waved to the crowd below. He was *surrounded by soldiers in grand livery and friends and family in royal finery.*

The young woman wilted as she saw this.

She ran away from the place at great speed.

She arrived at the lighthouse.

She climbed to its highest level.

She then jumped off, right into the sea.

The waves carried her limp body.

A man on a boat saw her.

He jumped off the boat.

He carried her unconscious body on to his boat and revived her, saving her life.

Assuming she had been possessed by spirits, he left her at a temple.

The temple priest performed a ritual, smearing vibhuti on her and hitting her with neem leaves to ward off the spirits.

A grand queen of some sort, who commanded everyone's obeisance, arrived at the temple for a darshan.

The temple priest told the queen about the mute woman.

The queen was pregnant at the time. She learnt that the mute woman, too, was.

She had her escorted into the royal palanquin and took her back to the palace with her.

The woman gave birth to twins in the palace garden.

The queen arrived and said she would raise one of the twins.

At first, the woman refused.

After giving it some thought, though, she decided it would be best for both children to be raised in the palace.

Leaving her newborn babies behind, she slipped away in the darkness, without telling a soul of her intentions.

She spent a very long time wandering the forest.

However, she ached to see her children every now and again.

She would hide among the thickets of trees by the riverbank.

The king, queen and children would go boating on the river often.

The woman would glimpse them from a distance, drink in the sight and leave.

Once, one of the children fell off the boat.

No one seemed to notice.

The woman waded into the water.

She saved the child and handed him over to his family.

Then, she plunged back into the waters and swam ashore, where she disappeared among the trees.

All these paintings, made with saffron dye, were startlingly accurate in their depiction of objects and people. Prince Arulmozhi Varmar studied each, as eager as he was astonished.

At the final painting, he turned to the woman and gestured: *I am the boy who fell into the river. You are the woman who saved my life.*

The woman, eyes brimming with tears, embraced the prince and kissed the top of his head.

She then ushered him to another corner of the mandapam, and pointed out another series of paintings. These were not incidents from her life. She used these pictures as aids, along with her gestures, to warn the prince of the various dangers that lay in his path.

Vandiyadevan and Azhvarkadiyaan had been observing the events from the spot where they were standing. The former felt more than once that the elderly woman's face somehow resembled Nandini's. Turbulent thoughts rose in his mind, as did several doubts. But this was not the right time to give voice to either.

Finally, the woman led them all out of the stupa and then began to climb to its top. Her flexibility amazed the three men. Vandiyadevan was exhausted from the effort, but persisted in climbing.

At the halfway point, they stopped and looked towards the city. Part of it was ablaze.

'Aha! The former palace of Mahasena Chakravarti is on fire!' the prince said.

'The place where we were sleeping?' asked Vandiyadevan.

'Yes, the very same!'

'If we had been asleep in there …?'

'We would have been Agni Bhagavan's next meal!'

'How can you tell from such a distance that it is the very palace where we were staying?'

'From the pictures that spoke to me inside the mandapam.'

'We didn't hear what they said.'

'That is no surprise. Paintings have their own language. It makes sense only to those who can understand that language.'

'What else did the paintings tell you?'

'Several secrets that my family has been harbouring. The paintings also asked me to leave this island right away.'

'May the language of those paintings flourish forever! Vaishnavare! My side has won!' Vandiyadevan said.

'Ilavarase! That is not all the paintings said. They said you must not sleep under a roof for as long as you are in Lanka. You must not pass close to houses or under trees. Isn't that right?' Azhvarkadiyaan asked.

'You're absolutely correct. How did you know?'

'You know the language of paintings. And I know the language of gestures. When your clan deity was speaking to you, I observed her facial expressions and the signs she made,' Azhvarkadiyaan said.

'Well, good for you. There's barely one jaamam left for daybreak. Let us sleep on the roof of this stupa for some time before we leave,' Arulmozhi Varmar said.

The next morning, the rays of the sun slapped Vandiyadevan awake at dawn. As if the events of the night had not been enough, arsonists and mute people and deaf people and bears that climbed trees and ghosts and Buddhist monks and bejewelled crowns had populated Vandiyadevan's dreams in a confused story that quickly lost its plot. Those images disappeared as he opened his eyes to the sun, leaving behind fear and uncertainty.

Vandiyadevan saw that the prince and Azhvarkadiyaan had already woken and were ready for the journey ahead. He hurried himself along, and the three men began their descent from the stupa.

They kept to the main roads as they wended their way towards the Mahamegha garden, at the centre of which stood the sacred Bodhi tree, a millennium and a half old.

Buddhist monks and devotees clustered together by the tree, doing their perambulations around it, and praying before it. Some had brought floral offerings. The prince bowed before the tree.

'Empires and emperors will vanish as they arrived. But this Bodhi tree stands testimony to the fact that dharma will always remain victorious and survive everything,' the prince said to his companions.

Even as he spoke, he looked about himself, observing everything. In one corner of the garden stood three horses with their grooms, ready for a journey.

The prince approached them and the three grooms broke into smiles of joy as they bowed low to greet him. The prince appeared to ask them a question. He then called to Vandiyadevan, 'It was indeed Mahasena's palace that was set on fire last night. These men were worried we had been killed. Their joy and relief on seeing us alive is quite uncontained!'

'It's true that the Bodhi tree has stood for a thousand and five hundred years. But dharma died a long time ago,' Vandiyadevan said to Azhvarkadiyaan.

'Don't ever say that again. For as long as I am alive, how can dharma possibly die?' the Vaishnavite replied.

The three men mounted the horses. They left the city of Anuradhapuram through the northern gate. The crowd that had gathered for the celebrations still teemed about, chanting and cheering, and so no one took notice of them.

About a kaadham to the northeast of Anuradhapuram was a town called Mahindalai.

'Emperor Ashoka's son Mahinda first set foot in this town, when he came here to spread Buddhism. How lucky he was. He didn't arrive at these shores to conquer, with an army and armoury. He didn't have to run and hide from men out to murder him by night either,' Arulmozhi Varmar said.

'What a horribly boring life he must have led,' Vandiyadevan said.

The prince laughed. 'You must never leave my side. When you're around, I can find moments of cheer even in hazard.'

'And moments of cheer quickly turn into hazard,' Azhvarkadiyaan said.

At that moment, a cloud of dust rose in the distance. They could hear the sound of hooves. Soon enough, they saw a band of horsemen, their spears glinting in the morning sunlight.

'Aiya! Pull your sword out of its scabbard!' Vandiyadevan warned.

NOTES

1. POONGUZHALI

1 Perhaps as an indicator of the increasing popularity of *Ponniyin Selvan* as a series, Kalki Krishnamurthy tends to break the fourth wall rather often, and calls the readers' attention to particular vignettes. This might also have been with filmmakers in mind. Eventually, the film rights for the series were bought by actor (and later Tamil Nadu Chief Minister) M. G. Ramachandran, popularly known as MGR. When Kalki speaks directly to readers, he also switches to the present tense. Although it is more common to do this in Tamil writing than in English, I have chosen to retain it in order to infuse some of the flavour of the original into this translation.

2 'Poo' is Tamil for 'flower' and one of the meanings of 'kuzhal' is 'curly hair'. The word 'kuzhal' has several connotations, referring to anything shaped like a tube or a reed, including the flute.

3 The four traditional landscapes in Sangam literature are kurinji (mountains), mullai (forest), marudam (fields) and neidal (seashore). Later, paalai (desert) was added to the list, and they are known collectively as 'ainthinai'.

4   One of the forms of Shiva.
5   One of the three revered Shaivite saints, along with Appar and Tirugnana Sambandar.
6   This note was written by Kalki in the 1950s.
7   Sea randa or zebra wood trees.

2. QUICKSAND

1   A story from the Ramayana—the rakshasha Maricha played a pivotal role in the kidnapping of Sita. He took the form of a golden deer that was chased by Rama at the behest of his wife. Maricha led him to the heart of the forest and then returned to his demonic form. Even as Rama shot an arrow and killed him, Maricha called out for help in a perfect imitation of Rama's voice, prompting the latter's wife Sita—who heard the cry—to send her husband's brother Lakshmana to his aid. In Tamil, the rakshasha and the form he took are often referred to as 'Maya Maricha' or 'Maya Maan', the latter meaning 'illusory deer'.

3. DELUSIONS

1   Elder brother's wife
2   An ancient unit of measurement, equivalent to seven-and-a-half naazhigaivazhi, approximately ten miles.
3   A story from the Ramayana. When Lakshmana, Rama's brother, was wounded in battle, the physicians needed herbs which could only be found on the Sanjeevi mountain, which at the time was a part of the Himalayan range. Hanuman volunteered to fetch the herbs, but identifying them was not his forté. Conveniently, carrying heavy objects and flying long distances was, and so he lifted the mountain and took

it whole to Lanka. Its herbs saved the lives of many of Rama's men and monkeys, but clearly no one thought to return it to its original location.

4   An ancient measure of time, estimated to work out to about twenty-four minutes.

5   A scroll made of palm leaf, used for writing letters.

4. AT MIDNIGHT

1   'Periyavar' literally refers to someone who is elderly or important. But it can also be used as a respectful form of address to an older person.

2   A raised platform on either side of the threshold of a house, where travellers—even strangers—could sleep without disturbing those inside.

5. AT SEA

1   A celestial being, a Gandharva who could have spent eternity making music but felt impelled to attack Indra—the king of the devas—instead, and got himself maimed for his pains. Indra purportedly twisted the Gandharva's head and thighs into his body. The Gandharva, ever pragmatic, pleaded for a way to be able to find and eat food. Indra then bestowed him with grotesquely long arms on which he could propel himself and a giant mouth embedded in his stomach so that he could eat. He would be freed from this horrific form and returned to his celestial body once Rama severed his arms.

2   In Tamil folklore, the kolli vaai pisaasu is a particular sub-genre of spirit—the ghost of someone who has died in a fire. It is said these spirits wait in trees and jump down on unsuspecting travellers. They ask the

travellers for fire, and if an unfortunate traveller were to respond, the spirits possess him or her.

6. AN ANCIENT RUIN

1 Of the nine rasas, loosely translated as nine emotions or overtures, the sringara rasa refers to love.
2 A female monkey.
3 An owl.
4 'Paavi' literally means 'sinner'. 'Sandaalan' could be read as a casteist slur, but it is typically used as a curse, perhaps a pejorative one. The latter is most likely in this case, since it stands to reason that the physician's son must be fairly high in the pecking order of caste.
5 Older brother's wife.
6 Indra's weapon, the thunderbolt.

7. 'SAMUDRA KUMARI'

1 'Vadava muga agni' literally means 'fire from the face of the mare', and refers to the mythological idea of a primal fire which has the face of a mare and body of flame and hides in the seabed, apparently under the south pole, for the right time to flare up and destroy the entire earth.
2 A corruption of 'Aro Haro Hara', used by Shaivite devotees to call to their lord for refuge.

8. BHOOTA THEEVU

1 'Bhootam' in Tamil has the same connotations as the word in Hindi—typically, a ghost, but it is often used synonymously with 'demon', and sometimes more in the context of its Sanskrit origin, to mean 'the past'. 'Theevu' means 'island'.

2   The outer part of a temple, around the sanctum sanctorum.
3   The equivalent of the plough asterism Ursa Major in Indian astronomy. It is named for the seven most venerated sages in Hindu mythology, Vishwamitra, Jamadagni, Gautama, Vasishtha, Kashyapa, Bharadwaja and Atri.
4   The Mizar and Alcor pair, or the horse-and-rider binary, are named after the sage Vasishtha and his wife Arundhati in Indian astronomy.
5   The Pole Star.
6   Snake Island.

10. ANIRUDDHA BRAHMARAYAR

1   Two different sects within Shaivism—Adi Shaivites are traditionally priests, while Veera Shaivites are followers of the Pancharyas or five acharyas, Renukacharya, Darukacharya, Ekorama, Panditharadhya, and Vishwaradhya.
2   The fourth of the Dasavataram of Lord Vishnu, where he appears as half-man, half-lion.
3   The sin of killing a brahmin—a reference to Rama's killing of Ravana, who was brahmin.
4   A horoscopic condition that bodes misfortune.
5   In this context, we can assume this to mean 'the right rituals', although 'sankalpam' literally means 'declaration of intent'.
6   Colloquial term for 'ruffian'. It is something of a pun, since 'thadi' means both 'stick' and 'corpulent'.
7   The term 'kombu' means both 'horns' and 'staff'. The idiom 'Thalayile kombu mulaichirucha?' which

translates into 'Have horns grown on your head?' is often used derisively to bring someone down a peg or two. The inference is that he or she is not unique in any way.

8 'Azhvarkadiyaan' means 'the devotee of the Azhvar'. 'Azhvarkadiyaarkadiyaan' means 'the devotee of the devotee of the Azhvar'.

9 Navidar is a caste, whose traditional occupations were those of barbers and midwives.

10 Literally, 'street play'. It is used pejoratively to refer to any kind of loud noise or commotion.

11 I've retained the original words mainly to showcase Kalki's love for wordplay. 'Tirukoothu' or 'Tiruvilayadal' literally means 'the divine game' and usually refers to one of the Hindu pantheon manifesting himself on earth to test the devotion of his worshippers, disguising himself in various ways and often provoking them to anger. 'Tiru' means 'holy', contrasted with 'theru', which means 'street'.

12 Literally, 'the devotee of the devotee of Adi Shankaracharya, who worships the Lord's feet'.

13 A reference to the tuft Azhvarkadiyaan wears at the top of his head. 'Munkudumi' literally means 'front bun'.

11. THERINJA KAIKOLA ARMY

1 The navaratna malai is the longest possible necklace—and, therefore, the most expensive—that can be fashioned with the nine precious stones. 'Malai' means 'garland' and so one may imagine that the necklace was about the size of a garland, which indicates just how wealthy the traders were.

2   This literally translates into 'The Five Hundred of Foreign Nations and a Thousand Directions'. 'Ainootruvar' or 'The Five Hundred' was a name given to groups of businessmen who plied their trade under the aegis of the Chozha empire. Those who traded within the land were called 'Swadesis' and those who traded overseas were called 'Nanadesis'.
3   'Padai' means 'army', and 'padaiyaar', 'members of the army'.
4   Literally, 'Idangai' means 'left hand' and 'Valangai', 'right hand'. These were terms used to refer to caste divisions. But one may infer from the context that they were speaking of the left and right flanks of the army, while Aniruddha Brahmarayar's interlocutor was the commander of the middle section of the army.
5   This is the title of the commander of the armed forces of a particular region. Prince Aditya Karikalan holds this post for the Northern Front, and his younger brother for the Southern Front, from which soldiers were sent to fight in Lanka.
6   In one of Kalki's displays of punning that are impossible to translate, the commander says, 'Oru kai paarkkirom!' which literally translates into 'We'll put a hand to it' and means 'We'll show them their place'. The prime minister goes on to say, 'A hand? You'll put three hands to it', and puns on the 'kai' in 'Idangai', 'Valangai' and 'Naduvirgai'.
7   The Velaalars were the dominant aristocratic caste in the era of the Chozhas. The members of the elite army would be abasing themselves by taking on the title 'slaves to the Velaalars'.

12. GURU AND SHISHYA

1 'Anbu' is the Tamil word for love or affection.
2 This chapter was written in 1951.
3 An ancient measure of land. One veli is equivalent to roughly six acres.
4 A typical Shaivite chant.
5 Although the word could be translated as 'tradition', I have chosen to retain the original because the word is typically used even in contemporary Tamil to denote a religious tradition.
6 One of the branches of Shaivite worship, in which the Vedas are given importance.
7 A term of respect typically used by Vaishnavites while referring to a man, similar perhaps to 'Esquire'.
8 Clearly, the preceptor after whom our prime minister is named.
9 A corruption of 'Nanda Vilakku', the lamp one sees upon entering the outer hall of a deity's shrine. The lamp is believed to be redemptive, and must never be allowed to burn out.
10 Abhishekam is the bathing of the deity with various liquids and semi-solids, ranging from milk to fruits soaked in syrup. The archanai is a ritual in which the priest recites the name, birth star and gotra of a devotee who makes an offering, in a bid to receive a personalised blessing from the deity.
11 The chanting of the various names of a particular god—this is typically done by Vaishnavites.
12 'Pillai' literally means 'son', but in this context, it could be interpreted as a version of 'My child'. The extended last vowel indicates it is an address.

13 A reference to Nammazhvar, who is also known as 'Sadagopar'.
14 The pasuram goes on to say that now that the Lord has entered his mind and seated himself upon his head, the devotee will never let him go and will hold on tight to his feet.
15 Meaning, 'He who wrote the Bhagvad Gita' and referring to Lord Krishna.
16 The Tiruketheeswaram or Ketheeswaram temple, located in Mannar in the Northern Province of present-day Sri Lanka, is believed to be the oldest temple in the island, dating back at least 1,400 years.

14. TWO FULL MOONS

1 The Tamil equivalent of Dussehra—the nine nights of the festival are dedicated in the Tamil tradition to the three goddesses who are consorts of the Trinity—Saraswati, Lakshmi, Parvati.
2 All these women are symbols of spousal devotion and chastity. Sita of *The Ramayana* is famous enough. Kannagi of *Silappadikaram* burnt down the city of Madurai as vengeance for the king having sentenced her husband to death on suspicion of theft. She may be perceived as a good wife less for the pyromania than for her love of a husband who whittled away his fortune on Madhavi, a dancer and his long-time mistress. Nalayini was married off to an old and cranky sage on the whim of her father, and bore much abuse from him, even carrying him to the house of a prostitute and waiting patiently outside until he was done. In return for all this, she was given a boon by her husband, and seems

to have made up for lost time by asking for five young versions of him in his stead. Perhaps because she stuck to the same man five times over, she is considered an icon of chastity. Savitri was married to Satyavan, whose return to life she negotiated with Yama, the God of Death.

15. A PRIMAL SCREAM AT NIGHT

1. 'Inji' is the Tamil word for 'ginger', but in Sangam Tamil, it meant 'city wall'.
2. The land was known as Naavalaanteevu—the island of Naaval trees. Naaval is the Tamil name for the jamun tree, and Naavalanteevu is the literal translation of 'Jambudvipa'. So, shouting 'Naavalo Naaval' would be the Sangam Tamil equivalent of 'Jai Hind'.

16. THE HALLUCINATIONS OF SUNDARA CHOZHAR

1. Modern-day Java.
2. As the gods were wont to when they were bored, Agni and Indra decided to put Sibi Chakravarti to the test. Agni took the form of a dove and Indra that of an eagle. The two descended on to a terrace of the palace and interrupted the king's navel-gazing to ask him for help. The dove asked for succour, shelter from the eagle who was all set to devour him. The eagle asked not to be denied his prey. Sibi offered to feed the eagle many times the weight of his prey. The eagle insisted nothing would be as tasty as the dove. The king said he could not let down a creature that had sought his protection, but could not let a subject go hungry either. The eagle reluctantly agreed to trade

the dove for an equivalent in its weight of flesh cut out of the king's right thigh. The king began to cleave his thigh, but even when he had cut it right to the bone, the flesh weighed less than the dove. Finally, he sat on the balance, and learnt in the stupor of his blood loss that the entire exercise had been the entertainment of an evening for the gods. As some recompense for his trouble, he would go down in history as the king who had all but given up his life to save a dove.

3   Manuneeti Chozhar had arranged for a bell to be placed in the palace accessible to every subject. Anyone who wanted to complain to the king could ring the bell. One day, the bell was pealing madly. The king rushed to see what the matter was, and found a weeping cow pulling at the rope of the bell. Her calf had been run over by a chariot in the palace boulevard. The king, wracked by guilt, decided his punishment would be to experience the cow's own loss and suffering and had his son run over in the same boulevard. As is customary in such cases, a member of the divine pantheon appeared and restored to life both the calf and son.

4   'Anbe Shivam' translates literally into 'It is love that is divine', meaning that love—in this context, affection, care, concern and consideration—is the ultimate form of divinity.

5   A terrace lit by the moon.

6   A reference to the infighting among the Yadavas, the subject of the *Mausala Parva* and the reason the Pandava brothers gave their kingdom up and began their long walk to Heaven.

7   An uncle, either one's father's younger brother or

cousin—as in this case—or the husband of one's mother's younger sister or cousin.
8 Literally 'older grandmother' or 'senior grandmother'—the older sister of a grandmother, or the wife of a grandfather's older brother.
9 There is some ambiguity here. Kalki has mentioned in earlier chapters that Arinjaya Chozhar had only two older brothers, Rajadityar and Kandaradityar. However, he has mentioned in several subsequent chapters that there was a total of four brothers. Our own secondary research suggests Parantaka Chakravarti had only three sons. Perhaps Kalki meant Sundara Chozhar was effectively fourth in line to the throne, since his grandfather was still alive. We have chosen to retain the original text because of the lack of clarity.

17. DO THE DEAD COME BACK TO LIFE?

1 Another name for Goddess Parvati. The Vishwaroopam is technically the universal form, but the connotation here is of a terrible form in which the deity in question has numerous faces and limbs and appears in both benign and fearful of avenging forms, typically encompassing all creatures and things in the universe, including the victims of the said deity's murderous rage.
2 This word means 'mute'. Later, we will meet a character called Oomai Rani. Readers might remember that 'oomai' was used as a pejorative against Senthan Amudan's mother. I have decided to retain the Tamil word from here on, so that the various connotations of the word may be known. In this context, the king uses it perhaps from pity, but predominantly as a statement of fact and nothing more.

3   This literally means 'most auspicious'. It is often used to speak of someone who is generous or considerate.
4   This word literally means 'sinner', like 'paapi' in Hindi. It can be used as a heartfelt curse, as it is in this context, or as a light remonstration among friends as Kundavai often does with Vanathi, saying 'Adi paavi'. For someone who was so in love with a woman to call her 'paavi' right after calling her 'maharasi' is jarring, and I wanted to retain that tone in translation.
5   Literally, 'The God of Time'.
6   A tall, ornate lamp made of precious metal, with provisions for six or more wicks.
7   Father's elder brother's wife, as in this context, or mother's elder sister.

18. WHICH IS THE WORST FORM OF TREACHERY?

1   In most translations of Indian mythological stories, the Trinity is commonly known as Brahma the Creator, Vishnu the Preserver or Protector, and Shiva the Destroyer.
2   Garuda, the vahana of Lord Vishnu, is considered one of the Azhvars or Vaishnavite devotees.
3   This harks back to a legend in which Garuda seized nectar from the Devas in a brutal war to fulfil the filial duty of freeing his mother from the snakes, whose king had demanded amrit as ransom.
4   Trumpets used in a particular kind of folk music.
5   Drums used in a particular kind of folk music.
6   A devotional poem dedicated to a particular deity, typically comprising ten stanzas.
7   An ancient instrument similar to the harp. Incidentally, Jaffna in modern-day Sri Lanka is known as 'Yazhpaanam'

in Tamil and named after the instrument. 'Yazhini' is a common name among Sri Lankan Tamils.

8   A heavy percussion instrument used mainly in Kerala these days, but a regular accompaniment in ancient Tamizhagam.

9   It was common practice in ancient Tamizhagam to endow war heroes, poets, priests and others with lands. These lands would be classified as either Iraiyili or Mutruttu. Both were tax-free. In the case of Iraiyili, the person to whom the land was given could use it for cultivation or other designated purposes, but could not sell or mortgage it. He was allowed to use it, but did not have ownership of it. Mutruttu land came with full ownership. The beneficiary did not have to pay tax on the land, and could sell it, but the buyer would have to pay a tax to the royal treasury in the case of a sale.

10 An ancient unit of measurement, equivalent to about one hundred and twenty-six kilograms.

11 An ancient unit of measurement, equivalent to 1.6 litres.

19. 'THE SPY HAS BEEN CAUGHT!'

1   A pejorative term since it refers to caste, the word indicates that someone is brutish, coarse and uncivilised.

20. A CLASH OF TIGRESSES

1   Ravana's oft-reviled son Meghnad is particularly popular in Tamil Nadu and Kerala. Apart from being a clever tactician and brave warrior, he was also said to be a powerful sorcerer. This could be the asset with which Kandamaaran is crediting Vandiyadevan here.

21. THE DUNGEON

1 In *The Ramayana,* the Ashokavanam is a garden in Ravana's Lanka, one of the most beautiful spots in the palace; Hanuman went on a ravaging spree in this garden soon after he had met Sita, who was kept captive there.

23. NANDINI'S LETTER

1 The Tamil word she uses is 'arasilangumara', which may be split into 'arasu', which means 'royal', 'ilam', which means 'young' and 'kumara', which means 'O Prince'. She seems to have deliberately used the word 'young' to signify that they are now related as grandmother and grandson, she having married a man of his grandfather's generation.

2 The word 'kumari' usually means 'daughter', although it could also be used to mean 'princess'. In this context, I've chosen to retain the original word since there is some ambiguity about it.

3 'Paadagi' literally means 'traitor', used here with the feminine ending. It could refer to treachery of any kind.

26. A DAGGER BAYING FOR BLOOD

1 This literally means 'When God is in a giving mood, the gifts will bring down the roof'. An English equivalent would be, 'When it rains, it pours'.

2 This is a literal translation from Tamil of a saying that has variants across Indian languages. The rough Hindi equivalent is 'Aap ke munh mein ghee-shakkar', which means 'May what you say come true'. In Tamil, the

saying is retrospective, suggesting that one should be rewarded for having predicted something correctly.
3 This is one of Kalki's puns. 'Nillu' means both 'Stop' and 'Stand up'. Azhvarkadiyaan is asking Vandiyadevan to stop talking, but the latter pretends to have mistaken it for an order to stand up.

28. THE ROYAL PATH

1 Gajendra Moksham is a famous myth from the Bhagavata Purana in which an elephant, on being trapped by a crocodile, shouts for help from Lord Vishnu, who appears and kills the crocodile. As the elephant prostrates before his saviour, Vishnu explains that in a previous birth, Gajendra had been a king called Indradyumna and was cursed to assume a lower form by the rishi Agastya over a perceived slight. This had delayed the moksha Indradyumna would have been sanctioned in his own lifetime under other circumstances, but would now be granted in his avatar as Gajendra.
2 The king Trishanku wanted to reach heaven in his earthly form, and was en route to having this wish fulfilled by the rishi Vishwamitra. This led to an ego clash between Indra—King of the Devas and Lord of the Heavens—and Vishwamitra. Indra tried to send Trishanku crashing down to earth, and Vishwamitra responded by freezing the latter in place and then creating a second heaven around him. The devas panicked and approached the rishi, begging him to stop. Placated by their abasing themselves before him, Vishwamitra stopped halfway, seemingly with no

concern for Trishanku, who was forever frozen in a half-completed heaven in the middle of the sky. This idiom is essentially used to mean 'stuck in the middle'.
3 This is an endearing Tamil saying with no real equivalent, *'Enna, kombu mulaichirucha?'*, which translates literally into, 'Has [s/he] grown horns?' The implication is generally that one thinks one is special, although why horns would endow one with such an ego, I cannot think.
4 A pallipadai is a memorial temple erected in honour of kings who had lost their lives valorously on the battlefield. The Tiruppurambiyam pallipadai was the site at which conspirators from Pandiya Naadu had met, as recounted in *First Flood*.

30. THE DUEL

1 'Paavi' is something of a curse word, meaning 'sinner'. Vandiyadevan, who was using the respectful form of address for Azhvarkadiyaan since he had first heard him sing a pasuram, calling him 'Vaishnavare' even when he was joking, has now switched to the informal and less polite 'Vaishnavane'.
2 'Asadu' is a uniquely Tamil word that signifies something of a cross between stupidity, stubbornness and naivete. The closest equivalent in English would probably be 'ass'.

www.ingramcontent.com/pod-product-compliance
Lightning Source LLC
LaVergne TN
LVHW010309070526
838199LV00065B/5491